My Mother's Shoes

SHIRLEY RUSSAK WACHTEL

ISBN: 1463674155
ISBN-13: 9781463674151

"Wachtel views her mother's remarkable life, first recounted in *The Story of Blima: A Holocaust Survivor (2005)*, through a creative new lens…Among Wachtel's adroitly rendered scenes of Jewish domestic and communal life, of wartime Poland and 1950s New York, are several small masterpieces; a baby is accidentally dropped and dies, an apple is menacingly peeled in a labor camp, ice melts under a woman's exhausted body in a Polish forest, a father weeps openly over his failure to provide, matzos are broken and challah is dipped. Wachtel entwines the singular and the ordinary with quiet lyricism…An evocative, moveable feast plumbing past and present with equal grace."

—Kirkus Reviews

"*My Mother's Shoes* is an important and significant book which beautifully articulates the joys, the sorrows and challenges that face the "second generation" of Holocaust survivors. As the generation of Holocaust survivors passes from the scene, the Jewish world is beginning to confront the issues that engulf the second generation. Wachtel deals with these issues in a sensitive, creative, yet realistic and factual way. It is not a pleasure to read, but it is important to read. A painful subject beautifully presented to the reader."

—Rabbi Chaim Rogoff, East Brunswick Jewish Center, NJ

"*My Mother's Shoes* represents a significant contribution to the literature of family, of grief, of loss, of the Holocaust and its aftermath for survivors. Wachtel's innovative form encourages the reader to enter the minds and hearts of its main characters and does what Aharon Appelfeld suggests, in *Beyond Despair*, art should do: '... constantly challenge the process by which the individual person is reduced to anonymity.'"

— **Dr. Laura Winters, Chair, English Dept., College of St. Elizabeth, NJ**

"Dr. Wachtel's memoir, *My Mother's Shoes*, addresses the issues of survival and the powerful impact of the bond between a mother and her daughter. Despite the horrors that Betty Russak experienced during the Holocaust, she had a unique perspective on life. Betty saw life as a gift and she transferred these thoughts and feelings to her daughter. This memoir gives us insight into how a mother's inner strength can positively influence her daughter. There was no self-pity in this relationship. This is the story of a mother who taught her daughter to embrace life. It is the story of a daughter's appreciation of her mother's special qualities."

— **Lawrence Danzig Ph.D (Clinical Psychology)**

"I read the excellent *My Mother's Shoes*...I think the story of Blima's survival during the Holocaust would be most appropriate. Incredibly, there are many students out there who have no idea that the Holocaust ever happened!!! Getting this story out to a very wide audience is something I would love to do."

—**John Langan, Publisher, Townsend Press**
(publisher of *The Story of Blima—A Holocaust Survivor*).

"The first ten pages made me weep; the following pages simply charmed and fascinated me. I wouldn't change a thing...I am grateful to have read it."

—**Janet Burstein, PhD., Drew University**

"I just finished this book. I'll say more later; I can't stop crying at the moment. I will say now that Wachtel is indeed a wonderful writer, and she has made her mother alive for me. I can see her and feel for her and rejoice with her. Poignant, powerful, mighty writing!"

—**Sallie DelVecchio, Associate Professor, Middlesex County College, NJ**

PRAISE FOR

*The Story Of Blima
—A Holocaust Survivor*

"Shirley Russak Wachtel does a remarkable job in telling the story of her mother, a survivor of the Holocaust, in the book *The Story of Blima*. The book is an excellent source for upper elementary and middle school students to introduce them to and learn about the Holocaust. The story is written in such a positive and unique manner, that the readers, both adult and student, become quickly associated with her mother, Blima. Involvement by students and educators in the book will assist in meeting the Holocaust/genocide mandate in New Jersey."

**—Dr. Paul B.Winkler, Executive Director,
New Jersey Commission on Holocaust Education**

"Wow! Shirley Russak Wachtel is a masterful storyteller. Blima is alive, riveting, touching, powerful, deeply haunting, and utterly masterfully told. I am grateful to have read it."

**—Yvonne Collioud Sisko, author of *American 24-Karat Gold:
24 Classic American Short Stories***

"I have read it and was very moved by it."

**—Roslyn Abt Schindler, Associate Professor and Chair,
Department of Interdisciplinary Studies, Wayne State University, MI**

"I just finished this book and I absolutely loved it. I can't wait to read the next book, *My Mother's Shoes*."

—Jennifer Sarhadi, Modesto Junior College, California

For my mother, Blima
and her mother, Shaindel

Bottom Row—left to right—Salusha, Brandl, Chanusha
Top Row—left to right—Miriam, Adele, Blima

1939

Acknowledgments

I would like to thank my agent, Ben Camardi, who never lost faith in my words and has stuck by me, no matter what. I also thank Gina Blume, my friend and publicist, for her tireless work in helping me to get the message out. So many of my friends have encouraged me in the process, but three individuals in particular have provided concrete suggestions for revision and generous praise which has kept me focused and determined. They are Marcie Ruderman, Donna Danzig, and Helena Swanicke. I am indebted for the support and assistance of my wonderful brother, Jack, and my cousins, Mark, Joey, and Shaindee, with whom I share this story. To my two most reliable readers, Emily and Jaime, I give my love and thanks. Of course, without the memories and openness of my beloved Aunt Ruschia and my Uncle Karl, this story would never have been written. Waves of gratitude go to my three children, Howie, Brad, and Charlie, whose love inspires me every day. And, finally, I thank my husband, Arthur, who was there from the start.

The journey of a thousand miles
begins with a single step.

—LAO TZU

Preface

On a warm Tuesday afternoon in April, just five days after my mother's death, I found myself seated on the leather couch in the family room, talking to my friend, Debra. Ours was an unlikely friendship with somewhat incongruous beginnings. On the recommendation of a good friend whose children she had watched for several years, I hired Debra as my house cleaner. Every two weeks she would come into my home to scrub floors, polish dressers, and wipe down the blinds. Over a period of years, however, her duties extended into areas neither of us would have imagined at the time. She listened with amusement as I related some witty remark my youngest had made, sighed deeply as a tirade of anger over my brother's impatience spilled forth, and hugged me when I could no longer contain the tears of frustration over the suffering my mother endured. Her placid open countenance was both a welcome confirmation of my own feelings as well as a salve. On this day, though, Debra's friendship extended its bounds, forcing me to view the relationship with my mother in a new perspective, a perspective that neither my closest friends nor those who had known my mother for years could provide.

Superficially, Debra and I could not be more different. Debra is an African-American raised in Barbados; I am a Caucasian American whose parents were Holocaust survivors. Debra was raised in a family of twelve children, whereas I have only one younger brother, and but a handful of cousins. Debra and her husband are raising three daughters in an apartment in Brooklyn, and my husband and I have three sons in a suburban home in New Jersey. Debra baby-sits, cleans homes, and attends community college part-time, while I have post-graduate degrees, teach college English, and write.

We have come to understand, though, that our commitment to family and education, and our shared aspirations for our loved ones have overcome any apparent differences. Yet, for the first time since we had known each other, Debra and I were now seated on the same sofa. She wore a gray cotton turtleneck and sweat pants, her thick dark brown hair tightly held behind her ears with a simple band, and when she leaned into me, her scent was a mixture of Windex and baby powder.

It wasn't long before we began to speak of our mothers. I told her of the closeness between my mother and myself, how we seemed bound by the same threads of fabric. I spoke of my mother's losses, her struggle for life in the concentration camps, her renewal in America, and the determination she and my father had for their children to have better lives. In retrospect, it had become clear that her survival against all the odds was not a mere accident–there was a reason for it. Her life, I concluded, was not one which could be summed up in an hour, or even a day, but was the stuff of novels.

Then Debra spoke of her mother. She wasn't small of stature, like my mother, but large and powerful. Yet she had also suffered heart-searing losses, seeing six of the twelve children to whom she had given birth lose their lives. She was a woman who was financially poor, yet resolved to see her surviving children flourish in America. Before she died four years earlier, she too delighted in the loving cocoon of growing grandchildren.

After we spoke of these abundant treasures bestowed by our parents, Debra asked if there was anything I needed. I explained how overcome, how truly overwhelmed I was with the kindness of family, friends, people who never even knew my mother. One friend, who rarely drove alone, had made the hour-long trip to the cemetery, and then presented me with not one, but thirty-six hard-boiled eggs, each representing a circle of consolation and renewal. There was another friend at the college who sent a note detailing the bond she felt with me, for she too had recently lost her mother, her best friend. And the professor who never knew my mother, yet whose sympathy was palpable, with words which did liberate me to go on. The classes covered, gifts of fruit, wine, complete dinners–the generosity at times too much to bear, my gratitude vastly insufficient.

When I pondered this aloud, wondering why people, most of whom had never met my mother, would be so purely kind, Debra's response was swift.

"They know you, Shirl. Whatever goodness was in your mother was passed down to you." Although the comment made me cry, something in me yearned for it to be true. I could never hope to approximate the woman my mother was. No matter what losses I suffered, I had not endured the immeasurable pain of her early years. Nor could I have had the strength to enter a new land where the customs, the language, even the way people drank their tea was different. Finally, I knew I would never have been able to raise a family without the unwavering support and compassion of my own mother. After all, I was never the totally selfless kind. I could not dress and feed a tired five-year-old as she lay in bed each morning, fold endless series of towels in a launderette and come home to cook each evening, sacrifice my own education, adornments, vacations, just so my children could thrive. No, I was tied to my mother, yet decidedly different from her.

But then Debra explained that it wasn't the daughters themselves, but the circumstances of our lives which made us different. They pour all the wisdom and love into us, and we take from it. Like us, they simply, she said, did the best they could. And momentarily I was reminded of the old aluminum colander with its bent handle which my mother used as a sieve for her chicken soup. Carefully, she would pour the steaming soup through the colander, and the bones and fat would lie within it while only the clear rich soup was collected in the bowl below.

Just before she left, Debra asked that I do one small favor for her. She turned to me and placed her large hand on my shoulder.

"That book you mentioned before," she said, her brown eyes still glistening, "write it."

And So

I like it best when she sleeps. When she sleeps, I don't have to look at her eyes. Her eyes are remarkable, you see. They are matchless, neither a subtle cornflower, nor the color of a dusky, rolling sea, nor even a silky lazy sky which settles comfortably over apartment buildings as children sit down to their suppers. Nor are they fantastic for the incomprehensible fact that neither of her children managed to inherit the particular shade of blue. No, they are unique because of one irrefutable fact–they speak. Through the years, they have spoken of many things, most predominantly, love. But now, now that they are the only voice she has left, I can't bear to hear them. Yes, definitely sleep is best.

Today the sun is pouring, pushing its way through the closed damask shades, which with little prodding, open. Sunlight, an unabashed intruder, falls upon her face, but her breaths come soft and steady, and her hands are motionless clenched upon her chest. I stare at the face, as I have the last four months, and I realize again how beautiful she is. Not the standard notion of beauty, but the kind accomplished by a mask of quiet serenity achieved only in age. I marvel at its smooth contours, and hope briefly that the powers of heredity bless me with the same fine skin one day. In fact, even with her chin sunken in like that, one can barely believe that she is eighty-three years old (give or take a year depending on the source).

I walk into the bathroom she never uses and wet a paper towel, which I then gently place over her forehead. She makes a few "puh" sounds pursing her lips, nothing more, as the towel caresses the furrows of her sweaty brow. I move the cloth down the willful nose, and as I take note of the bump in its center, I am surprised that I no longer feel the twang of guilt upon its discovery. The thin lips are expressionless and covered by pathetic little patches of crust. I make a mental reminder to coat them later with Vaseline.

She wouldn't like people seeing her this way, without her dentures, mouth swallowing up the thin lips. Once, she accidentally broke the false teeth, and she cried for a whole day. But they wouldn't allow even the teeth in this place. So I put the dentures away, or maybe I threw them out altogether. At the base of her neck are sprinkled the freckles of childhood along with a couple of moles, to which she is prone, and I lightly cover these too with the cooling wetness. Finally, I squeeze the last of the tap water onto the top of her head, and with my fingers I comb back the remaining hairs, straight and thin, like my own. She is almost totally gray now. There were times, as recent as a few months ago, when I would squeeze the Clairol Herbal Golden Brown onto her head, as she simultaneously pinched her eyes tightly shut. I can still smell the stinging odor of peroxide in the air. I watch as a single droplet of water, not hair dye, escapes onto her left eyelid which flutters as a petal would when brushed by a spring breeze. Standing back, I watch the rhythmic movements of her breathing, her chest barely rising beneath the sleeveless yellow flowered sundress with buttons (they all have to have buttons) down the back. The dress isn't even hers, having somehow made its way into her closet, not an unusual occurrence. She is too tightly swaddled today beneath the beige flannel blanket, and someone has casually thrown an afghan over all, a patchwork of dancing pinks and grays. In the bed, buoyed by round sacks of air, she is at once a presence and an unimposing picture of fragility. No longer able to look at her, I turn away.

Photographs line the window sill, the TV stand devoid of TV, the dresser, the large bulletin board in the corner. Reminders of a life lived, the pictures are present in almost every one of the rooms. They are all the same, yet each is different. In this room, there is one of my wedding, twenty-five years ago, another, more recent, of her and two brothers, a black and white posed one of me and Jack, he with a striped rubber ball in his hands, I with a gray ribbon, then a scarlet red, wound around a ponytail. Jack's face is round like my mother's, mine long like that of my father. I am missing a tooth. Most of the photographs, though, are of the grandchildren, five in all, and all boys.

"No princesses," she would often say, "only kings." Every so often I hold the largest photo of all five directly in front of her face, and I point to each one.

"See, there's Howie. He's at Georgetown now..." and finally, "little Sammy, remember?" I say, calling him by a Yiddish endearment meaning "lightning bug." As I point to each one, sometimes I think that I see one of the blue eyes begin to willfully tear. But each time, I dismiss the notion, reasoning this a natural physical reaction to the dryness in the air. And I convince myself, I pray, that she is no longer capable of crying.

Today, there is silence. The creak of the double doors perpendicular to her room is less frequent than usual, and the lighthearted bantering of aides more distant, muted; even the screams, which rattle periodically through the corridors, are quieted now. All silent save for the steady cranking of the cogs rhythmically churning the liquid, which resembles a kind of noxious chocolate milk, into the plastic tube. Down beneath the crocheted dancing afghan, sneaking further, further underneath the too tightly wound beige flannel and sundress into the soft yellow putty which was once her stomach. Nourishment. Life—no, I correct myself—existence. She exists with every whir of those cranky cogs. To camouflage the sound, I place a cassette into the radio by her bed. Written across the edge it says: *Favorite Jewish Melodies*. Immediately, the sturdy voices sing out; I visualize young strong Israelis dancing with banners through fruit-laden orchards. *"Shane vidila voona, lichtic vee der shtaren...Sweet little one, light as the stars... Fin Gott a mitunah, ost der mer tsi gui brangt...From God a blessing you have brought to me."* It is her favorite song, a tune which has always brought tears to her eyes. Now, her eyes are shut.

Yesterday was different. I found myself walking down the hall with its too pristine white tiles, shining golden oak chair rail, sedate salmon-colored wallpaper with the look of suede on which were placed at regular intervals, pictures—a Jewish woman praying over candles, a couple dancing under the *chuppah*, an abstract of a hillside in Israel. It was all too sanitary, too ordered, and I hated it. My high heels clicked against the tiles as, like radar, I followed the high-pitched whining sound which had reached my ears just as I stepped out of the elevator. My pace quickened as I walked past her room with its neatly made bed. Finally, I saw it. The back of the special narrow wheelchair with the inclined seat, the pole adjacent to it, and one skinny white arm with clenched fingers stretching into the empty air. The whines bore no resemblance to the strong, round tones I knew so well—those comforting tones which even in anger could wrap themselves around you and make you feel that nothing was ever or could ever be bad again. Nothing like this mutant cry which was an unnatural pitch, a hybrid borne of fear, of pain? When I faced her, she looked up at me, straight into me, and then altogether through me. She screamed again.

I stood up straight in front of her, my eyes going to my own skirt, a cotton blend of black and white Swiss dots. Somewhere inside my brain, a small egotistic voice murmured an unspoken question. *"Do you like my outfit?"* Of course, she had always loved polka dots, and so she would smile appraisingly, check the hem, and have me spin like a teenage ballerina.

"Zaya shein...Very nice," she would say with a smile, and then she'd ask, *"Viful?...How much?"* She'd have to see the shoes, too.

Bright black pumps with very high heels. She certainly would have approved.

Indeed, the voice in my brain is a child's voice–still demanding to be noticed, appreciated–now drowned by an insistent whine. She knows only herself, reasons an older voice, submerging the child.

I approached the nurse's station where I was greeted like an old friend. My tone, lighter than usual, inquired about her last dosage of morphine. I was told that the last supplemental dose was given forty-five minutes earlier. Her tolerance was building.

The sacral wound, which is delicately often referred to as a "bedsore," rests precariously close to the anus, and is much smaller, I am informed, than when she first came here. Big enough to put a fist through, they had said, yet packed with bullets of pain. The morphine reduces the pain, which is often agonizing, but as her tolerance rises with each day, so does the dosage. It is a horrifying but unavoidable cycle.

Often, walking down the hallways (those further away from where she is stationed), I overhear the familiar banter between mothers and daughters.

"I picked up my new dentures today, ma...See?...How about some more water?" or "Lucille, you should really go to a doctor for that constipation problem." "I'm eating roughage, mom. I'll be all right."

Sometimes, hearing it all brings a momentary smile to my face. I am definitely the youngest offspring here, as far as I can tell. Senior citizens with back pains and canes often drop by to visit their elderly parents. As I walk past, feigning oblivion, I wonder who will care about my dentures, my eating habits, my polka dotted skirts when I get older.

But, even here, you have to laugh. Indeed, emotions always hit highs or lows. There is no moderation, the subtle niceties of time having long fled this place where gentlemen wear diapers which emerge from tweed pant waists, and women go dentureless.

You have to laugh. Once, a woman in a wheelchair took her shirt completely off. And although there was nothing about the old lady's body that could be recognized as womanly, one nurse running toward her joked, "Save it for when you can get paid for that, Sadie." On another occasion, one of the patients was sitting in the TV room, where none but the attendants pay attention to the flickering screen. She was screaming, "I need something...I need something!" and being ignored by the overworked staff.

"I'll tell you what you need!" screeched a hag with the profile of a *baba yagar*, the mythical witch which so often scared me in childhood. With raised fist, she ominously wheeled herself, rubber baby doll in hand (many of the patients have these) toward the woman.

"You need to be quiet!" she screeched, approaching until a tall aide with mounds of curly black hair promptly wheeled her away.

There are times, though, when the conversation is less dramatic, as when I overheard one patient, sporting a trim white bun, an alligator pocketbook resting on her lap, insist to her friend, "But I *do* love my husband...It's just that I can't *remember* his name..." As I said, you have to laugh if you're going to return to the world outside, if you're going to have any kind of normalcy.

When I came back to her, she was calmer; the morphine was beginning to work. I could tell that she was partially awake despite her closed lids, because the tremor in her hand, more distinct of late, was again present. I tried feeding her some applesauce, which she sucked slowly, every so often smacking her lips.

"Remember how you loved to eat apples?" I prod, recalling the way she would carefully peel away one long circle of skin with the edge of a knife, then slice the white fruit into thin wedges, making sure to core the brown spots and save one thick wedge for the dog.

"I can tell you love this," I say, trying to catch the sauce which has begun to drip down her cheek and onto her bib.

But, that was yesterday. Today is better. And so I wait until the Jewish song ends, and another begins. This one is about someone dear being more precious than all the money in the world. And then, for no reason, I begin to cry.

I place my cool cheek next to her warm one, thinking again how this time with her has become both the worst and best part of my day. My tears cover her cheek, which I kiss, murmuring, "I love you" over and over again, as if the force of the words could infuse her with some power. A lifetime of unsaid "I love you's" sail up into the air and burst like so many bubbles. But she doesn't wake, and her eyes remain shut, speechless. Sometimes, I wonder if I'll have the heart to leave her, the strength to return. But, of course, I do, I must.

As I look through the window past the front yard into the parking lot where cars are neatly lined in rows, I suddenly remember that I have to get back home. Charlie will be home soon, and he will be needing a ride to Hebrew school, Brad will be calling for a ride from basketball practice, about thirty student essays needed grading, and a stop had to be made at the butcher shop if there was to be any supper tonight.

I begin to button my coat, and as I bend down to place one last kiss on the forehead of the sleeping woman, suddenly my body is gripped by an old fear. When I leave, no one will know her. No one will know my mother.

SECTION 1

Europe

BETTY

Silent as a sunbeam
You come when I am sipping coffee
You slip through my open window
How many years? How many years?
You come when I am sipping coffee
You come when I am at the mirror
How many years? How many years?
Your hand a veil brushing back my hair
You come when I am at the mirror
Pushing my way through a crowd
Your hand a veil brushing back my hair
I feel your arm weaving through mine
Pushing my way through a crowd
Driving alone I turn on the music
I feel your arm weaving through mine
And hear your laughter echo,
*   stirring melody like a golden spoon*
Driving alone I turn on the music
When I pray you whisper at my ear
And hear your laughter echo
*   stirring melody like a golden spoon*
When I dream it is your face which flickers
*   across my eyes*
When I pray you whisper at my ear
This world offers no escape, no exit sign, no secret door
When I dream it is your face which flickers
*   across my eyes*
For you come sometimes even in my smile, my voice
This world offers no escape, no exit sign, no secret door
I turn and write a poem, a word, words
For you come sometimes even in my smile, my voice
And I am afraid to linger in the moment
I turn and write a poem, a word, words
Gratitude is no longer mine to keep
And I am afraid to linger in the moment
All sent in sighs, flowers at the doorstep
Gratitude is no longer mine to keep
Silent as a sunbeam
All sent in sighs, flowers at the doorstep
You slip through my open window.

Blima

"My name is Blima," I answered, handing the young girl at the counter a box of fine round rolls, "it means flowers." But she just quietly reached up, held the prize against her chest for a moment, and skipped off, her long platinum braids bouncing behind her.

I loved talking to the children who would come into the bakery each afternoon when school was done. Their coat pockets jangling with coins from their parents, they would stride proudly into the shop, survey each row of baked goods— long tan sourdough breads dripping flour like snowflakes, dozens of *ruggelech* winking at them with chocolate and prune eyeballs, and corpulent jelly doughnuts puffing red bubbles through their centers. Then each child would make a great show of consideration and point one tactful finger at the showcase. Sometimes, if I was lucky they would talk to me. The *shiksas* and *shaigitzes*, the Christian boys and girls, were especially curious about the short, dark-haired Jewess behind the counter. They asked why the bakery was closed on Saturdays, what the narrow peg, the mezuzah, meant, and why my head wasn't covered by a scarf or *sheitel*, like so many of the women they'd seen. I, in turn, would ask about the way they worshipped, why their Jesus was considered a savior, what foods they gave up for Lent, questions I would never have dared ask their parents. The children, for all their show of being masterful bargainers, would answer generously. And in this way, each learned from the other.

It does not make me proud to say that this is the closest I have come to an education, having left the *chidah* after the eighth grade.

Not that I really cared much. Most girls my age, younger even, were already in a *shedach*, a match, and some even had one or two children. And although I too had a beau, I was too busy at the shop to fill my head with such *narishkeit*. Tante Rachel made sure to remind me of that each morning just before she slid the last of the steamy goods onto the shelf and went into the back room for her nap. Not many others could have tolerated her as much as I, and I guess that's why Mama chose me and not my sisters to work for her. But Tante Rachel had a broad, olive face and slits for eyes, like the Hungarians who were moving into the neighborhood, and I didn't much care for the way she shook her toothpick at me when she was trying to make a point. Worst of all, she wouldn't let me have any more of the poppy seed muffins, so I grew accustomed to eating the black bread instead. She complained about a shortage of poppy seeds in Dumbrowe, and with Purim coming next week, the customers would be banging on the windows looking for their sweets. So I learned to eat the black bread, which wasn't so distasteful even without butter, even if it was one or two days old and the moldy parts had to be cut away.

Tante wasn't really so bad. After all, she did let me eat the coffee cake crumbs which were still sticking to the counter at the end of the day, and she did teach me how to make the proper change, and tie a fairly serviceable sailor's knot to the tops of the white boxes. Besides, she was my mother's sister, so what could I do?

I stood on my tiptoes and peered over the window at the far end of the shop. Half of a sun blinked like a golden eye behind the mask of a gray cloud. It was as if God Himself were pulling in a rope of dusk coloring all of Dombrowe a melancholy purple. Soon the street lights would silently assert themselves on each corner, and mothers would be hurrying their children to the table while young couples giggled and whispered as they walked briskly to dance halls in town. I wiped my white palms across my apron which I quickly untied, but not before taking one last piece of black bread, careful not to cut the end piece which, if old wives' superstitions came true, would mean that I would be bearing a son in the near future. I could wait for that!

I placed one thick piece of the hardy dough in a bag, and, after hesitating a moment, added the end piece for Masha, the cat. As I was putting on my coat, the two bells on the glass door sounded, signaling Adele's arrival.

"Blumke! So I am waiting outside and going to *shtarb* from the cold already. Let's go!" I motioned for her to wait as I buttoned my coat and said good-bye to Tante, who looked up from her newspaper and, pointing her toothpick at me, reminded me to lock the door.

When my sister Adele and I walked down the street, we looked like two princesses gliding on a cloud of snow. Certainly, I never felt that way alone. In fact, I most often wanted to sneak into the corners of my house and observe everyone's comings and goings like a quiet bird. But when I was with my sister Adele, my favorite sister, her magical aura enveloped me too, and I felt, if not superior, at least like I was somebody. I tried to keep step with my sister's long strides as I rushed alongside her. She threw her head back and laughed, and as she did so, her raven curls leaped happily.

"I tell you, Blumke, you are slow, slow, slow,!" she admonished. I looked up at her, a scowl washing across my face.

"So who works as hard as I do in this family? You certainly do not."

"Well, of course, you were always the best child," she quickly retorted, giving me a sidelong glance and laughing again. I couldn't be too upset with Adele for long, though. She was simply too endearing, too beautiful. As her older sister, my affection for her was like a satin sheath, covering any core of envy in my heart.

Again, I inspected the lovely round face. Even without the powder and cherry rouge, Adele was stunning. She had piercing chestnut brown eyes, not pale blue ones like my own, and hers were coyly concealed by long dark lashes. Her nose was a little upturned dot centered in her face, belying her own Jewishness. This feature too was unlike mine, which was too prominent, too bold. The mouth, oh, her mouth, was embraced by full jewel-red lips which always, to me, seemed parted in laughter. And finally, the skin had an ivory sheen which glowed free of indentation or mark. Such was the skin young girls dreamed of, knowing that when the elder years crept upon them, the early bloom of youth would forever be in their cheeks. Adele was such a one; no matter what, she would be forever young. Just a touch of scarlet on each cheek completed the picture of perfection. Yes, Adele was perfection. Small wonder that last year she had come in first place in the local beauty contest.

We crossed the large road quickly, careful to skirt the round black cars which heedlessly zoomed and honked down the street. Sometimes young men in tweed caps would stick their heads out the window and whistled or shouted obscenely at the pair in matching long brown coats with lamb collars.

"They always think we are twins," said Adele, kicking her long booted legs higher as a wolf whistle resounded behind us. I pushed my chin deeper into the warmth of my collar. How many times had I wished to be a twin to Adele or Miriam, or Brandl even. But no, the fates had not been so compassionate as to allow that, or even permit me the luxury of being inside my own womb, for that matter. Froyim was my twin. Even under my heavy coat I could feel the bumps rising up my arm, just thinking of him. Froyim–the yellow-haired lizard who was a head taller than I even at birth, and who has tortured me, it seems, from the moment of conception. Of all the boys, it was he who looked most like our father, and I suppose he thought resemblance enough to give him the authority to lord over us all, and me especially. "Blima, where are you going?" "Blima, don't be out too late." "Blima, watch out for the boys, they are all snakes, you know!" Wherever I went it seemed as if Froyim was walking in my shadow, an eternal sentinel.

He even had the gall to give me his picture, telling me to keep it always in my wallet.

"Remember that wherever you go, my eyes are on you, Blima," he said, handing me a shiny new photo. No smile in the picture, but I could see the secret laughter behind those gray eyes. My tormentor!

I have heard of bonds between twins: similar tastes, attitudes, and emotions. But the bond I had with Froyim was forged with iron hemp, and through the years it wound tighter around my spirit.

"Did you hear that one, Blumke?" Adele's melodic voice shot me out of my reverie.

"Hear what?"

"Why, that tall boy over there, the one with the checkered cap," she said, pointing her chin slyly toward the left.

"Do you think I care what that boy was saying, or what they all say, for that matter? Adele, remember that we were raised as respectable girls. At least I know that I am."

"Oh, we all know how good you are, Blumke. And if we forget, we have Mama to remind us. *Beste kind*– the best child you are among us all," she mocked, but her chestnut eyes twinkled merrily, without a hint of malice. Before I could protest, she continued, "But tell me, are you so good, so respectable with Smulka?" she exclaimed, her open smile giving way again to full-blown laughter.

Already I could feel the heat of a blush, spurned by her teasing, come rising up my cheeks.

"Of course I am, and I could not be otherwise. You know very well that–" but before I could finish speaking, Adele removed one delicate hand from her fur muff and boldly placed it on my bosom.

"Why, you are!" she howled as she gave each breast a firm pat, "You are still binding them!" Again, I could feel the heat rising, this time up to my earlobes. I bit my lower lip to stop myself from crying.

"Really, Blumke, you would think that you are a China woman in the nineteenth century, only instead of binding your feet to keep your femininity, you are pushing down your breasts to become a man. This is Poland, and it is 1939, Blumke! 1939!...Tell me, how do you tie them, with Tante Rachel's baker's cord?"

I swallowed hard before I could answer. Only Mama and my sisters knew of this desperate action, which I had begun four years ago when I turned sixteen. Yet none of them could understand how it felt to stand at four feet nine inches and have heavy breasts which pointed half a foot out as if to say, "Here we are!" They didn't know what it was to have men bow their heads in reverence as their eyes crawled over your chest. Nor could they guess what it felt like to squirm uncomfortably as male friends, cousins, even strangers would reach out brazenly as Adele just had, and glide appraising fingers over my breast as if it were one of the loaves of bread displayed in Tante Rachel's shop.

"Never mind about why I do it, Adele," I retorted, gaining strength as I felt the warmth on my face slowly descend, "You just be glad that you don't have such problems."

"Besides, I added, grabbing her arm as we crossed another busy street, "Your mind shouldn't be on me or men, or anything but helping Victor tonight with the children."

"Ah, yes, Blumke, you are so right," she answered, shaking her wild curls again. As she took my free hand and placed it into her own muff, my sister's eyes were bright with reflections of the streetlamps which now glowed fully ablaze.

"You are always so right, and always so *good*."

I sighed. If Adele only knew the times–the many times– when I wished I hadn't been quite so good.

✡ ✡ ✡

Zalman was only two months old when he died. To be totally truthful, I hardly even remember what he looked like. Straight brown hair over a round reddish face, like any baby. I don't even remember why Mama placed him in my arms that day. I do know that I was only a child myself, no more than six. I suppose he squirmed a little in my arms like babies do, and I became afraid, and so I dropped him. It didn't take long for Zalman to die once his head hit the concrete at the bottom of the stairs. No one ever blamed me for it, though, not even Mama. After all, I was only a child myself.

Adele and I finally caught view of the massive hill leading to our brother, Victor's, house. It was still snowing, and we knew there would be hidden patches of ice the closer we got, so we steadied ourselves against each other and dug in. It was already dark, and our figures in the snow cast long shadows as we approached, ghosts against the clouds.

Victor's house, tiny as it was, sported a welcoming facade, its wooden porch stacked with bridge chairs extended beyond the width of the home. A series of green shutters provided all the protection of wrapping paper against the elements, which were constantly threatening, and the house itself seemed to shiver as it stood in the center of a circle of angry leafless trees.

I knew our journey was almost done when I could feel the gravel hidden beneath the snow turn from soft popcorn kernels to nuggets so hard I could feel them even through the soles of my heavy boots. One low-beamed porch light cast a narrow yellow ray onto the bridge chairs, making for an eerie setting like that of some tense drama which was about to begin. Anyone who didn't know the family inside might have been hesitant to enter on such a bleak and endless evening. But already Adele and I thought we sensed the tempting aroma of our sister-in-law's chicken soup, a mélange of garden vegetables and one young, pale yellow pullet. By the time we reached the front steps, five-year-old Salusha and two-year-old

Chanusha were already running toward us, hatless, winter coats secure over but one of each of their arms. The admonitions of our sister-in-law, Ruschia, went unheeded as both girls jumped upon me, demanding to know what I had brought them from the bakery. I reached into a deep pocket of my coat and brought out the brown package Tante Rachel had given me that morning. The warmth of the four miniature Linzer tortes had dissipated hours ago, but each remained intact like a cold coin within the bag. The children quickly grabbed the two tortes I handed each of them, and stuffed them into their mouths. First, Salusha, then Chanusha extended chubby arms to embrace me, squeaking, "Danke, Tante Blima, danke!" and, as an afterthought, turned to the pretty aunt who had been waiting her turn expectantly.

"Salusha! Chanusha!" a voice rang out angrily, as each child quickly stuffed the remains of torte into her mouth, hurriedly sucking the powder off her fingers. Inside, my oldest brother, Victor, and his wife Ruschia, were already getting into their heavy lamb-lined coats.

"You are more than half an hour late," scolded Victor as he gave each of us a quick kiss and hug. Not stopping to listen to our protests, he quickly turned to a brass trimmed mirror in the hallway, and ran a small comb through his hair and mustache. I don't recall a time when my brother didn't have a mustache, although of course there had to have been one. It was the same with his characteristic rotund belly which proclaimed his love of both food and life. Straight out like a woman five months with child! I often envied my nieces having Victor as a father, for his generosity and high spirits were infectious, and of course his two daughters were the prime recipients of that philanthropy.

In Victor's house, none felt a stranger, and my brother was rewarded in turn with what everyone agreed was an abundance of fortune. It was said that Victor was born with a gold spoon in his mouth, probably just an excuse for others to deny his business acumen. Whatever ventures Victor would enter would invariably prosper. As a youngster, he had taken a job pouring ten-pound bags of coffee and tobacco into small metal cans then quickly worked his way up to assistant manager of the shop. His latest enterprise was a small china store, and he and Ruschia were now on their way to a new source of inventory, one which promised renewed supplies of the finest silver cutlery. Victor never worried about the future, which he pursued with an optimism which promised basketfuls of not only spoons, but riches. And, most of the time, it turned out just that way.

Ruschia was holding her daughters' powdery fingers under a fast running faucet.

"Of course, you must finish your soup and chicken," she murmured, "but how can you, now that you've eaten your dessert?" She planted a firm kiss on each child's forehead, reminding us where to find the meat plates and cutlery, as if she had to.

Once my brother and sister-in-law had gone, Adele quickly proceeded to set the table as I doled out the steaming soup into brown earthen bowls. Before I sat down, I made sure to set aside the chicken bones, saving them for a personal delicacy later in the evening when I would suck tender morsels clinging to the bone. The rich sweet soup was appropriately hot, and it coated our throats. Once more, I reminded myself to ask Ruschia for her recipe. Her soup, I had to admit, was better even than Mama's.

After a dinner of chicken, new potatoes, and corn, we bathed the darlings and put them into their bed. Since an evening frost in Dombrowe was strong enough to rest in the blood, Adele reached up to the top shelf of the linen closet and pulled out a heavy white quilt which she tucked under the sides of the mattress. Ensconced tightly under the huge snowdrifts of covers, only two squirming dark heads were visible. As I gazed at the smiling countenances of my nieces, which always appeared as if they were conspiring to some mischief, I wondered which of the two was the prettiest.

While Chanusha, the younger one who possessed heart-shaped lips and long black lashes, did seem the easy answer, Salusha's's porcelain face radiated a quiet intelligence. Naturally, the question was nonsensical, for each was quite beautiful in her own way. Then I remembered something Mama often said when we children would pester her to name her favorite. Holding up one hand in front of us, she would ask, "Which finger is most important to me, and which can I do without?" Of course, we couldn't answer, and so she would shoo us away, calling us "sillies" as she turned to her ironing. But just the same, with the two angelic faces looking up at me, it was difficult not to wonder.

As I kissed each of my nieces goodnight, my heart, I admit, yearned for a daughter of my own. But I would never cut off her hair, as my sister-in-law had done. Each wore a cap of dark brown locks, so short they almost could have been taken for boys. No, I resolved, my daughter would have very long hair all the way down to her shoulders, just like a girl. A very feminine girl. And strong. Independent. So many of the things her mother was not.

Shirley

I was born afraid. At first, of course, my fear wasn't some amorphous thing trembling within me, but had a very definite face. It
was the face of the *babar yaga*. Every child knows her well. She is
the hag with one tooth, a pointy chin, and big red warts all over
her face. She who rides around on a broomstick and visits little
children when they don't finish their dinners or won't go to bed
on time. Sometimes, though, she visits them on very dark nights
when everyone is sleeping, or when they turn around and don't see
their mothers. The *babar yaga* is not the same for everyone, though.
My brother, for example, had the boogey man, a stooped creature
who walked with a limp. But it's all the same thing.

I don't think I ever really got over my fear of the *babar yaga*, but
just added to my panoply of terrors as I grew older. It all got down
to one fear which began, I think, with the navel–losing control.
Unfortunately, I felt as if I were losing control most of the time,
floundering, if you will. It is no wonder, then, that my very first
memory is of a dozen (maybe only two or three, but it seemed like
a dozen) adults restraining me while someone coated my throat
with medicine. I don't recall having trench mouth at all, but I
clearly remember the cure.

The next major event when I remember being ambushed by
the fear monster occurred less than a year later, and when I was
quite healthy. It was at my Uncle Kalman's wedding where I was
to be the flower girl. I had prepared for the event for months in
advance, choosing an aqua colored satin dress and a matching hat

in the shape of a heart. I even practiced throwing rosebuds with little pieces of crumpled up paper. I wanted so much to make a good impression on my new aunt who was quite beautiful, and my young uncle who even went to the trouble of buying me a rubber doll dressed as a bride. All I had to do was walk down the aisle by myself, throwing rosebuds from a small basket. By myself. Just as my parents took their seats in the synagogue, I could feel a trembling crawl from my toes to the top of my head. Then the tears came. My mother, slightly frantic, summoned my seven-year-old cousin Marcus to my side. "Do I have to?" asked the nervous page boy, as he was quietly being cajoled. Today, I still have the photograph of myself wide-eyed and scowling, and my cousin Marcus biting his lip, as onlookers grinned widely. I am sure that I received much more attention than the bride.

After I experienced these traumas at age three or four, fearful episodes began to multiply rapidly. Once, when I was in the third grade, I visited the Bronx Zoo with my class. Somewhere between the aviary and the bear cages, my partner and I wandered into a cave to see the lizards. When we emerged, our class was nowhere to be seen. My partner, an outspoken girl with red pigtails, remained perfectly calm and suggested we retrace our steps. I, on the other hand, ran frantically from one zoo maintenance worker to the next, dragging poor Peggy along with me.

"Do you know where Mrs. Ganz's third grade class is? From PS 165?" I asked hysterically, my face sweating a deep crimson. After receiving only questioning looks from the puzzled workers, I finally saw my teacher waving to us from the top of a hill. It took me awhile before I could stop hyperventilating, though.

Another incident occurred when I was selling Girl Scout cookies in a building project, not far from my home in Brownsville. My friend, having convinced me that elevator pulleys were none too sturdy, pulled me toward the stairs. We decided to start with the top floor and work our way down. But upon reaching the sixth floor landing, we discovered that the door had no knob. "The painters must have taken it off," reasoned my nine-year-old chum. But I was already flying down the stairs, trying every door at each landing. By the second flight, I began to bang hard with both my fists against the knobless metal door. "Hey, we're trapped in here! Let us out! Let us out!" I screamed. Finally, the door was flung open by a frail elderly resident. No sooner did I glance at my friend with relief than the door slammed shut. "You kids are making too much noise!" I heard as both the voice and the woman faded down the hall. Quickly, I ran down the stairs which led to the lobby, and began banging all over again. The tears only felt hotter as they streamed in rivulets down my cheeks. One of the painters quickly opened the door, and we fairly jumped at him in our haste to get out. I suppose we gave him something of a scare, but he couldn't have been more scared than I. No one could.

I eventually learned to internalize my hysteria. Since my family somehow managed to move into crime-ridden neighborhoods where people were always being robbed or otherwise molested on the streets, and moved out of them just as the rapes and murders began to occur, I learned to become both paranoid and streetwise. My brother who was five years younger but slightly taller than I, would wait for me at the bus stop on early winter evenings as I got home from high school. In addition, I learned to walk in a purposeful manner when I was alone and cross to the other side of the street when I saw someone lingering ahead. As cautious as I was, two things happened which awoke such a fear in me that I virtually tried never to find myself without a companion.

I was only about nine when we lived in a brownstone in the Brownsville section of Brooklyn, another neighborhood which was on the verge of changing from bad to worse. It was an unusually warm spring evening, so my neighbor, Freddie, a Puerto Rican boy about my age, and I decided to sit outside on the stoop. Freddie had gathered a pile of pebbles and wanted to see which one of us could throw them the farthest. I told him that I would rather just watch him. He was only hurling the pebbles a few minutes before a couple of Negro girls came into sight across the street. As luck would have it, one of the pebbles hit the biggest girl on the ankle. She glared at me.

"Whitie, you tryin' to hit me, or what?"

I must have turned whiter than I was already, and instead of answering her, I quickly fled through the doors to my apartment upstairs. I don't know what Freddie did, but from the events which transpired the next few weeks, I am sure he didn't confess. It turns out that Sylvia, the victim, was not only in the fifth grade, two grades ahead of me, but a gang leader with a thirst for vengeance. She and her pals followed me home each day threatening to beat me up. As I said, I was streetwise even at the age of eight, and learned to always walk down Hopkinson Street amidst a crowd of people. As the numbers thinned out, I would slip into a barbershop where I knew the owner, and escape through a back exit. It didn't help that my best friend at the time was a large chubby Negro girl named Elizabeth. She was just as afraid of Sylvia as I was. Eventually, summer arrived and by the next year Sylvia had already graduated and lost interest.

The second incident which occurred the following year was even more terrifying, if that can be believed. It's the kind that gets nervous parents only more nervous when they read about it in papers. It occurred at the peak of the afternoon when shoppers were busy filling their carts with peaches and bananas or arguing prices with oily fishmongers. There were also kids walking the few blocks from school to have tuna fish or peanut butter and jelly sandwiches at home. I was one of them. I was only two blocks away from home when a young man with a clipboard approached me.

"Excuse me, young lady, are you from the neighborhood?" I nodded, too timid to speak.

"I'm doing a survey on apartment living, and I really need some-one to help me. It'll only take a few minutes." He smiled pleasantly. I really didn't want to, but already the man was holding onto my arm and taking me inside the nearest building. I think God must have been especially attentive that day, because once in the lobby, the man let go of my arm and began walking ahead up the stairs. He cocked his head with a wink, and summoned me to follow him. I was paralyzed with fear, but only for a second.

"I think I hear my mother calling me!" I said, and ran out the double doors. I know that I had never and probably will never run that fast again. I didn't pause to look back, but quickly shot up the stairs and blurted the whole thing to my mother, who was standing at the kitchen sink. A detective came over later that afternoon as I recounted the details with a cover over my head. From then on, more than ever, I knew that bad things would happen.

Much later, the bad things always loomed closer, waiting for me like predators. They were even more ominous now that they not only lay in wait outside, but also stirred within me. I was prone to periodic panic attacks. I still shiver when I recall the geology lab exam at Brooklyn College when I froze as words began swimming like black schools of fish before my eyes. The professor allowed me extra time, and I ended up with a "B," but had to endure the stares of my classmates until the end of the semester. Then, a few years later shortly after I married, the pain in my stomach had me counting the days till my demise. "I want to have babies!" I cried, "Will I ever have babies?" For a brief, very brief moment, I even contemplated flinging myself onto the subway tracks at the Kings Highway station. It turned out to be a hormonal imbalance.

You might say, then, that fears have dominated most of my life. I never really stopped to analyze why or how. All I knew was that no matter how afraid I was, or how bad things got, there was one person who could make it all right. My mother.

Blima

I had been holding them in for so long that, finally, almost as if by a will of their own, the words had to come out.

"I'm not pretty, Mama!"

She glanced over her shoulder at me, holding the cotton rag midair, as if it were a baton.

"*Narishkeit*, such foolishness," she said under breath, and continued making long oval faces on the dusty gilded wall mirror.

I was supposed to be helping, but there I was folded into the yellow armchair by the window, my face pasted against a small hand mirror. Mama was right. It wasn't like me to be so introspective. But like a bird which had been caged too long, sometimes I allowed my mind to squeeze through the bars and feel the light summer air ruffle my feathers, my secret wishes escape into the breath of day.

"Who says it, who?" she blurted, like an inquisitor.

"Everyone remarks on Adele, the beauty queen, after all. Miriam is a mother herself, and Brandl, the baby, oh how sweet, how adorable!"

Mama let the cloth drop momentarily at her side and cast me a look of disappointment.

"But, Blimala, you are—"

"I know, Mama, so good! Always the good one!" I lay the small mirror carefully on the dresser, ran my finger around the border of tiny pink flowers, and scowled. How I would have liked to smash it on the floor into a million pieces, and I would have, if I weren't so afraid of the seven years of bad luck it would bring.

"Mirrors tell the truth, Mama," I whispered, and without my knowing, let fall a single tear. But already I knew I had begun to test her patience, and the idea entered my mind that she would fling the dirty rag at me in a fit of temper. Instead, she came over and sat on the arm of the chair at my side. She picked up the hand mirror gingerly and placed it so that both our faces were held in a single reflection.

"Do you see?" she said, staring into the glass, "Now, who is the pretty one?" A familiar vice gripped at my heart as the tears unleashed.

"But…but of course, you are beautiful!"

"No, Blimala, it is you who are the most beautiful of all. See? See your eyes, their own blue, like your father's. Like the lake, from when you were children, do you remember?" I bit my lip trying to recall the soft shimmer of the lake at the home of my cousins, where we had so often played in summers, the lake reflecting the aqua tint of a descending sunlit sky.

"And the nose?" she continued.

"Oh, no, it is too big! Too big!" I squealed, cupping it with my hand.

"No, not big, but proud and dignified. There is no shame in it," she said, delicately removing my hand.

"See the mouth?"

"Too small, thin-lipped like an old grandma!" At this she laughed, a deep outburst like a sudden thunderstorm which comes rumbling up from beneath the clouds. Much like the laugh I would have one day.

"A grandmother? Oh, like me, you mean?…Ah, no, Blimala, here again you are mistaken. Your lips are sweet and delicate and truthful. And yes, much like my own."

"And the freckles? Can they be removed, Mama?"

"Freckles? Spurts of sunshine, that is all." She sighed, and I felt her eyes move patiently away from the mirror and wash slowly across my face.

"Don't you see how much we look alike? Only you are much, much prettier. You are the best of me. And if that is not pretty enough, then what am I to say?" She placed a soft arm around my hunched shoulders.

"Besides, what is pretty, anyway? Eyes? What matter the color as long as the ones you love can see themselves shining inside of them? A mouth? Wide or narrow, so long as it speaks the truth. And the truth is that you of all my children are most like me. In looks, perhaps. But more importantly, here," she said, wiping the back of her hand across my forehead, "and here," placing it now against my heart.

"These are the places where we are most alike." She hugged me then, and resting in her arms, I never wanted her to let go.

Using the back of the armchair for leverage, she got up abruptly, grabbed the old rag, and proceeded to clean the bedroom dresser. I arose, placed the small mirror aside, and took hold of the broom handle. It took the two of us most of that cloudy afternoon to clean the rest of the house.

I don't recall ever discussing the way I looked with her or anyone after that. And in a few more months, I wouldn't even care.

When I woke up that morning, the first thing I did was run to the window. I parted the long tweed drapes just in time to see the sun spilling forth like a giant yellow egg yolk between the whites of thin clouds. It was a day like any other, and yet there was something electric, intangible at my fingers which rested on the window sill, an impending breeze in the sparks of air dancing around my head. Even before it happened, I knew *Zayde,* grandpa, was going to die.

I got dressed quietly so as not to wake my sisters. As I pointed my foot forward to slip it into a nylon stocking, Masha padded tentatively over and sniffed at my toes. After securing the stockings to garters, I bent down to pet the Persian who had already begun growing too heavy for her own good. She mewed softly under my touch then curled her round body and bushy golden tail between my ankles. I lifted her up, kissed her cold black nose, and smiled as she tried to regain her balance on the waxed wooden floor. As I brushed the yellow strands off my hose, I watched Masha's tail slip out the door toward Zayde's room. In a few minutes she would be lying next to the soles of his big feet, and the plaintive mewing would begin again. It was an odd circumstance, considering Zayde had always shown nothing but bitter distaste for the creature, and Masha responded by careful evasion at the sound of his sharp cane against the plank boards. Mama always said cats and other animals had a sense of the ominous; dogs paced before earthquakes occurred, birds fluttered as skies darkened before a storm, and cats howled like frightened children before the catastrophic. Perhaps that was why Masha had been sleeping at Zayde's feet the past few nights. Or maybe she knew that he was just too tired to notice her anymore.

I was no more than half a block away from Tante Rachel's bakery when I knew something was wrong. A small congregation of shopkeepers, some still wearing their aprons, had gathered in the middle of the gutter. I was not yet within hearing distance, but I could see some pulling at their beards, others gesticulating wildly. And there was something else. As I neared the scene of activity, I noticed a peculiar light emanating from the facades of some of the stores. Nearer still, I realized that it wasn't a light at all, but a yellow scroll plastered haphazardly to the outside of each window. "JUDEN" it said, boldly black on yellow. This shop is owned by Jews.

I pushed through the cadre of store owners and turned left toward the bakery. Underneath the shameless sign sat Tante Rachel, looking round and small like a two-day-old roll. Only a soggy flowered handkerchief held a clue to her despair.

"What is it, Tante? Why are all the people so angry? What is the meaning of these signs?"

Tante spread her palms before her as if she could find the answers in their lines. It was a few minutes before she spoke.

"Hitler's Nazis," she said softly, still gazing down, "It had to be. Did old Weinberg, the fish seller across the street not predict this? First one town, then another, and finally Dombrowe. It was only a matter of time."

I sat down on the bench next to my aunt, or rather slumped suddenly, succumbed by the impact of her words. Nazis. I had heard the name, even seen them once or twice zooming by in little black cars like bothersome insects. Froyim had warned me of them. He had heard stories of assault, thievery, even kidnappings by this group. They met in dark clubs where they saluted each other and vowed allegiance to a vociferous little man, a painter by trade, called Hitler. His power had grown steadily in the last few months, as people in cold little towns like Dombrowe checked their pockets to find only the seeping of hope, the dust of frustration. These men, he warned, these Hitlerites, could be dangerous. They had some plan they spoke of in these smoke-filled clubs, a plan for the country, the world. A plan which did not include Jews.

"Lower your head if you see one of them walking toward you with a grimace on his face," Froyim had admonished just the other day, "and if he begins to smile, run as fast as you can."

Of course, I ignored my brother's dire warnings as I had all his other hysterical, unsubstantiated worries about my welfare. After all, I was not a political person like my younger sister. Only twelve, Brandl had once pushed herself between two soldiers in order to snap a picture of the grand hero saluting in that peculiar way from the top of one of those insect vehicles. I, on the other hand, much preferred keeping company with the warm sudsy water with which I scrubbed the floors, or the silent combs used to straighten the knots out of my younger sisters' hair. Froyim and Brandl could have their speeches, their meetings, their protests. I just wanted my life.

But now it was different. The Nazis were no longer part of some ephemeral fairy tale, no longer confined to underground clubs, to angry words whose power faded as soon as breath touched air. They were in my world now, on the window of the bakery.

After about an hour of listening to Weinberg's curses and Mrs. Korsky, the seamstress's hysterical wails, Tante Rachel placed her hand on mine.

"Go home now, Blimala. The goyim will be too arrogant or too afraid to come in now. And the Yids, well, I don't think they will feel much like buying cookies today. Best to go home."

I nodded and moved forward as if to stand. But sitting next to Tante, her taupe cotton jacket against the sleeve of my dark woolen coat, her rough hand, veins bulging, atop my own small rounded knuckles, I was unable to move further. And so we sat, for a long time, like two gray pebbles watching giant clouds roll across the darkening sky.

By the time I returned home, Zayde was already dead. When I walked into his room, I saw Mama's head buried against his feet, where Masha had lain only hours before. I could see the outline of Zayde's long powerful body beneath the thick plaid blankets, looking as strong as I remembered, except for his head which was hidden now by the thick fabric. I had never seen a dead person before, except for little Zalman. Zalman. A tiny ball of flesh, as soft as dough with eyes of blue marble. Every so often he would emit a high-pitched squeal like the sound of the black cars that sped by more frequently now. And I would blow up one of the blue balloons we kept in a kitchen drawer and wave it in front of his face until he became so mystified he would eventually drift off to sleep. Then, since Mama couldn't abide the popping noises in the house, we children would run outside, loosen our grip, and watch as it sailed high above the tops of chimneys, clouds, and into the vast horizon. Now, Zalman himself seemed as mythic as that blue balloon. But, Zayde, well–that was a different story.

If it were possible for one human being to embody life's energy itself, that person would be Zayde. In spite of the fact that he was a central figure throughout my life, I knew little of him. Yes, I knew he had a long beard of gray steel coins for as long as I can remember, that he was a rabbi once and later owned a shoe store which he passed on to *Tata*, our father, and that he loved the taste of herring and onions. But beyond these things, I knew little, not even how he had become blind. Each evening until I started working for Tante Rachel, I would hear the sound of his stick tapping against the concrete long before he reached the front door. As the eldest girl, I was to make sure his glass of hot tea with lemon was set on the table before he entered, and I would have his woolen plaid blanket ready to drape over his knees after removing his heavy black boots. He never spoke to me then, or hardly ever. Occasionally, though, he would place his huge hand, with nails precisely trimmed by either Mama or myself, on my head, and murmur, "*Danke, shayna maydel.*" *Thank you, beautiful girl.* A warm current would go through my entire body then, for I knew that he never addressed my sisters, who were far prettier than I, in such a way. And even though I knew he was blind and saw me as no more than a shadow, if at all, I believed his words.

Like everyone else in the family, though, I also feared Zayde. Part of the reason was that we didn't know him very well. But what we did know inspired awe. He had worked as a rabbi, salesman, train conductor, even a boxer, and survived the deaths of a wife of forty years and five children. He had lived with us for fifteen years, and spent all but the last year of his illness attending *shul* in the morning and helping my father in the shop each afternoon. He was fairly silent at all other times, except on Shabbat afternoons when he would gather my *Tata*, three brothers, and other *hassids* from the town around the metal kitchen table and regale them with stories from the Talmud between bites of Tante's sponge and honey cakes. Sometimes, late at night, I would pass by his room and notice a soft light coming from within. With the intent of shutting the door, I would enter slowly only to see his back rhythmically swaying, his head and shoulders covered by the faded blue and white tallis. Once, and only once, I heard him cry out in the fervor of his prayer, "*Surala*." Sarah, the name of my mother's mother and my grandmother.

My mother looked up from the blanket, now soaked with her tears.

"Blimala!" she exclaimed, reaching both her arms toward me, "Zayde is dead!"

"I know, Mama, I know." I said, returning her warm embrace, letting her dampen my cheek and loosened hair with her kisses and tears. I took both her ivory delicate hands in mine, and not knowing what to say, added, "It is better for him now, Mama. He is at peace."

"Better for him, but not for me. Not for me, Blimala!" she cried, flinging herself across Zayde's stiff motionless legs. It was only last week that she had asked Tante Mima, my father's older sister, to consult her book of dream interpretations, for Mama had been troubled of late by dreams where she is drowning. But Tante Mima had forgotten to do the research, or maybe she saw something ominous in the interpretation, and only now did I understand.

I remained standing, waiting for Mama to look up, brush back the strands of my hair or fix my collar But she only lifted her head briefly, her eyes still fixed upon the blanket, and directed me to wash up and run down the block to the *shul* so that preparations could be made. Tomorrow would be a burial.

I did not walk into the bathroom, though, but headed straight for Mama's bedroom. This was my first real encounter with death, and I shirked from the thought of Zayde no longer coming home to pat my head or swaying in silent prayer before an open curtain. Most of all, though, I feared the change in Mama. I needed her to make sense of it all, to tell me that yes, it would be all right today, tomorrow. So, instead of running to *shul*, I quietly slipped off my boots, turned down the covers, and found the indentation of Mama's body still in the sheets. Then, as I had done so many times before, I molded my body into that spot. And when I could smell the lilac of her hair, the peaches in her skin, I closed my eyes and took a long deep breath.

✡ ✡ ✡

Almost as if in a dream, I felt myself falling in slow motion and head first into the open grave. From the heavens, a voice, my father's I think, screamed out. And then all was black.

When I awoke, I found myself in an old wooden cart which just minutes before had been used to transport Zayde to his eternal home beneath the dust. Mama was pressing smelling salts against my nose with one hand, as she stroked the top of my head with the other. A few feet away, I could hear my sisters arguing.

"Did I tell you not to let her stand there?"

"And could I force her to stand in the back–don't be such a child!"

"Fine. So now you see we almost had two in the grave, because you can't watch anything but your own manicured fingernails!"

"Better keep watch on your own son, Miriam. I am sure he will be obedient to your every word."

"Adele, perhaps at age two he is more of a *mench* than you. If only you–"

Abruptly, the argument ceased; no doubt my sisters caught sight of *Tata's* stern eye. He had only to turn his head, and he commanded the will of an entire household. For Mama's part, she ignored the whole affair.

"Blimala, *bist bessa?* Are you better?" I nodded, assuring her that I was. Only when she saw the gradual return of color to my pallid cheeks did we venture off the cart into the bright sunshine. A strong breeze was blowing, and I pulled my cotton kerchief tighter around my head. These fainting spells had become more embarrassing than worrisome of late, and I disdained the public attention which often accompanied them. I reassured them all that it was only a touch of the old anemia, exacerbated by the lack of a proper breakfast in the morning, until all but Mama turned back toward the gravesite and the men who were all now swaying in prayer. Mama kept tight hold of my hand.

When we walked silently back to the row of cars, I was oddly thankful for the diversion my fainting spell had created. Only the mark of heavy tears was streaked down my mother's face, and for the moment she had ignored the self-pity spawned by her sorrow. Turning oneself to the task of life lessens our self-reflections, I thought, as I glanced at the tightness in her eyebrows.

One of the neighbors was already there when we reached home, and she came running outside with a pitcher full of cold water to pour over our hands. Except for the covered mirror and an eerie silence which had descended over the household like a shroud, it appeared that all had been readied for a party. Platters of herring, salmon, and various vegetable salads lined the dining table; huge whitefish, their bellies neatly seared from head to fin, lay in beds of dark green lettuce, the open eyes of the fish assuming a ghostly glare beneath the crystal chandelier. In the center stood a giant bowl of perhaps three dozen hard boiled eggs, all peeled, naked, white, and cold to the touch. Once inside, we were beckoned immediately to place them in our mouths. The circle of life must continue. I bit into the softness of the egg as I watched my mother, father, brothers and sisters do the same, and I had to admit to a certain feeling of comfort. Zayde was no longer with us, that was true. But here we all were eating eggs together just as we did almost every morning, in the same way that the sun would rise from the gray of dawn each day. Each day no matter what. I washed down the yellow green yolk with a glass of sweet tea.

As the men went into the living room to pray, more neighbors slowly filtered into the house to pay their respects. Each person stopped in front of Mama and, as was the custom, said a prayer in order to comfort her. A group of about ten women encircled her, encouraging her to eat and drink, for the sake of her children if not herself. And before long, I was even able to catch the hint of a smile wash across her face as she munched on a thick slice of buttered *challah*.

The children, as they are inclined to do, took the time as an opportunity to play hide-and-seek amongst the rooms, and eventually their laughter and squeals drew *Tata* out of his prayers and into the kitchen. Adjusting his eyes to the light, he turned his massive head to each of the four corners until his vision suddenly fell on my youngest brother, Kalman.

"Is this a party, or what? Do you think this is a playtime for you and your friends?" Kalman remained as if glued in the corner, pushing his chin against his chest.

"No."

"No, what?"

"No, *Tata*. Not a party."

"Of course it is not a party. Remember, God sees all. You of all people should know that."

"Yes, *Tata*. I'm sorry, *Tata*."

When *Tata* had left the room, Mama turned her head to the frowning child, beckoning him with one finger. Immediately, he ran to her, and wrapping him in her arms, she kissed each of his brown eyes which were already glistening with tears. I watched as Kalman soaked up the love which emanated from her bosom like a roll takes in the full taste of gravy once dipped inside. As he inclined his head into the pit between her breasts, one could still see the baby he was, in spite of the fact that in just over a year he was to be a Bar Mitzvah, and already he had begun to accompany *Tata* to the front pews of the *shul.*

"*Kind, kind,*" Child, child, Mama now murmured, as she often would, smiling down at him from her place with us on the balcony as Kalman glanced already with envy at the frills of the woven *tallit*, the prayer shawls, to the right and left of him. He lifted his head, finally, and again I could see the golden brown curls dance across his forehead, the crinkle of a smile appear in the corners of his eyes, the almost too perfectly etched face; a beautiful child foreshadowed the man he would one day become. Kalman. The youngest boy, the last to be a Bar Mitzvah. But a whole year to wait. Yet–in a year, who knows what could happen?

I couldn't find my shoes. I had spent all morning looking for them, in the closets, under the sofa, behind the cartons of Passover dishes, in *Tata's* armoire where he hung the *tallit* even. I had questioned my sisters, asked Mama if she had perhaps borrowed them or lent them to someone, all in vain. More than anything in the world, I hated losing things. I grew frantic, began tossing scarves, books, trinkets into the middle of the floor. Beads of sweat fell like raindrops from my brow, I ran from room to room, my eyes darted north, south, west, east, back to north again. I forgot how to sit. I forgot how to speak. I screamed. In short, the search had demonized me altogether.

Mama came running in. Laying her eyes on the demolition in front of her, her hands flew to her head.

"Blimala, what have you done?"

"My shoes, Mama. The new ones *Tata* gave me for Helen's wedding. The blue silk with the little white bow and the skinny heels.

I can't find them. I've looked everywhere, and I can't find them at all!" I threw my hands up into air and fell back into the bed, utterly desolate.

Mama shook her head and gave me a sad look.

"Blima, I am surprised at you. Over shoes you go so crazy?" she said, stooping to pick up a pink striped scarf.

"But you know how I hate to lose things. And how I always, always have everything in its place. It's Adele and Brandl who–"

"I know all that, many times I know it," Mama sighed, impatience creeping into her voice, "But I also know how smart you are. When you lose something, you must think and don't go running and screaming. You just sit down calmly and think." She picked up a heavy dictionary from the corner of the room and handed it to me.

"Fine," I said, returning the book to its place on the shelf, "But it matches the dress so nicely, and besides, *Tata* had to order it special, and–"

"And so? *Tata* can order again. You go to the store and look in the catalog, and he can order again. Besides, you will find the shoes before that. We are not looking for a needle here, but shoes. Blima, Blima, this is your worry? Better to worry about other things."

"Very well. You're right. They have to be here someplace," I answered, trying to restore a sense of calm to my voice. As I stooped to retrieve the rest of the shoes and skirts scattered on the floor, I thought about the "other things" Mama said we had to worry about. Sickness. The family businesses. The Nazis in the streets. Neatly folding a kerchief and placing it on a closet shelf, I shut my mind to all that. I thought it best to worry about the shoes instead.

That night, I turned slowly as Mama drew chalk lines across the bottom of my new dress. I still hadn't found the shoes, but was wearing a pair of Adele's new spring ones which had the same type of heel. Mama hummed Jewish melodies as she worked.

"Mama, do you think this neckline makes my bust look too big?"

She looked up exasperated, and just shook her head. Satisfied, finally, she placed her tape measure in an apron pocket and stood up. Wiping her hands on the apron, she brusquely pulled up the shoulders of the dress and gave the scalloped neckline a yank.

"*Zaya shein*," she murmured to herself then stooped down again with a bunch of pins in her mouth. Mama looks round and small, I thought, as she labored at my knees. Like the childhood teddy bear I kept in my closet and secretly pulled out during heavy rainstorms. Her bust was full, her hips ample, and stretched over all was the whitest skin, untroubled by the brown sprinkles which I had inherited from God knows where. In character, though, we were alike, at least I hoped so. We never walked, but ran as if pursued by time. We embraced rarely, but when we did it was with a spontaneous surge of emotion, like a waterfall. People sometimes said I looked like her, but I didn't think so. Her bright eyes danced under sparse brown brows, but they gleamed brown, not a dull blue like my own. And they crinkled in the corners like fallen leaves when she laughed, which was often. Her nose was strong and average, but her smile, though thin-lipped, was always full and genuine between cheeks that glowed brick red without even a touch of rouge. Mama's hair, when not pushed beneath the *sheitel*, fell straight chestnut and vibrant to her shoulders when she loosened it at night. Her maturity gave her an aura of beauty which none of her daughters, not even Adele, could touch. Of course, she didn't realize it at all. She never even looked in a mirror.

Ruschia walked over to assess my outfit. She circled me appraisingly.

"*Shein!*" she exclaimed, kissing the tips of her fingers. She made me feel good. Ruschia always told the truth.

"And the bust?" I asked, giving the neckline another yank.

"A little cleavage is good too. At least you got," she laughed, handing Chanusha a coloring book. Ruschia was sweet. No, she was more than that. She was wise too. She, Victor, and the girls had formed a habit of visiting our home at least twice a week, so it was that she became as a sister to us. Well, actually, she had always been a part of the family before she even married my brother. Ruschia and her sister Sophie were our second cousins, and when they lost their parents it was only natural that a marriage be arranged between Ruschia and the eldest cousin. Mama and *Tata* had to sign the permission certificate, being Ruschia was only fourteen. I was glad no one had arranged a marriage for me, although I secretly hoped I could one day love Smulke, who was tall, blonde, and perfect, the way that Victor and Ruschia loved each other.

"Let's hope they will be married," Ruschia murmured, almost to herself.

"What?"

"Just a minute." She finished writing Chanusha's name with a purple crayon.

"Your friends. Helen and her gentleman. I hope they can have their wedding."

"What are you saying? Why would they not marry?" I asked, growing agitated.

"Well...Look, Blimala, I do not mean to frighten you, but you know how it's been lately. In the streets, in the stores, and how they look, make eyes, and laugh when we go into the synagogue even. And that Hitler, well, you can read the papers for what he says about us. It is just...just hard for us now, that's all I mean." She turned back to the coloring book and stared some seconds at it, as if to find meaning in the pages.

"Well, I just don't believe it is as bad as all that," I retorted, moving uneasily on the pedestal until Mama, pins in her mouth, shot me a cross look.

"You know of my friend Rifka and her beau, don't you?," Ruschia said dully, "The laughing and name-calling was bad enough, but when the two were exiting the synagogue first time as man and wife, one of the *gonifs* snatched Moishe's hat right off his head.

Then another had the audacity to step on Rifka's train that her mother made from her own hands. I didn't see, but heard, that an egg flew at them from God knows where. Fortunately, it missed. I tell you, Blima, these are uncertain times now. Just so you know."

"So it is, Ruschia, but a name is just a name. And what is a hat or an egg? For the foolish ways of idiots we should stop our lives? Run to England, to America?" I shot back, "This is not for me. I'm not ready to give up my life just yet." I looked down at Mama who rose from her work with a look of something I couldn't quite make out. Removing the pins from her mouth, she eyed her handiwork intently.

"Let's pray to God everything will be okay."

From the armchair, Ruschia looked up at her mother-in-law, searching her face.

"Mama," she asked, "Do you think it will be okay? I mean everyday they taunt us more, everyday they restrict us more. There are even rumors they are grabbing Jews from the streets. Do you really think it will be okay?" Mama smiled at her benevolently.

"I believe in God. I have to believe."

In the months since Zayde's death, Mama had been troubled each night by dreams in which he came to her, his hands open, imploring like a beggar. So real was the phantasm that she would sometimes wake in the middle of the night and run to his room and check the bed. In the morning, she would place coins in the dusty *pishka* which, since Zayde's death, had been placed on top of the refrigerator for charity. But still, the next night he was there again.

Mama helped me down from the pedestal. Suddenly, we were shocked upright as a high-pitched whine shot through the air. It took only about a minute for us to realize what it was, and we ran into the kitchen. The golden-haired Masha lay coiled on the windowsill and between screeches was furiously licking the residual frost off the window. She had taken to these screeches of late, some-times at dawn or just as the darkness would descend, and no one could quite figure it out. She had left Zayde's bed soon after his death and spent most of her days at one window or another send-ing up these desperate whines, no... cries, really. They sounded much like human cries.

It was useless to tempt her with food, even her adored tuna, and she only yowled louder if we tried to get her to go outdoors. Perceiving it was useless, we left her. Eventually, she stopped.

My feet had begun to hurt in Adele's shoes. I hurried toward the bedroom to remove them along with the dress so Mama could begin the sewing, but just before I turned into the hallway, I was stopped by something. In the parlor sat my father in a high-backed upholstered chair. He was reading the paper and frowning beneath small gold-wired spectacles; the curls of his black beard brushed the page. On the floor stretched out to his left were Kalman and Brandl playing a game of checkers. Brandl smiled in a mischievous way as Kalman, twisting a lock of hair, pondered his next move. Sitting on the couch with a big bowl of purple grapes between them were Victor and Ephraim, arguing as usual over a point of business. Victor, always easy-going, would laugh as Ephraim would jump up with wild gesticulations and bend toward his brother in an attempt to use his height to enforce a point. Underneath a giant window with emerald green drapes was Adele, who had just learned to knit, and was lost in concentration over a stitch in a winter sweater she was creating for one of Miriam's children. Seated on the gold brocade chair, every so often she patted her thick black hair swept elegantly in a chignon, her dark brows lifted imperiously over long dark lashes. She looked like a queen. On the little end table where she laid her rolls of blue yarn was a black and white photo of Miriam, her two children, Adele, Brandl and myself taken in front of the house last summer. Over all, above *Tata's* chair, a portrait of his great-grandfather, dressed in black with beard down to the waist, surveyed us all somberly.

"Blimala," *Tata* motioned to me, "turn on the light." The lamp, one of three in the room, was covered by a tiffany shade decorated with apricots and oranges. Switched on, it cast a stream of pale yellow light into the room. And for a moment, just a moment, I felt myself suspended in its ray. I floated, led by the light, into the room where the others, my family, formed a classic tableau. How neat, I thought, how ordered my life is. All in place as it should be. I let the light seep into my brain, circle and warm it. When I turned toward the bedroom, the dots of light danced before me.

I removed the dress, hung it on a padded hanger, and sat down on the bed. Masha padded quietly in, mewing softly. I picked up the cat and stroked her slowly on my lap. My eyes carefully taking in each corner of the room, I resigned myself to the loss of the shoes.

Betty

I have new shoes. They are white with black polka dots and a small red bow. They have high heels of maybe two inches. I bought them at the Florsheim on 13th Avenue, so I think it was a good price at fifty percent off for going out of business. I wear them with the black skirt I have with the red circles on the bottom, and I don't look like such a *greenhorn*.

My daughter, Shirley, is playing in the front with her friend, Susie. They play the hopscotch, and Susie sometimes takes my daughter to teach her jumping rope. It is still sunny now, but soon Chiel will be back from his work at the factory. It is good that he works again, but he is never happy. He does not like working for somebody. He wants to be his own boss. Okay, I tell him, so I can go to work also, and that way we can save for a piece of business. Just like when we first come here in '48. The neighbor, Rhoda, already said she will watch my daughter, no problem. But he is so stubborn! Ah well, he is a man. He wants to do everything himself, and wants no help from Victor, who owns his own business, or Kalman who will be owning and managing a boarding house after the marriage. I really think he does not want me to work because I make more money than him. When we lived in Manhattan with Victor and Ruschia, Mr. Silverstein paid me seventy dollars a week. Two months later and he is paying me one hundred and twenty so fast are my hands. He said it was worth it for a good worker of coats, which I am. I told him I learned this at the camps, but my English was not yet so good. Mr. Silverstein said it didn't matter about my

English, and he knows Yiddish, anyway. Chiel is a good worker at
the uniform factory too, but not so good as I am.

Chiel comes home, and Shirley jumps into his arms. He is
Shirley's favorite I know because she stays on his knee all the night
and tells him what she did in the daytime. Her Yiddish is perfect,
but more and more she is answering us in the English which she
learns from her friends. She knows more than me already, but it
is harder to learn when one is older. Besides, is she not a true
American citizen? Is that not the reason why we waited three years
to see her born?

"Guess who I saw today?" says Chiel, taking off his jacket.

"I cannot think, who?"

"Yaacov, from the *lager*. You remember, the friend I smuggled
some pots for. I never knew he is living right here in Borough Park!
He fell upon me crying like a *meshugana*, saying if not for me he
would not be here. Thank God, and all of that."

I put some pieces of chicken and fried potatoes with some
applesauce on Chiel's plate first. Then I cut up a small piece for
Shirley to take with the applesauce. She will not finish, and the last
few pieces I will have to put in her mouth. For me, I like the bones.
I never throw anything away.

"How many such people you run into already, Chiel?" I say, sitting down last, "They all love you because you are a hero."

"What, hero! It was wartime, and I was just doing what I could.
I am a man, that's all."

"Well," I say nibbling the meat off of a tender drumstick, "in
this house I think you are a hero, anyway."

After dinner, Chiel puts on the television, and we watch Perry
Como. I love him the best, and sometimes when I am cleaning, I
even sing *"Hot diggity, dog diggity, ooh what you do to me. It's so new
to me!"* Shirley laughs when I do that. Or sometimes I will sing
*"Sugar in the morning, sugar in the evening, sugar at suppertime. Be my
little sugar, and love me all the time."* That one is from the sisters on

Lawrence Welk. At night, when I put Shirley in the bed she likes to hear the *leedles*, the songs from home. She is listening to *Shein Vidala Voona* and the other lullabies since before she had one hair. I think that is why she is a singer. She is such a talent!

While he watches Como, Chiel sits down with his notebook and does his homework for the next evening. Since he is in the English school, he is learning so many words! He can even write many sentences about whatever he wants. Sometimes, he reads them to me because I am just reading the *Forward*, and that is not much of a help. He writes: *"I have a little daughter named Shirley. I love her very much. When I come home from work, she gives me a kiss. I am happy to see her."* His English is so good!

After he is finished, he takes Shirley on his knee again and asks her to sing for him. She jumps up and waves her arms like a real singer. She sings, *"Oh, my Papa, to me you are so wonderful..."* which she hears from Eddie Fisher, *"Not one could be so gentle and so lovable... Oh, my Papa, to me you are so good!"* Shirley says Eddie Fisher is handsome, but not so handsome as her daddy. We clap our hands, and Shirley does a little dance.

I am so lucky to have her, especially because she has the name of my mother, *Shaindel*, which of course is *Shirley* in America. Even from the beginning, she was a beauty. Her head was perfectly oval because she was born from a Caesarian section. Only Ruschia knew about my maybe needing a cut before Shirley was born, but she was always quiet because she did not want to scare me. Well, I am happy the baby was that way because she was perfect and pink. But she cried a lot, and still she does. Thank God Ruschia helped me during those first few months! Chiel always says, *"a maidel fiert da reidel"* or, a girl spins the wheel of children in a household. He says that, but doubts we can afford another.

I look at my daughter bouncing up and down for her father, and I can see almost all her straight red hair has turned a blonde. It is too short to put in a braid or a ponytail yet like Chiel's youngest sister used to wear. Chiel thinks she looks most like her, and I tell her this even though we have no pictures. I think she will look like an angel with the hat she will wear that is shaped like a heart for Kalman's wedding. Shirley sings the song over and over again. Somebody wants to put her on the radio, even. But I think she is too tied to me to do it.

Finally, Chiel stands up and sweeps our daughter into his arms. He kisses her cheeks and pinches her behind.

"You are the best!" I say to her.

Later, after I bathe her, I am sitting on the couch unraveling a new spool of white thread to fix a hole in Shirley's anklet. I tell Chiel about the chicken farm Victor and Ruschia are thinking of buying in Lakewood, New Jersey.

"Maybe we will go there for something too," I say.

"Maybe," he murmurs, settling into his armchair.

This is good, I think. Now I wonder what he will say when I tell him I am pregnant.

Blima

It was spring on the last day I saw my mother. I was returning home early from Tante Rachel's bakery, another day when even to run the ovens and overhead lights didn't make opening worthwhile for all the meager business that was taken in. Wishing not to let the goods go to waste, Tante had sent me home with armfuls of brown rolls and still warm loaves of raisin bread. I could smell the full raisin-scented sweetness as it mingled with the fragrance of newly-cut grass. It was the first day when one could say with some certainty that the new season had arrived, after months of biting cold where sidewalks had deceived the unwary with paper-thin sheets of glaze underfoot. How I longed to remove my old blue woolen coat, but I simply lacked the agility to carry it and keep the breads intact. Besides, I could already see the concrete stoop and little patch of grass which signaled home. I quickened my pace.

From here, everything goes. I think I heard the sound of boots from behind. I think I felt the narrow patch of air, someone's breathing sliding down my neck like a black veil. I think I saw a flash, a car and then the clowns, so many clowns, emerge like the flickering of a Keystone Cops movie. Only then I became a part of the crazy film, and my arms, my legs, were no longer mine, and I am lifted. Lifted away by a will stronger than mine. Mama. Mama in slow motion. She is on the stoop in her blue apron with the birds, her hair wrapped with a white cotton kerchief. Her hands fly to her head and out into the stiff air. "BLIMA!" she calls. She is running. "BLIMA!" But I am flying through the air in someone else's body. A package rolls soundless. The delicious scent of spring which had encircled me only a moment ago has vanished, replaced by the stench of raisins which now bores into my skull like bullets. I turn my head. I see her. "BLIMA!" The stoop fades–the sidewalk. "BLIMA!" My senses go numb as the Gestapo push me into the wagon where others, with bowed heads, wait. "BLIMA!" Only the sense of hearing remains. I see the hands–her hands? The blue apron with the birds chasing after me. Only the hearing remains. "BLIMA!" The kerchief becomes a cloud, and the birds soon fade from the sky. "BLIMA!" Her hands reaching out. So close. Is this when the past became the present? Or did the present become the past? All the yesterdays frozen in one moment to be repeated again and again. All the todays swallowed up by the past, the only reality. Nothing else matters. I turn again and see only the trees thickening in the distance. "BLIMA!" And then the nightmare begins.

Betty

I am in a pool so blue like the color of my own eyes. I look and look, but I cannot see the end of it. Like an ocean, but with all kinds of people jumping and swimming and talking all together. They do not speak slowly, so I cannot understand what they say. But some of the women in the flowered bathing suits smile as they walk by. All of the children smile at me. Children always smile.

America has so many hotels! Chiel says it is too hot for going to Coney Island. I don't think so. I like to go on the boardwalk, and we take Shirley and Jackie on the rides. The slow rides are very good for them, and Chiel and I stand and watch our children in the seats next to each other. Jackie is only four and on a small rollercoaster which is faster than I would like, but he is not scared. He puts up his hands and waves them, and I yell, "Hold on, Jackie! Hold on!" But Shirley holds him good, and makes a face. She is a *"boyak,"* a scared one, like me. When they come off the ride, Jackie is laughing, his round face like a balloon. Shirley still does not smile, but takes Chiel's hand and wants to go. Shirley looks like a real *Americana* now, with the red Wrangler shorts and a red and white plaid shirt with ruffles above the belly button. I put the red bow on her ponytail, so everything is a match. She wants clothes everyday, like a model. She asks Chiel and he says okay. Not me. I think she will not know the worth of a penny even.

We go then for knishes. On the boardwalk you can get every kind of knish you want, not just potato. Jackie eats a blueberry one, Chiel and Shirley take cherry cheese or even with the pineapple, and for me, I like the kasha. After everybody eats, and Jackie usually has another one, we go for the ice cream that we have to eat fast. I need plenty tissues to clean up Jackie's face. He wrinkles up the nose and moves around, but I put some spit on the tissue and wipe his face clean. Then we take the D line back to Brownsville. When we get home, we put the fans on again, and the children take a cool bath. I have to put the lotion on Shirley and Jackie. Shirley likes to get red like her outfit, but she does not like so much the burn. She never listens. In the nighttime, the white sheets are so cool like an ice pop next to the skin. I close my eyes and hear only the whirring song of the fan in the window. I recognize the melodies it sings. They are from my home.

But here in this Normandy Hotel, it is so different! All of the hotels in the Catskills are like this, with air conditioning in the lobbies and even in the rooms. On the walls there are even pictures of fancy people riding in carriages. All around, if you want to buy, there is plenty. You can buy the makeup which I do not wear, except for the lipstick. Or you can buy very fancy costume jewelry, like Chiel used to sell in Lakewood. They have pins like ducks and spiders, and even tigers with green stones for the eyes. If you want a beautiful satin scarf, you can get the fanciest in light pink with blue horses on them, or even a gold one with orange stripes. Some people even buy bathing suits, and I don't know why they would not just bring one from home and save the money. Chiel says he wants to buy here a short terrycloth jacket, but I say it is too much. He has plenty towels in the hotel.

Also, you don't have to worry about eating here. They put Chiel and me at a big round table with dishes of pickles, peppers, and sauerkraut. They put out the challahs and the rye breads then you read from the menu so big like a sign. You say what you want to the waiter, and he brings enough for the whole table. If you do not like the goulash, he will bring you the salmon. If you finish the salmon, he will bring you a whole other one. Who can eat, then, the desserts of éclairs and big chocolate cakes? But some people have eyes bigger than the mouths. The waiter and the busboy *kibbutz* with you like they are friends. The people at the big table also kibbutz even though they are strangers. Most of the people are *landsmen* from home, and some are rabbis with the beards. Soon, Jackie comes back from the dining room special for children, but Shirley most times stays with us. After we get up slowly with full stomachs, we walk a little under the trees. Then there is a big show with some singing.

I think my lilac flowered one-piece bathing suit is nice just like the ones they have in the store. It has good cups that hold me up and do not show too much. The silky part even covers the tops of my legs, which is good because even though Chiel says I have pretty legs, he does not like the men to look on me. The big flowers with the twirling white stems are blue, almost the same like the pool.

Here, in this pool, I am not so much afraid. I can go step by step, but the water is so like ice that my skin lifts up when I take every step. I wait a long time until the ice melts and I am in the water just up to the waist. Chiel is holding Jackie's two hands, and Jackie is laughing and kicking. Maybe he will be a swimmer, but Chiel and I are not. I am too afraid, but in this water I can walk and soon it is like a mattress, very cool. I fix the white rubber cap on my head to make sure my ears are covered. Then, like the other women, I dunk just to the shoulders. Aah, this is the best.

I call to Shirley, but she shakes her head. She is still sitting on the side of the pool, with one toe in the water. I wave to her.

"Shoiley, *kim aran!* Come in!" She shakes her head. "No, I will take my time. You go ahead, Ma." She likes to answer me always in English now. I think she is forgetting the Yiddish. I turn away from her, but do not see Chiel and Jackie, the pool is that big. Now I am completely comfortable. I walk a little bit and dunk again. "Aah," I say, motioning to a woman with puffy yellow hair not yet wet. She nods her head, smiles with wide red lips, and keeps walking. The heavy water pushes against my legs as I walk, and when I look down, I can see my toes in the blueness. I dunk a few more times, splashing the water on my face. All the people look cloudy now, and I see one thing not too far away. It is a white twisted rope that is so long it stretches from one side of the pool to the other. I put my hand on it. Then, I lean against the rope so that I can dunk again. But instead of holding me, the rope pulls me down under the water. Water fills my eyes and sneaks up my nose, and I stand, coughing. But the rope pulls me down again. I push harder on it so I can stand, but I squint and close my mouth this time as I go under again. I push on the rope to stand, three, four times. But every time I go down until I feel myself drowning with all the people standing and laughing around me. Up again, I open my eyes wide, but nobody sees me. I go under and under. And then I feel a hand on my arm pulling me up and away from the rope. I stand up and take a deep breath. When I rub the clouds of water from my eyes, I see my daughter. My Shirley.

Blima

I am walking in the snow. The girl in front of me falls, and I bend to pick her up, linking my arm through hers. "*Shnell!*" someone yells, and we quicken our pace. Although I can no longer feel my hands, I push a strand of hair covered with spurs off of my eyes. I walk.

The sun pierces a path of bright yellow for us through the forest, and we follow it. At times, I feel we are ascending into the heart of the sun itself, without thought, hearts beating, feet always moving. It must be past noon now, for I can see the remnants of the heavy snow we endured over winter have begun to melt, leaving tired limp circles around emerging twigs. I wonder briefly what has happened to the sweet scent of spring I felt only moments before, but then the thought melts quietly like a snowflake. Some of the girls have begun bending and plucking the buds quickly, out of the watchful eyes of the soldiers. They push the bits of green into their mouths then munch slowly, eyes on the yellow path. Never do they miss a step. I forget the round white potatoes and warm *cholent* from my mother's table, and think only of my empty yearning stomach and how delectable those green buds look.

"You," I whisper to the girl whose arm is linked in mine, "I will get us some of those twigs right there. Do you think you can walk alone for a moment?" She lets her head fall in a nod of sorts then opens her mouth to speak, but only a dry cough comes out. Then, she looks me full in the face and I can see she is just a girl of no more than sixteen or seventeen. I slowly disentangle my arm from hers, keeping up the steady march. When I see her steps are in line with the rest, I lower myself and allow my arm to brush across a patch of fledgling twigs, and like a swooping bird, gather them into my hand. I link my arm in the girl's again and press a few of the twigs into her hand.

"Eat," I whisper. And the two of us consume our precious snack, tough and covered in dirt, as if it were a marvelous slice of honey cake.

Somewhere, a shot rings out. It is the third time we have heard the sound since beginning our march. But already we have learned not to stiffen or cry out, having witnessed the butt of a rifle slapped across an older woman's back for doing just that. So instead, we let the ripple of what—astonishment, fear, disbelief—ascend through our own bodies as we keep walking. Imperceptible ripples within mortals moving forward like a muddy river.

It is dark now and, forgetting, I look next to me so that I can link my arm through Adele's for warmth. Hanging onto my elbow instead is a sad piece of flesh that was once a woman. I am tired too but I walk. Now, it is all I know.

I remember yesterday. It seemed like hours that I had been sitting next to the soldier to my left and a girl, a phantom at first, to my right. Heeding my twin brother's warning, I kept my eyes riveted to the floor of the car, strewn with pieces of tissue and cigarette butts. As the cold metal of the soldier's black Lugar pressed against my hip, I was grateful only that I still wore the coat covering my body, my eternal shame. I swallowed the wad of saliva long stuck in my throat, and tried not to think, to numb my senses, as my mother's screams become indistinguishable from the sirens which blared now from every direction.

Only once in my life had I been on a train, perhaps when I was but five or six, just when the stamp of memory begins to take hold. It was on a trip to Berlin with my father, for some business.

A new inventory of shoes perhaps. I remember the exhilarating rush of wind as we poured into the car with the others, all fine people dressed in hats of black fur and carrying mysterious leather briefcases. When I fell into the soft fleece seat I felt like a queen in the throne as *Tata* patted my knee in a familiar way, and the conductor punching our ticket winked at me and asked in a most charming manner if this was my first trip. I settled back into my throne and watched the lush landscape as it drifted lazily past my window...

"*Aruf!*" the commandant ordered as we climbed up into the train, although this vehicle bore no resemblance to the locomotive of my memories. No plush seats or avuncular conductors would appear on my second trip into the hinterland. These vehicles, I soon realized, were only cattle cars with frightened figures, all women, huddled in each corner of the wooden box. Women once flattered by men who stepped aside when they entered a room. Girls adored by a Mama and *Tata* who tucked them securely into bed each night. No, no longer women. Now, each one of us was a Jew. And that, we would soon find out, meant we were less than animals.

Only when enough of us had filled the space until, I think, it could hold no more, and we heard the last "*Aruf!*" the last "*Shnell!*" did we allow ourselves, finally, to exhale. The door creaked abruptly shut.

I was clinging to a protruding wooden beam in one corner, praying I would not faint, when I heard my name called.

"Blima? Blima Weisstuch, is that you?" I turned to the mass of women in front of me, but was unable to find the source of the meek voice.

"Blima...Straight in front. It is me, Clara. Your schoolmate from the *gimnasium*. Rebbetzin Linbraum's class?" I saw a skinny arm emerge from the amorphous crowd, and I grasped it firmly, pulling it toward me.

"Clara. Do you know me? Clara Reitman from Dombrowe," she announced, a hint of a smile flickering briefly across her face.

I looked into the eyes of my friend and immediately recognized the phantom who had been sitting next to me on the ride to the station.

"Clara? Why, I–"

"I knew you did not recognize me with the hair," she said, reaching up to touch a crown of blonde curls, "Colored it last year, you know. And the baby fat, well, that is gone now too!" she added, patting her flattened stomach.

"You though, Blima, look exactly the same as when we sat next to each other in the seventh year class...It *is* good to see you!"

She inclined her head toward mine, and whispered conspiratorially, "I noticed you right away when they pulled you in, but I dared not say, you know...the guns."

I nodded. It was good to see an old friend from home, and I clasped her to me like a sister.

"Do you have any idea where they are taking us?"

No, I shook my head as I bit into my lower lip, regretting every time I closed my ears to the warnings, regretting for the hundredth time that day, my own willful blindness. Clara touched my hand, "Don't fret over it. They would have taken us no matter what."

Had she heard of others, like ourselves, being captured? Had there been correspondence with families? Clara, it seemed, was as blind as I had been.

"No one I know, of course. And certainly no one from Dombrowe." But she had heard stories of girls grabbed off the streets, as we had been, or from inside shops, schools, even hospitals. Was there word? No one knew. It was difficult, almost impossible, to hear of news within the town. And no one knew, of course, if the Semitic-looking man standing on line behind you for a loaf of bread was really a traitor. And the other towns? They might as well have been across the Atlantic for all we knew.

After one hour, or perhaps two, the train screeched to a halt, and those sitting against the walls of the car felt their bodies and hearts move upward simultaneously as all eyes stared intently at the door.

"*Shnell! Mach shnell!*" The barks reached our ears even before the doors ground open. Hopes of an arrival at a destination, wherever that might have been, or better yet, a rest stop, were dashed as another twenty or so women rushed into our car.

"Where do we go now? There is no more room!" came the desperate cry from the rear. A Nazi hoisted himself on board like an ominous beetle.

"*Vas?*" he demanded, brandishing a silver pistol. No one dared speak. He stood some minutes peering into the crowd as, heads bowed, we squeezed tighter against each other. Although my German was faltering at best, I knew enough to discern his next words as a threat. The car, if we liked, could be made lighter by a few at this very moment. Then in my head, right behind my ear, I heard the echo of my own voice and a horrifying realization. *He is liking this.*

As he spoke, my eyes froze only on the pairs of shoes moving toward me. High buttoned. Brown. Leather boots. Alligator. Chunky wooden heels. Maroon with fur trim. Where had these shoes been headed before ending up here on the dirty straw-laden floor of a cattle car?

And then, a word.

"*Bitte, capitan...mine boach..*" Please, captain, my stomach. A black Lugar rises into the air and shivers briefly. A sound pierces the car and we women move up as one body. For a moment I feel, impossibly, that we are going to fly upward. If only. There is a scream only from the speaker who falls against some of the others in the back. The rest of us are silent.

I dared not look at the fallen woman, but kept my eyes to the ground. Some minutes later, I heard movement, a shuffling of feet, as a few of the others propped her body in a corner. I glimpsed her shoes, high-buttoned, a scuffed oxford brown. The German bellowed an animalistic note of triumph next to me, and I could feel his putrid breath against my cheek.

Don't faint now, Blima, I thought to myself. Blima, don't faint.

✣ ✣ ✣

Not knowing is perhaps the worst thing which can befall a person. To know a thing for a certainty even if it is tragic brings a sense of doneness, a sense of peace. But not knowing slithers into the heart like a silent snake making every blood vessel quiver with anxiety. Today I know where I am. But tomorrow? Last week I was standing in my mother's kitchen peeling potatoes as she placed them into a pot of boiling water, one by one. Yesterday, the same hands were reaching out to me as I sped away in a car to the place where I am today. But where exactly is that place? And where is my mother? Will I know my way home back to her? Is she even at home? Am I to be lost forever? Perhaps it is best not to think at all.

I have been walking since we left the train some hours ago, I know not how many. My thoughts keep returning to the high-button brown oxfords and even though I never knew her, I can feel the tears coming into my throat. I squelch them for I know already the cost of crying. Instead, I focus on the ice land which stretches in its monotony ahead of me as well as behind. An ice land, still barely touched by spring, whose barren tree limbs fold amongst themselves like white spider webs as we obedient flies push on below.

I have lost Clara, but already I feel her presence somewhere in the forest behind me. I keep moving my feet and learn to forget the gnawing pain in my belly that is hunger. The twigs which have supplied us with nourishment up until now have vanished as I believe we draw closer to our destination. Every so often a woman falls. She is either shot or remains there on the ground with no child's hand to stroke her forehead, no comforting words of *kaddish* for family. My companion on this interminable tread was one of those. So I ignore again the biting hunger which grips me now and then. I only know to move forward.

At last there is a clearing, and I hear a soundless sigh of relief, not for reaching who knows what, but for at last being able to stop. I see the sign as we rush through barbed wire with spotlights and guard dogs and Germans, sentinels on all sides. What are they afraid of? A group of women with withered bones and empty spirits? The sign says "Grunberg." It is as I thought. A forced labor camp somewhere in Poland. I am a prisoner and the year is 1941.

I stand in front of a German woman commandant who doesn't smile. Without a word, she peels my blue coat off my body as I hurriedly tug the watch off my wrist and pull on the simple gold chain on my neck until it breaks. Quietly, I thank God that it is not summer, so the small diamond ring Smulke gave me only last year slides easily off my finger. Those who are not so lucky must endure the barks of the soldiers as the pathetic women struggle removing a ring from a swollen finger. I toss these possessions onto a growing mountain of valuables. That is the least of my problems I think as I am pushed along to a table where another female guard, also without a word, grasps my arm and quickly tattoos a five-digit number on it. I smile inwardly. So now I am no longer Blima, but a number. Can it be that Hitler's plan for the towns to become "Judenrein," free of Jews, has actually come to be?

But I have little time for speculation as I am pushed on again, my hair severely shaved, my pink cashmere sweater and woolen plaid skirt changed for a white blouse and black skirt bigger than I by two sizes. Somewhere in all this I lose my shoes. On my feet are wooden soles with pieces of canvas stretched across, coverings really, and also two sizes too big. I move on.

Finally, and it can only be thanks to God, we are placed in small bunks filled with straw. There are perhaps fifty of these in the barracks, and I find myself in the middle one. I glimpse the girl below, only a few years younger than I. She is hyperventilating, and when I see her arm extend, I reach out and encircle her wrist with my hand. She begins to cry silently. *"Mama, ve bist du?"* she whispers, calling for her mother. I squeeze the wrist and have not the strength to do more. We have all lost our mothers here.

It is black in the barracks except for the bright yellow beam which periodically shoots through the small windows and sprays the room with light. We sleep, but our dreams are restless and troubled. Always my mother is running after me, arms outstretched, always the SS pulling her back, pushing me forward. Her screams waft through the limpid air and encircle me. "Blima!" she sobs relentlessly until I awake.

Battling the sleep from my tired eyes, I hear her, yet it is no longer my mother's voice which calls my name, but another.

"Blima! Are you sleeping?"

I look up and see only another head with brown stubs bobbing above. But the voice is a familiar one.

"Clara?...Is that you?"

"Yes, Blima, I thought it was you I saw before, but I was too afraid to speak...What luck, no?"

I can hardly retain my joy, but can only emit a fractured sigh.

"I slept so until I thought I would never get up. But, I don't know, I am afraid to sleep, afraid to be awake. What time do you think it is now? Those bastards took the one gold watch I had from my girlhood. And then, of course," Clara's voice cracks here, "the hair... Why would they take the hair, Blima?"

"Lice, I think," I answer, touching my own shorn scalp. I peer through the window on my left only to view pitch blackness, and I think even hell has its fires.

"Perhaps it is one or two in the morning, I don't know," I answer.

"They will wake us in a few hours as soon as one stream of light comes through the horizon, so we'd best get to sleep."

"Clara?"

"Yes, Blima?"

"How do you know, I mean do you know what is to happen to us? Besides the hair, there are the numbers..."

I could feel shifting above as Clara moved to a sitting position.

"There are others here who know. Do you remember Sala and Annie from the *gimnasium*? I was walking with them in that damned forest. They have received news of others in these camps. It is not so bad as long as you are willing to work. They told me, in fact, that they came voluntarily." Voluntarily? This was not to be believed.

"No, Clara. How can that be? You saw with your own eyes that woman on the train. People dropping like flies on the ground..."

"I tell you, Blima, that this will be a paradise compared to the uncertainty of staying home. Who knows what is in store for the others?" I wasn't sure what Clara meant, but I didn't want to think about it then.

"Clara, what do you mean we will be okay if we work? What kind of work?"

"Any kind. Digging ditches, washing out their pots of sauerbraten, whatever they demand. Remember, when they ask if you can do it, just say yes. Think of nothing else."

I hear Clara stretch out on the straw and know that I will soon hear the steady breathing of her sleep.

She spoke of not knowing what was to be back home. Not knowing. The not knowing can tear someone apart, Mama would say when *Tata* would arrive home too late from the *shul* or Rabbi Perrinsky would keep Kalman an extra hour for Haftorah study. I turn in my bed hoping to turn away too from the thoughts of home which plague me now that I have stopped moving. It is then that I hear the soft crinkling sound from beneath my shirt, and I remember. Thrusting my hand between the binding and the brassiere, I pull out several photos. I spread the small pictures out in front of me. To think I had almost forgotten them! Weeks ago, having heard that the young people were being abducted from the streets, I grabbed the store of family photos which had been in my keeping and placed them each morning beneath the bindings across my chest, close to my heart. Just in case.

I look at them and know that I will look and look again each day that I remain here for however long. Mama always said that when the memories fade, as they surely must, all we have are the pictures. And here they were, all with me again. The four sisters; Adele, Brandl, myself, and Miriam with the children, all smiling in front of Cousin Louis's home in the country. No, Adele as always is not smiling, but gazing up laughing open-mouthed at some secret joke. Another shows Victor, Ruschia, and their sweet cap-haired daughters in formal pose. In still another there is Kalman bundled in a short coat, leaning against the stoop in front of our home. Even the despicable Froyim is there in the photo he admonished me to keep always. I am, for the first time, glad I did. There is also a small photo taken by Brandl, of Hitler himself waving from a car. I search his face for some answer, but seeing none, put it away. I can feel my breathing coming easier now as I gaze over each photo. They are all here. All except Mama and *Tata* who arranged to have pictures of their progeny, never themselves. No matter. Mama's face, they said, was stamped upon my own. And her spirit, I knew, had long been within my heart.

I return the photographs to their hiding place beneath my blouse and push my face into the straw. With the hours till daylight waning, there is but one thing I know for certain in this uncertain world. Tomorrow I must work.

Shirley

My mother could unknot things like nobody else. Things like necklaces and pieces of string. She would just take it in her hands, and the recalcitrant thing that had frustrated me for hours would unknot to a smooth line almost magically. She could also make a thing that looked like a sack fit to perfect proportion with her needle and thread. She always said that everything on me looked great and, eventually, it did.

I knew from the time I could walk that my mother could do that for me, smooth things out. Mommy didn't want me to have a minute of frustration or unhappiness. I didn't realize until many years later that she did it for herself as much as for me. But maybe some of the things she did were a little overboard. Since my first whimper at being alone in bed, I was allowed to sleep with her. How I loved curling my body into the slope of her back and warming my feet against her smooth ankles! Needless to say, my father was not much in favor of this idea. I guess they must have had many arguments, but I never quite got it since they usually spoke in Polish when they didn't want me to understand. Instead of being cajoled back to her marriage bed, my mother would assign my father to the couch. When I was eight, I received a white French Provincial bedroom set, and I would spend many hours at the vanity with a huge mirror which folded back to make it a desk. I would sit long nights looking into the mirrored vanity pretending I was painting the cheeks of my collection of fifteen or so dolls which usually loitered along my dresser, under the bed, and in the corners. My bed, however, remained untouched. I was content, for the next couple of years at least, in the soft space of my mother.

This dependence touched on other areas of my life. Although I was toilet trained at an early age, I still required my mother's assistance in bathroom matters until I was past four. Once I began school, my mother took note of the difficulty I had waking up each morning. After a few minutes of calling me, she would pull off my pajamas (she called them *pashamas*) and dress me for school. Then, as I was still rubbing the sleep from my eyes, she spoon-fed me hot Cream of Wheat. Afterwards, she pushed me into the bathroom, wrapped me in a coat and scarf, handed me my Cinderella lunch-box, and sent me to school. Up until we moved back to Brooklyn, she even accompanied me to school, bundling up my compliant little brother for the walk across the park in Lakewood. When my straight brown hair became long enough, she added braiding to the regimen. She would stand behind me pulling and turning the strands into a smooth, shiny plait. She would pull so tightly on my scalp that often I would return home plagued by a headache. Special occasions when I wore my hair in a ponytail were no better. Nevertheless, I was proud of my hair, which was almost always longer than anyone else's.

Surprisingly, my mother could even help me with schoolwork. My drive to learn English made me a precocious reader, so books were never a problem. But when it came to math, the numbers all seemed determined to float haphazardly in my brain. But Mommy and Daddy were quick with numbers, drilling me again and again, sharpening pencil after pencil. In third grade, cursive handwriting became my nemesis, and my fingers steadfastly refused to adhere to the proper slopes and curves. So, again, Mommy and Daddy would sit on either side pressing their hands on the back of mine as I squinted at the wide-lined paper, tears rolling down my cheeks. Many years later, my mother would remind me of my problems with handwriting, adding, "And see what a good writer you are today!" She could never quite understand the difference between the physical act of writing and writing prose.

All their protection couldn't shield me from illness, though. During kindergarten and first grade, I missed about a third of the year with colds and sore throats. Even if I had a sniffle, I was kept home. This is because my mother would remind me that when I was a toddler, she would stay up day and night with me, for fear that I had polio. She wasn't taking any chances. Once, a doctor urged my mother to have my tonsils removed, a common operation for young children during the '50s. "She has to be in the hospital?" Mommy asked. Then she asked me what I thought. Today, my tonsils give me no problem at all.

Mommy often asked my opinion on what she considered *Americana* affairs. Many Jewish girls are sent to a yeshiva or Hebrew school here. Did I want to go? I attended public school. What about these camps that all the children go to? Sleep away, of course, was out of the question, but after I tried one year of a YWCA day camp, I nixed that too. My parents didn't try to convince me to learn to swim either. I was much too afraid and, besides, neither of them had ever learned. When I objected to taking swimming, a prerequisite for graduation at Erasmus Hall High School, my parents got me doctors' notes which would exempt me from swim class and wearing those horrid bathing suits, a different color for each bra size. For the semester prior to getting my notes, the red of my bathing suit matched the crimson of shame seething inside me. They also agreed when I, at age eleven, insisted that I absolutely was not getting braces on my teeth, in spite of the fact that a canine tooth arrogantly overlapped my front incisor.

While most parents assert that they know what's best for their children, my parents relied on me for the right thing to do. Or maybe they really did know. But if it caused their daughter a moment of anxiety or pain, it simply wasn't considered. Not until I had my own children did I finally admit that I hadn't always known what was best. So, at age forty, I got braces, became a Bat Mitzvah, and learned to swim.

When I was about fourteen, I visited my Aunt Naomi for a week in the country, upstate New York. There, I helped her take care of her two little ones while Uncle Kalman worked weekdays in the city. My cousins, Joey and Shaindee, were little, four and five, and acting like it. It was already the end of my week, and my aunt was packing lunches for my Uncle Kalman to take back with him. Of course, the kids were pestering her. But what she said to them astounded me.

"Your father comes first. I love you, but I love him more, so wait your turn." At the time, I couldn't understand how a mother could love a husband more than her flesh and blood. I just thought children always came first.

But there were times when I didn't get what I wanted. When I would walk in late or become petulant over buying something we could not afford, Daddy would point to his belt. He even used it a few times, like the time I yelled "Shut up!" to my mother. Mommy's wrath was worse, though. She would screech at us and come toward us with both hands swinging. Even though her anger was as intense as a flame, it just as easily extinguished itself. The worst of all was when they would yell at each other, fighting over who would be the one to die first.

But I accepted all of this. What I found most difficult to accept was my mother's asking *me* for help. The first time was when she took her citizenship test. I was only ten, but knew enough to assist her with the names of the Presidents and dates of the battles in the Revolutionary War. On the day of the test, I could see her looking toward me as she struggled with the answers. I wanted to, but I couldn't. I just couldn't help her.

Blima

Four AM. A shrill whistle shocks us awake. We jump down from our cubicles and line up for *appellplatz*, roll call.

"Pinch your cheeks," someone whispers, and word goes down the line. We pinch until it hurts and pray for the tinge we had only days ago to return. When the woman commandant turns to inspect the others, we wait, shoulders back, standing tall. Looking at the girls opposite us, I surmise we are a sorry bunch.

The commandant must be a man, I think, for I find no trace of femininity, no softness in her long face. Her dark hair is cut short and her body is tightly wrapped in a thick coat with gold buttons. In one hand she holds a whip, in the other a leash holding a large German Shepherd she calls Otto. I am amazed that someone took the time to name him when we ourselves are but numbers. As the commandant walks down the line for inspection, I try to glimpse her eyes. But I am unable to discern a color. If steel can be muddied, I decide finally, they are that. Certainly they hold no clue to a soul. When she walks past me, I avert my eyes.

She sits down with the dog beside her and begins to call numbers. I have never memorized mine, and I quickly look down. "44703." The girl, Manya, who has been assigned as our leader pulls out any girl who dawdles. We suppose this is better than facing the whip, for us and for her.

"44703!"

I jump forward as if by a spark and join the others. I don't know if hearing my number is a good thing, but then our group of about twenty-five begins to march toward the main barracks where I can already smell the cooking of bean soup. When we enter, my hopes are born out. I am given a portion of bread and a cup of tasteless bean soup. The black bread is not like Tante Rachel's on the eighth day even, I think. Yet I devour both quickly as if they were manna from heaven. Only much later do I think I must not rush so, for the food hits my stomach ferociously. I must learn to eat more slowly, not savor exactly, but give my system a chance to digest properly. We go to the toilet, mere holes in the ground, and relieve ourselves. We are given ice water which we pour quickly over ourselves, happy at last to be clean. And then we march.

The sun, the same sun I would see from my room at home, rises full and proud over the mountains. The air has a crispness from the last traces of winter's frost which still cling to it and I swear, as we march, I see particles of silver dancing in the distance. The mountains, first a dusty blue, emerge from the clouds. As we draw closer, I see each hillock ringed by the promise of green, and I take solace in the fact that the earth is still here. I try not to think of my swollen knees, the tiny pebbles beneath the wooden soles which attack me mercilessly with each step. Earth is still here, and so is the sun. Everything is the same, and for a moment I see myself walking up the steps to the home of my parents, coming to the door. My only worry is that it will be closed.

A girl three people in front of me trips on a pebble and the lash comes swiftly down. I see her standing up and marching again as if bothered only momentarily by a fly. The lady commandant in the heavy boots laughs and calls her a stupid cow.

We arrive at the factory where there are two women overseers. One is short with sacks of ruddy flesh on her cheeks and under her chin. Her short white hair is sleeked away from her face, giving it the appearance of a tennis ball. She walks up and down the rows of girls with much effort, and when she stops in front of me, I notice a nervous tick at the side of her right eye. She smiles, and it is the first time I have noticed this simple gesture in anyone of authority. She even tells us her name, Helga, and assures us, another grin overtaking her face, of our good fortune in being chosen for this labor.

But it is the other overseer who inspires fear in me. She is tall, taller than any of the girls or the guards, for that matter. Unlike Frau Helga who wears a simple blouse and long skirt, Frau Gizella wears a jumper with huge pockets. The pockets seem to be full, and I can see what I believe to be a thick rope emerging from one of them. Her platinum blonde hair sits atop her head like a crown. The rest of her features are Aryan in nature, the high brow, upturned nose, and blue eyes not unlike my own. From the moment I enter the factory, the eyes never leave my face.

"*Canst du niyen?*" she asks me the same question she has asked of other girls down the line.

I remember Clara's words and swiftly reply, "*Yavol, Commandant.*" I have no clue how to sew even a sock, but here I tell her I can. The black sewing machines wait ominously in row upon row of the vast factory. If only I had watched Mama more carefully! If only I had paid attention. If only...

The girls who say they have no skills are led out of the factory through what appears to be a long tunnel until I can no longer see them. We sit down, each of us who remains, at a machine with a pile of sturdy brown tweed uniforms, perhaps thirty in all. I lift the spool of thread and take it to the bobbin. It slips from my hand and rolls to the floor, but no one notices as I quickly retrieve it.

One of the girls has been found out, and I watch as Frau Helga stomps quickly toward her and grabs her by the neck. The pity was she had no hair to be pulled.

"*Was ist los mit dir?*" Frau Helga cries, dragging her toward the door through which the others had disappeared. The girl, a skinny one of no more than sixteen, has learned and makes no sound as she proceeds down the long tunnel. When the doors have closed,

Helga rubs her chubby hands together as if to cleanse them of some vermin.

"*Arbeit mit azin!*" she snickers, eying each of us. Work with iron. I must learn to be iron.

I return to the thread and bobbin, which I somehow master. I am trying to position a collar to be sewn at the neck of a uniform when suddenly I look forward and see two huge pockets before me.

Frau Gizella places large but surprisingly smooth hands on the machine, bends her head and peers directly into my eyes. I remember the rope in her pocket, and for a moment my heart stops.

"*Danna numa?*" she asks. She wants to know my name, but I immediately recite my number.

Gizella closes her eyes and shakes her head slowly. The other girls have begun their work and take no notice.

"*Danna numa,*" she repeats. I swallow. I try not to look at the thick blonde eyebrows which shadow her eyes.

"Blima. Blima Weisstuch."

"*Fin ve best du, Blima Weisstuch?*"

"Dombrowe, Madam."

She considers this a moment.

"*Dombrowe. Ich vice nicht dus land.*"

She has never heard of my town, and I sit frozen before the machine, unable to take up the collar.

"*Canst du niyen, Blima Weisstuch?*" she asks, her voice lower.

I nod, even though it is clear that I haven't a single notion of how to sew. She stretches her massive hand forward as I ready myself for the pull at the neck. Incredibly, she begins to regulate the bobbin and fix the collar in the proper place. The girls' heads are all down as she straightens herself to full height and, with not another word, walks away.

I begin to sew.

Shirley

I have always felt outside the door. At first, I couldn't understand why. But from before I could even comprehend my own mortality, I understood that my family was set apart from others I knew. Yes, my parents did tell me that we were different, special. There was a reason for all things, but there was a force set apart, endowed by a holy light, which gave us life. And yet, instead of basking in its glory, I found myself cringing. It was as if my family had emerged from a burning building, and I could still smell the fire in the air.

My parents were different from others in many respects. For one thing, I was the one who assumed the burden of language. I was constantly correcting my mother, who said *"orangin* juice" when she meant *"orange* juice" and *"chocolata"* when she meant *"chocolate."* Even meals were out of the ordinary. On Friday nights, we would have a treat of her chicken soup with our meal, but usually it was just a plate of boiled chicken or top of the rib, some fried potatoes, and Mott's Applesauce for dessert. The only salad I had ever heard of was coleslaw. Italian night consisted of slowly boiled meatballs and Ronzoni spaghetti with a couple of squirts of ketchup. Chinese was chow mein from a can to which my mother added some noodles. Her specialties were dishes like *kapushnak,* a mixture of slowly boiled meat, potatoes, sauerkraut; and *cholent,* a stew made of beans, meat, potatoes, and other ingredients which had to cook for eight hours. Once in awhile, we would have *kishka,* some fat stuffed in a membrane. But only on special occasions because it wasn't so good for Daddy. We especially liked when my

father came home and would go to the sock drawer and remove a
Hershey bar, which he would dole out in pieces to my brother and
me, saving a small block for himself. For her part, my mother plied
us with leftovers, which were never thrown out. When my brother
and I refused to eat the crust of our rye bread, my mother would
cut it away and wrap it up to be eaten later. Even the tiniest slices of
chicken were packaged in wax paper and put into the refrigerator.
"When I was in the forest, we would eat the leaves," she said.

Outside in the public, it was worse. My mother would navigate
Pitkin Avenue like a tourist, surveying each window, getting lost
on every corner. If we were in need of an appliance, or even say, a
man's suit, my father would try to bargain the price down. I would
huddle next to the front door as my father would "handel" in a
loud voice, and make a great pretense of leaving before the embattled merchant would call him back. Sometimes, he wouldn't get
called back at all.

We derived our culture from a TV set, not a museum. Skating,
piano, and other lessons were an extravagance. So were fancy
soaps, baseball games, deodorant, sanitary napkins, and the theater. To be alive was to sleep and eat, and sometimes go to Coney
Island. These were our lessons.

At age eight, I discovered eating out. A pizza place opened up
two blocks away, and sometimes, after much pleading, I was given
a quarter to buy a slice. I would race the two blocks until I smelled
the fragrance of garlic and tomato in the air. When I walked into
the shop, I could already see the heat sailing in waves as it emerged
from the large steel oven. Placing my order, I waited at the counter while watching one of the pizza men make huge red swirls
with a giant ladle onto the dough. Then, after wiping his sweaty
forehead with a muscular forearm, he would grab generous hand-
fuls of cheese and throw them onto the sauce and dough mixture.
After, he would lift the wooden slab in his huge hands and slide
the whole pizza tin into the oven as gracefully as a magician. It

was like nothing I had ever seen! I would eat the whole slice right there, and when I was finished, I would throw my napkin into the garbage pail full of cheese strands and half-eaten crusts.

Since I was in public school, I was allowed to eat at the cafe down the block with the other kids, but only once a week. Sitting on the stool at the counter, I ordered the burger special which, to my disbelief, actually came inside a bun. On top of the burger was a large dill pickle which to my delight tasted even better than the sour ones I was accustomed to. On the side of my plain white plate were thick, not overly burned, french fries, with one large slice of beefsteak tomato sitting on a tuft of lettuce. I finished it all, letting the juices flow freely from my mouth onto the plate. I even finished the little paper cup filled with coleslaw. And I enjoyed every bit.

My mother knew about the pizza and even the burgers, but it was a long time before she found out about the fried chicken. I was only ten, but old enough to help a neighbor two doors down with her two young children. Her name was Angela. She was young, slender, and pretty, and she made the best fried chicken in the world. Not boiled, not baked and cut into little pieces, but tossed in a white batter and fried in bubbling oil. Angela would stand at the oven in her apron, turning each piece with tongs as I stood behind. At lunch, she would always have a chicken leg dried with a paper towel waiting for me. Coming home, I felt like a traitor as I licked the spices off of my fingers. But as I sat eating my sliced brisket and cup of applesauce, hearing my parents laugh too loudly over a TV show, argue too boisterously over money, I decided against telling. Years later, I did tell my mother about the fried chicken, even encouraged her to make it. But she never did make it as good as Angela.

This feeling I had of being different, a thing apart from others, was only enhanced by our frequent moves as my father went from business to business. When I was very young, I didn't realize that people could live in one place all their lives. As I grew older, I became envious of the friends who nonchalantly came home to a place where the indentations of a crib still remained on the carpet, where the pencil marks on the closet door for each year of growth were numerous. I was born in Borough Park, and my first memory is of my mother down on her hands and knees scrubbing the linoleum as if she could erase it altogether. Sometimes, when I close my eyes, I can still smell the pungent odor of the bleach which drifted outside as I jumped rope with my friend, Susie. After my brother, Jack, was born, we moved, and I began kindergarten in Lakewood, New Jersey. We had a much more spacious apartment there, and my father had a new job selling costume jewelry in a flea market conglomerate. I think I would have enjoyed country life, judging from visits to my Uncle Victor's chicken farm nearby. Once, I got the chance to stand in the coop watching the chickens dance away, all feathers and frantic clucking as I stamped my feet. I even learned to tell the difference when choosing between the white and brown eggs. But after learning that our building had been sold for renovation, my father folded up the business and we again moved, this time to Brownsville, Brooklyn. There, Daddy and a partner went into a luncheonette business. And, after reading a passage for the principal, I was placed into the top third grade class. But by the time I was halfway through the fifth grade, my father had an offer of a launderette in Flatbush and, once again, we moved. It was to be my longest stay in an apartment until I graduated from Erasmus Hall High School, and Daddy bought a candy store close to Kings Highway. That was my last home until I married four years later. But Mommy and Daddy soon retired and moved yet again.

Always being the new girl, the outsider, made me gravitate toward others like myself. My best friends were Anne, the girl whose face had been disfigured by a dog, and Cindy, the girl who had been burned in a fire as a toddler. Most of the other students, I soon learned, didn't much like new kids. Especially not if the kid was the shortest one in class or had the longest hair, as I did, coming into a new elementary school in the middle of fifth grade. Up until then, the most popular girl had the longest hair. Teachers with the best intentions often aggravated my feelings of isolation. My sixth grade teacher once pulled me and another youngster outside the room to tell us that we had not made the "SP" class, the one that skips a grade, but had made an enrichment class instead. The whole class knew, and I could hear them tittering as we walked back into the room. I ran home for lunch in a rainstorm that afternoon, and cried all the way. It was the same teacher who boldly announced to the raucous students, "I wish you could all be like Shirley. She is the quietest one in this class!" My ears still tingle whenever I think of it.

An outsider. I close my eyes, and night after night after night like pages in a book my dreams are written. One dream, an echo of a lost time, returns. It is the first day of school, and I am late. I enter the room only to find out the class is over and I have missed the most important day of all. I have missed my chance. And another dream, like a ghost's breath. I come home, home to my parent's door. But the locks are in place, and no one hears me. So I remain ringing the bell, screaming, screaming. Still outside the door.

Blima

Every day is the same. We awake with the first glowing shards of light, stand in the still cold for *appellplatz*, rush to the main barracks for our meager portion of bread and soup, and walk the miles to the factory where we shiver in our thin blouses and skirts even in the midst of summer.

One day, I am sitting at my machine quietly working on my fifteenth uniform within the hour by the clock on the wall. To my left are the uniforms I have completed with collar and buttons, to the right another stack of perhaps twenty which await. As I set the bobbin moving with my foot on the pedal, I suddenly feel the old hunger return. This time it does not pass, but grips me like a savage claw at the heart of my diaphragm. Before I have time to lift myself from the seat, a thin stream of yellowish liquid shoots out of my mouth. Frau Helga, twitching and grinning, comes running toward me on her thick legs. Before she reaches me, as if from heaven, I feel a long arm grasp my shoulder from behind.

Gizella calls me a dirty cow and rushes me to one of the toilets. For a moment, I think she is going to put my head in the slimy waste, and I feel myself gagging. Instead, she releases me and with one hand delves into her deep pocket. Again, I prepare myself for the tightening of the rope, but what emerges stuns my senses so that for the first time since my arrival at Grunberg I feel a fainting spell come upon me.

A chunk of thick rye bread floats before my eyes. I have not seen such a one since the first days past Pesach when Tante Rachel would bake them special for the family. I cannot believe I failed to catch its scent before it hit the air.

"Blima," she says, remembering my name, "*Ess dus broit yetz.*" Eat this bread now. She thrusts it into my hand and I hurriedly gobble it up. It is hard and does not have the sweet taste of the baked goods from home, but when it reaches my stomach it is at once a soothing balm. Gizella waits until I have swallowed fully and proceeds to throw water on me as I scrub my blouse and skirt.

"Blima," she says again, "*Host du mitter?*"

She asks for my mother, and I feel the tears well up in my eyes. I had not thought of my mother in months, submerging the image of her face deep within me, along with my own fears.

Gizella bends toward me, taking my face between her long fingers, and for the first time since I am here I see kindness in someone's eyes.

"*Du ben ich din mitter,*" she says, and kisses me on the top of my head. I cannot quite comprehend what she has told me, and I can only stare stunned into her blue eyes.

Here I will be your mother.

Gizella pushes me out and begins screaming, dirty Jew, sick cow. Next time you will really learn your lesson! I sit down in my place where they have added more cloth to the pile on the right, and like the iron I have become, pick up the next item.

From that day forward, each morning I would receive a portion of bread from Gizella's deep pockets. I would thrust it into the space between my breasts, beneath the cherished photos which I still carried with me, and later consume the prize in the toilet area. Once or twice, when a girl became particularly ill or gaunt-looking back in the barracks, I would slip her the bread I had saved, telling her that I had kept my portion from the morning's breakfast. Glad to satiate her hunger, she never asks questions.

The commandant of our barracks whose name we never knew but whom we called *Herr,* or mister, for the masculine way in which she supported her carriage and inclined her head directly toward you, has a disgusting habit. Just as the last shift of workers arrives and we are all falling into our beds, she stands at the door of the barracks, holds up a large red apple so that all can see, and bites slowly into it. It is a difficult thing to explain to those who sleep at night with a fullness in their bellies how this simple act can be a form of torture. But for us girls who once knew the sweetness of an apple, the sight is as a panoramic vista might first appear to a man regaining his eyesight after years of blindness. Some of us turn away, but as we press our ears into the straw we can still hear the crunch and imagine the taste of the juice on our tongues. Those of us who do look, see her peel the apple slowly, letting the red skin slide off the whiteness like a party ribbon undone from a package, lazily curling toward the ground. We see the apple slowly diminish to its core, which she passes to Otto who attacks and finishes its heart whole. Then, upon Herr Commandant's instruction, Otto tentatively approaches the skin on the floor, sniffs once, and swiftly sucks that in too.

One night after Herr Commandant bites into her apple, she is abruptly called away, leaving with Otto and the apple still in hand. The ribbon peel lies on the floor twisted in circles like a bright red rose. There is perhaps a minute of silence, a tightly packed silence of concentration such as the minute before a child is born or a man is put into the earth. Perhaps a dozen girls dive upon the floor in the same instant, pulling the apple rose apart. There is a scratching of faces, tearing of clothes, pushing and twisting as each girl tries to get her share of the peel. Who knows, perhaps I would have been among them if not for the extra bit of bread I sequestered each day? The peel is devoured immediately by some, while others climb hurriedly up into their cubicles to save their treasure, hiding it for now within the blades of straw. One girl, though, remains on the floor as she tries on hands and knees to insert a thin finger between the planks from which a sliver of peel peeks like a tiny worm which raises its head to the sun. The rest of us are too astonished to cry out when the door silently opens and the sole of Herr Comandant's boot slams into the girl's squirming hand. Just as quietly, she releases the leash holding Otto. The dog goes for her extended arm as the girl rolls herself into a small fetal position. Her screams ring through the barracks as the rest of us remain fixed as stone, our mouths set in grim lines, our eyes dry as sand. When the screaming stops, the commandant says merely this should be a lesson to us, and pulls Otto out through the door.

After fifteen or twenty minutes, the wounded girl manages, with the help of Clara and the others, to get up off the floor. She looks down at the planks which had been wiped clean with the girls' skirts, and now hold blotted patterns of dark red. I can see a long scratch, inflicted by someone, stretch from the temple to her mouth. Her mangled arm hangs loosely as Clara tries to bandage the open gash with her own skirt. The girl whimpers as she climbs up to her cot, and the rest of us turn over and try to sleep. Not that night, nor for many nights after, do any of us touch, or even have a taste for, the short red peels buried within the straw.

Clara is inconsolable. It is she who marked the girl, Lydia, with the scratch. It is she who is responsible for snatching the lengthiest peel from her hand. It is she who caused Lydia to search between the planks for the tiniest scrap. It is she who allowed her friend, her co-worker, to be found out and viciously attacked. And it is she who caused Lydia to be selected for the next transport to Gross-Rosen. I try to tell her to be iron, that Lydia is strong still and will survive whatever is placed before her. Does she not remember the dozens of uniforms our friend would place from the unfinished to the finished? Surely, Lydia will find her way out of the darkness.

One morning, Clara does not get up for the *appellplatz*. She is quiet in the straw, but I know the reason. She hopes to be sent to Gross-Rosen as a non-worker. But she forgets Herr Commandant who stands at the door with a salivating Otto at one side and the viperous whip at the other. She forgets the obstinacy of the chubby girl in the next barrack who was whipped not by the commandant, but the *kapo,* the group leader, a determined woman of perhaps thirty years of age, ordered to do the deed. I look at our young leader, Manya, who stands with her head bowed, and I know too well that before Clara carried out her plan, the lash would break them both. I can no longer be silent.

"Myer!"

The cry comes the second I make up my mind to utter it, and all eyes turn toward me. The name has met its purpose, though, as Clara, recalling her five-year-old brother in the wheelchair, resolutely steps down from the bunk and takes her place with the rest of us. Herr Commandant casts me an insidious look and Otto emits a low growl, but neither advances toward me. The only movement in the barracks is my thumb, which trembles involuntarily against my side.

I am a good worker and the fabric flies like a hummingbird from pile to machine to floor. I am no longer sorry that my work is not at the end of the tunnel where, I have since learned, girls sit on massive rocks in the sun and rain, packaging and tying boxes for the garments. The job, even with its hazardous exposure, captures my desire only until my hands learn to twist themselves into the right places for the buttons, the collars, and hems. My small foot flies upon the pedal until I am one with the machine. Without a word, Frau Helga grasps each finished pile and hobbles them over to a table in the center of the room. The lack of comment is tantamount to praise, and I know that my value as a worker seals my security tighter each day. Sometimes, when each machine is occupied with the arrival of more workers, I am placed with the finishers. Here too my fingers learn to spin the needle as trimmings and cuffs attach themselves to place. My eye pierces the needle like radar as thread sails sweetly through a parallel eye. I am iron, I say to myself.

It is not my value as a worker, but Gizella's abiding love for me which keeps my mind alert and my heart at a steady beat within my breast. Once, I ask her why she has chosen to help me and not the others. She smiles and shakes her head. It is my small stature, a will that she can see behind my eyes, she does not know. She confides too that she is a Catholic and abhors this irrational hatred of Jews. Yet, what choice does she have but to be here? She is here because she must be iron, but also because of her obligation to humanity. Right now, I am her humanity.

I do not think I could survive without my Gizella, or the songs from home the others and I sometimes sing because we are human and demand a lightening of the spirit, or the correspondence from home, which grows more infrequent by the year. Our letters home are monitored, but even if they were not, my family would know that my mind is occupied in work, I sleep well and deeply, and I grow fatter each day. I tell them of the soft beds, the warm rolls, and the many fine friends here. I do not tell them about Gizella, my second mother.

For four years I am surviving. But each day I feel will be our last one before the door to freedom opens, for sometimes I hear the bombings from the advancing Russian armies drawing closer. While there is a thin sense of relief, of impending light, there is also a feeling of dread below the surface that somehow we too will be blasted toward oblivion along with our enemies.

There is a fire over the mountains on the day Gizella takes me aside and, along with a piece of bread, hands me the photographs I gave to her long ago for safekeeping.

"Blimala," she whispers, "Tomorrow will come a transport and you will be on it."

"Where? Why? Where am I to go? Is my work not good enough, Gizella?" I ask, feeling each beat of my heart through my chest. She takes my forearm and runs her fingers across the numbers on it.

"No, Blimala, your work is perfect, of course. But the *wehrmacht* wants to evacuate this place, all of Gross-Rosen, in fact. They will be dispersing us all, even me."

"But, without you, Gizella, what will become of me?" I sob into a hanky, ashamed to be crying tears over this woman who is not my mother.

"Do not worry, dear daughter," she says, "We will find each other after the war, for this nightmare will be at an end soon. I feel it in my bones." She clasps me to her as some of the girls working nearby catch sight of us, but Gizella seems not to care. The stains from my tears are still on my shirt the next day when we line up for the journey to Bergen-Belsen.

We set out on a day when the frosty stillness hangs in the air, a plate of ice dangling above our heads. I hear one of the officers give the date to another. January 21, 1945. I etch the date mentally and count each page of time with the rising of every blue sun. The mountains, and with them Gizella, rescind as we march into the forest whose mysteries we have yet to unravel. In another time, this passage would have been an adventure. For us, it was movement, always forward without thought, another day of waking up alive. On any other day for any other people, the pristine scenery would have infused us with hope and wonder. Any other day, in any other time, but not for the walking shadows which we have become.

Our journey is longer than the last by many days, and each day brings a new horror. Of food there is little or none to speak, and the harsh winter trees hold but small pleasures in their silent store. Our nourishment comes from the dry leaves, remnants of the short autumn, or a nut left behind by a frightened squirrel. When we are lucky, it snows, and we take piles of it in both hands, pushing the white ice into our mouths, drinking in its sweetness. By day, we walk on broken shoes, some of us on pieces of cloth which we wrap around our ankles. By night, we sleep on sheets of ice which, warmed by the heat of our bodies, causes us to awaken in pools of water. Those of us who no longer have the strength to walk, fall. Those of us whose skin trembles with the cold and whose heads are consumed by the fire of illness also fall. And, the others who aren't sure if they can stand or keep apace, are shot. Sometimes, when the guards become bored and wish to taunt us, they make us walk a straight line, a near impossibility. They shoot bullets on either side of the line and mock the losers, the ones who collapse, the ones whose fear has left them in the second before they die. Other guards amuse themselves by having us run races then they force the losers to dig ditches for the dead. Throwing the last skeleton into the hole, the worker falls upon the corpse with a sudden shot to the back. Dead or not, he too is buried. Needless to say, the same fate awaits those who try to escape. And those of us who are able to still stand are left to wonder if perhaps these are the lucky ones.

For women, it is particularly difficult, as the male guards constantly remark lasciviously on our breasts, our thighs. We hear stories of rape, sadistic torture of girls as young as nine. But we here do not worry on that count, for starvation has robbed us of our monthly bleeding, and our skins have acquired a sickly ashen hue. My breasts too have shrunken, as I find myself tightening the bindings which hold the pictures to my chest, tighter and tighter. Men and women we once were, what we are now I cannot tell.

Sometimes, there is not the time to bury the bodies and we march past them, covered only by the tall bare trees and our own despair. When a sharp wind comes through, it blows against our bones and scatters us like rambling leaves further into the thickness of the forest. I pass one sister coaxing another off the ground, a son urging his father to eat a piece of saved bread, a mother holding back the hair of a sick daughter as she heaves yellow water into the earth. As for me, I walk with the stars and the saplings as my companions. Clara and the others have disappeared, and I tell myself it is good to be unencumbered. I tell myself it is good to be alone.

And I am alone, for even the fear which has been my silent ally these years, has deserted me. It walked off one day with Magda, I think. Manya, the frightened young girl thrust into the position of kapo. Manya, who dared look a soldier in the eye and was grasped one night in the woods as she urinated into a dirt hole right next to me. I could have been the one taken, but I wasn't. It was Manya who left, and in the darkness of the leafy trees, my fear too slipped silently into the shadows. As I watched the ruddy-faced boy-soldier emerge alone from the forest, rubbing his hands and spitting hard into the ground, I knew what I had to do. What I had to do was live. Live just one more day.

Eleven days and nights we march, and we arrive in Bergen-Belsen on the twelfth day. There is no sense of jubilation, no dancing except for the ones gone mad which, of course, is a justified way to act when the world is turned on its head. They dance as we enter the doors of another prison. No jubilation. But a sense of completion, yes. Perhaps now, after all, we can sleep.

I am sent to Lager C, in this place where I later learn there are a total of thirty-two blocks of 1000 each. Of order there is none, nor is there work in this holding camp, which is just as well, for I am beyond exhaustion. Although I yearn for a change of clothes, glad for the chance to feel something clean against my skin, I find only a pair of cotton socks and slide them onto my numbed and swollen feet. I look around at the breathing skeletons where only the mad have the capacity to laugh or cry. None are young and none are old in this place called Bergen-Belsen. And few are even alive.

No one seems to be talking much. But I notice that those already here have big bellies and round cheeks, so perhaps there is a meal to be had, after all. But I soon hear the woman next to me tell another that starvation has caused bloating in most of the inmates, and food here is scarcer than even the places from which we came. I stretch myself against my portion of floor and sleep for days.

I wake to scratching noises and turn to see a mouse sniffing at my behind. I jump up and run, I don't know where. No one seems to notice me, so I find another piece of floor and cautiously ease myself down again. But a stench so foul that it is indescribable again fills my nose, making breathing difficult. Yet I do sleep for I don't know how long until, in a dream, I hear my name whispered.

"Blima...Blima, wake up."

Perhaps it is Clara or the Devil himself. Fighting sleep, I open my eyes wearily. I see proud dark eyes in a gaunt face. I see Ruschia.

Betty

The door opens and lights start to pop. I can see nothing but little pieces of light before my eyes, but when the fireflies go away, I see my brother with the camera. Victor always with the pictures. Blackie, the cocker spaniel, comes over, smelling everybody and wagging the tail. I push Shirley and Jackie into the apartment in Rego Park so everybody can kiss them and say how big they are growing. This is not for too long, because soon comes Kalman and Naomi with the little ones, and everybody makes the noises about them.

This is an extra special one for the family because the three cousins from Toronto have come with their wives, and already they are making the jokes so that I laugh with tears coming from my eyes even.

"Have some *arbus*," says Ruschia, passing a bowl of chick peas with pepper so everybody can eat. I take a couple only, but Chiel takes them in two hands. He always likes the spicy.

"Ruschia, I see you have already the picture," I say, walking over to the pictures which are already on the wall after the party here only two months ago. I think I look too fat in the photographs, but I am sitting so no one can see how short I am. That is good. The other pictures, with the children no longer here, are in the bedroom.

"Very nice," I tell her, tapping the one with all the children cousins sitting on the round velvet couch, "Your Marcus is so handsome!"

"Thank you," she says, putting out more *arbus* from a jar, "soon he will graduate high school, you know? Oh, the time flies!" I nod, agreeing, and sit down next to Yankel, the middle one from Toronto. Right away he puts the arm around me, and gives my shoulder a squeeze. "Oh, Blimala, Blimala. *Vus machs du?* How are you doing?" he says, kissing my cheek.

"Oh, you know. I am healthy, what can I say?"

"Oh, healthy, healthy, I can see. Yes, you are!" squeezing again. I look over at Chiel, who is taking still another handful of *arbus*.

Then Yankel begins with the jokes, and I laugh so much that again the water is coming from the eyes. I take a handkerchief from my pocketbook and push it to my eyes. I have to breathe very deep now because of the laughing. And everybody laughs too, Yankel's cross-eyed wife and Froyim and the tall one. Even the dimples are coming to Lazar's cheeks and the quiet smile is with his wife, the *shiksa* who is more Jew today than I am. I look to Chiel who is smiling also and taking more of the *arbus*.

We sit at the dining room table with the chairs, also a velvet brocade, but so clean because of the good plastic. All in the breakfront are the good pieces like dancers and butterflies that Victor and Ruschia brought from Germany. Very fancy behind the glass. I have also, but not so many.

Ruschia puts out the *petah*, the jelled calf's foot with the lemon in the middle. I squeeze more lemon on it, and I see Shirley already takes another piece. She also likes the spice. But Ruschia pushes two more on her plate, saying she is too skinny yet. We fill the glasses with ginger ale and celery soda.

"You have *orangin* juice?" I ask, trying out my English. Everybody laughs.

"*Ahhrange* juice," Victor corrects. They think I am still too much a *greenhorn*, but I learn the English from the neighbors mostly and customers who come to the launderette. Not everybody goes to school.

The chicken soup comes, and it is so hot still I feel my lips and tongue burn. But when it comes into my middle, it warms me up and I feel again like a baby. Ruschia still makes a better soup than me, even though she it was who gave me the recipes. I think she puts more different kinds vegetables.

Victor cuts up the turkey with two big knives, giving the big legs to Kalman and Chiel. Then the potatoes and the carrots, and very soon we are all licking our hands, so good it is.

"So how is the cleaning store?" Kalman asks, adjusting his young son's napkin.

"Good, good, thank God," Victor answers, patting his big belly before putting another piece turkey in the mouth.

"Victor, you tell everybody who came into us this week?" asks Ruschia, smiling.

"Oh, I almost forgot!" Victor takes away the gravy from his mustache, and sits back. "Somebody very famous. Well really, somebody who works for somebody very famous."

"Who? Who was it, Uncle Victor?" the children start asking.

"Well...." he says, giving the big smile, "You know the Beatles?"

"The Beatles!?!" screams Shirley, who is usually quiet, "Paul McCartney? Did you get his autograph?" Victor laughs.

"Well, I don't know who this Paul McCartney is. But I know he has a clean jacket now. Somebody brought the jacket into the store. The Beatles, this man says, were in the hotel a few blocks away."

"That's right," says my daughter, "they just sang at Shea Stadium. How cool!"

"Well," nods Kalman, lifting his daughter down from the chair, "that is the good thing about having the store on Madison Avenue. Only bums come into the boarding house uptown where I am." Victor laughs again. That is Victor's luck, always the gold spoon in the mouth. Last year, he was on the show Candid Camera. A man came in and asked if he cleans pants. Of course, said my brother. So the man took off his pants, put them on the counter, and walks out.

Victor doesn't care. But later, they say he is on the Candid Camera. Then we all watch Victor on the television.

We get up from the chairs because we are tired from so much eating. The little ones play with coloring books on the floor, and with Blackie, the cocker spaniel who is getting old and cannot see already. Shirley and Sophie's son, Sidney, who is also sixteen like Marcus, go into Marcus's bedroom to look at his awards. He shows them too the lists from the show College Bowl that he keeps. I don't know what this is about. But Jackie too follows them inside. He is always behind his sister, but she calls him a pest. So what if he follows, I say.

I go help Ruschia with the dishes. I am not afraid to put my hands in the water, so hot it burns the skin. Not like the *Americana* women. They go for the lotions and manicures. Such princesses, such *pritzas*! Ruschia and I talk of the *landsmen* and the women's things, and the *kinder*, the children, of course. When we wipe the hands, we go inside and hear Victor asking Chiel about the launderette we have in Flatbush.

"Business is okay," says Chiel, and nothing more. All the time they have to ask him. If not, he doesn't talk. They are *your* brothers, he says. He does not tell about the heat so hot from the dryers like being in the desert, and the loud banging from the extractors too so that Chiel already cannot hear so good. I put the clothes from the bundles in the machines then take them out. The wetness makes more wrinkles in my hands and, now, even when they are dry, the wrinkles stay. The delivery boys that Shirley and the friends talk to are slow and do not always show up, but they are better anyway than the one that robbed us. We make the few pennies, and we have more worries from the customers and the mice and the water bugs in the basement that Chiel kills with the thumbs. All for the few pennies. But Chiel does not tell them that. He just says business is okay.

We have the sponge and the honey cakes and some of the rainbow cookies with marzipan. Then the purple grapes and the oranges and apples. The hot tea in glasses warms us, and the fruit cools us off. Very refreshing. But Ruschia brings more sweets, the chocolates from Switzerland that are very delicious. Shirley says she is on a diet, and again everybody laughs. Children are so ridiculous.

Ruschia surprises us. She brings out a gift which is a 14-carat gold bracelet with a charm for Shirley, who just had her thirteenth birthday. The charm shines like the first golden star in the night, and it has three candles on a birthday cake. The candles have three blue turquoise stones for the flames. I see she takes my daughter on the side when she gives her this. But Shirley only says thank you quietly. She thinks it is like a charity because they have money and we do not. She gets this idea from Chiel, who thinks my brothers are always having deals while he works in the launderette. I say so what. After all, they are entitled.

After we take the subway back to the apartment, I am taking off my clothes when Chiel comes up to me with a smile.

"So, you had a very good time tonight, no?" he says.

"Yes, and such a meal. Always Ruschia makes like this," I answer.

"And the company?" he asks, still smiling, "The company was also very good, no?"

I do not know what he means. "It was all right," I say, putting on the nightgown.

"Especially Yankel, no? Very funny man! Don't you think so?" He is so close now I can smell the chocolate still on his breath. I do not answer, and turn to go to the bathroom. But Chiel takes my cheeks between his hands and squeezes them hard. Never before has he hurt me, and I see he is mad.

"Oh, yes, you like your Yankel. A very, very funny man! Why don't you go back with him to Canada so you could be laughing all the time!" He lets go of my face and pushes me away. He is stopping himself, I see.

"Chiel, you are *meshugah!* Yankel is my cousin, my first cousin! And he is a married man! What is the matter with you?" I yell back.

"You are right, Blimala. I am *meshugah.* I saw nothing of his touching you tonight! I saw nothing of your laughing and laughing! You are right. It was all a dream in my mind."

"Chiel, stop the nonsense, please. You are talking crazy. No sense!" But I am yelling too loudly, and Shirley and Jackie are already standing like statues at the bedroom door.

"You know, maybe it is best if you do go to Canada with him. Why should I stop you, you are such a good wife...You and your brothers and your secrets and your laughing. You can all go back. I can take good care of myself!" he screams, taking long steps across the bedroom.

"Go ahead, I said. Have a good time. I am not so funny as Yankel or your brothers. I am not such a businessman either!" He is screaming, but I hear a gargle, and soon I realize he is crying too. I turn away from his face and see now Shirley and Jackie holding each other.

I cannot talk to Chiel now. I will talk to him tomorrow in the morning. I will tell him not to be afraid, and I will tell him I love no one but him. I will tell him that for me, he is like the air that I breathe to give me life. I will not tell him what Ruschia told me in the kitchen. That Victor saw someone he knew walking in the street last week. He talked to the man and found out it was Smulke. Smulke, still alive.

Shirley

My mother and I never spoke about sexual matters. At age twelve when my time came to have "the talk," Mommy simply looked up from the dishes one day and asked if I knew how babies were made. It was really more statement than question. "Yes, I know from my friends," I said hurriedly. With a definitive "Good!" she plunged her hands further into the bubbles, my cue to bolt out the front door. And that was all she needed to know. That simple exchange confirmed that I had been right all along, right in never telling her my secret.

When I was nine years old, I was sexually molested. He was a neighbor, the son of our building's landlady, and only a teenager himself. Jay never threatened me or told me to keep it a secret, but just the same, I knew I could never tell anyone. Just like I could never tell anyone about the thoughts I had of strangers and coercion and lust when I would lie in a darkened room by myself rocking back and forth.

It began quite innocently, as these things often do. Mrs. Wexler, our landlady, was an avid baker, and would sometimes invite my mother and me next door to sample her brownies and coffee cake. Jay's brother, Ted, was always away taking classes at a nearby college, but on late afternoons Jay would be sitting at the kitchen table doing his homework as our parents conversed. Mrs. Wexler would try to draw him into the conversation, but Jay would only look up out of the corner of his eye, grimace, and continue working. That is until the conversation turned to animals, and she made Jay show us his pet hamsters. My mother squealed immediately and covered her eyes. She was intensely afraid of hamsters and mice, considering them all rats. Rats, she said, were horrible and reminded her of war and death. I didn't ask any questions, and neither did anyone else, as Jay returned the furry creatures back to the cage in his room. Only a month later, my mother would get the scare of her life when she opened the oven to place a brisket inside, and one of the hamsters greeted her with a squeak. She ran into her bedroom and promptly fainted on the bed. She actually fainted.

But I thought the little animals were rather cute, and I marveled at the way they could secret food in pouches at the corners of their mouths. Having never owned an animal, I found them all fascinating. All except the cockroaches and water bugs I would find in the bathroom sink at night when I turned on the light. I despised those.

But my interest in the hamsters quickly waned when I followed Jay into his room and saw a giant fish tank filled with exotic freshwater fish. I was dazzled by the serene white beauty of the angel fish, the diabolical intensity of the slender black swordfish, the quickness and flash of the neons, and the wormy craftiness of the catfish which feasted in the gravel below. Sensing my enthusiasm, Jay began to explain the peculiarities of each of the fish, and when I had to go home, invited me back to see them again. Anytime I wanted.

Anytime turned out to be only a couple of weeks later when my mother began to help my father with the after-school rush at the luncheonette on Sumner Avenue. She usually would take my brother with her, so that I found myself in an empty apartment. I quickly finished my homework, and when the loneliness would begin to envelope me like shadows leaping out from every window, I would remember the invitation and the fish next door. Jay was a congenial host, and even when his mother was out, would offer me some of her chocolate chip cookies. Then, we would go into his room where I found more than an animal sanctuary. It was a like a magical treasure chest, truly. Once I found one precious item, igneous rocks and shells from the beach, I would discover another.

I had visited Jay perhaps three times when he handed me a new gift to peruse, a large picture book of the earth with transparencies which added land formations and color to each page. As I stood looking at the book, Jay came up behind me and placed his hands on my shoulders. Then, after about a minute, I felt his body pushing against my back and the top of my buttocks, as his fingers tightened on my shoulders. I could feel him going down slowly then lifting his body against mine. He began going faster, and I could hear him breathing hard into my ear as his hands dug into my shoulders. As he did this, I pretended to look at the pages in the book, as if nothing was happening. The indigos, aquamarines, and slates so serene only a moment before, began to dance and merge frivolously before my eyes. As the rubbing at my back became faster and stronger, the shades of earth danced more frantically, taunting me until I had to squeeze my eyes tighter to command the blackness that would take me away. Finally, they stopped as I felt Jay shiver and suddenly release me. After a minute, Jay would turn back to me and show me his coin collection or the colorful kaleidoscope he had sitting on the shelf, as if nothing ever happened.

After the incident, I returned to watch the fish and handle the artifacts in Jay's room. Again and again, without a word, Jay would come up behind me, place his hands on my shoulders, and go up and down. Occasionally, he would ask me to turn around while he did this. But I felt uncomfortable with his body hard against my belly and my hands at my side, no book or seashell to hold. He tried to cajole me to face him with promises of drawings and playing cards, but he would usually back down if I steadfastly refused. More than one time, his mother would come in without warning. I am sure she suspected something, but Jay would always turn away from me quickly with a shiver. Only his long red fingers held a clue as to what had just occurred.

I was never really afraid of Jay when he molested me in this way, and I certainly never enjoyed it. But I continued coming back to his room because of the secret, something very personal and private which was all my own. I stopped going there the day Jay gave me a drawing he had just finished, and I wrote his name on it. For some reason, unknown to me, he grabbed the drawing out of my hands, crumpled it up, and threw it in the trash.

"Don't you ever put my name on anything again, hear?" he growled, glaring at me angrily. I just stood up, faced him, anger and hurt burning in my eyes. I walked out of his house and never returned.

Of course, I never told my mother about what Jay had done, and certainly not my father. When people are burned once, you can't ever hold a match to their face again. I am sure, though, that psychologists would say the trauma accounted for my sexual inhibitions as a teenager when I refused to play "spin the bottle" or even let a boy put his tongue in my mouth. I was born at the end of August, and the boys quickly slapped me with the nickname "Shirley Virgo, the Virgin," even though all of my close friends were too.

Besides making me ashamed of myself, the experience with Jay somehow made me more determined. I had tripped off the path once, and I couldn't do it again. As the child of my parents, whose stories I had already absorbed into my consciousness, if I stood very still, I could almost feel their tales circulating in the blood within me. Almost like a mission. I knew I had to justify what they had endured and my own reason for being their daughter, for being here. Even if I wasn't quite sure what it was at the time, I was confident that it was something viable. If only I could capture it like an elusive firefly between my two hands.

I knew what it wasn't, though. It wasn't singing. I had heard the tale my parents loved to repeat of how I would sing "Oh, my Papa!"

in a loud voice when I was only three. How Mommy even took me once to the radio station, and the manager said sure, I could be another Shirley Temple, I even had the name! But I couldn't leave my mother's side, not even have her a few feet away as I sang into the microphone. And thus, my career ended before it ever began. I didn't stop vocalizing in the bathtub, though. And even when I was in kindergarten, my teacher once wrote on my report card, "Shirley loves to speak and perform before the class." I thought it ironic even then that she had no clue how my heart fluttered inside when I attempted to start a conversation with one or two of the girls in my class; the velvet bows in their hair glared at me, the navy blues and crisp reds of their plaid pleated skirts swirled around me, mocking my every word. It was much easier to be up before a class, not like having to talk to one individual girl who didn't even smile when she passed me in the hall. Like all other children, I thought I was the only one who ever had dreams.

It was in the same year of my shared secret with the next door neighbor, that I first began to understand what my mission would be. It was centered not on stage, but in the world of academia, which I tenuously was on the verge of mastering. All my long hours spent practicing writing with my parents had begun to pay off, and I loved to write in long flowing lines. But it wasn't enough to just admire the lines, they had to mean something. So I would stare out the window and simply think. Think of the old lady hurrying by on a frosty day, or the single droplet of rain lying on a leaf and slowly falling to the sidewalk with a splat. And then I would write. Poems just like my best friend, Elise, and I had copied once out of a children's book from the library. In seventh grade, the English assignment was to write about an inanimate object as if it were alive. So, finding the courage, I wrote a story about a day in the life of a piece of paper. And when Miss Miller returned it, I knew I had found my mission. I would be a writer.

Blima

I thought I had not tears to cry. But I do. The water flows from my eyes in rivulets for I had already forgotten what it was, even for a moment, to be happy. Ruschia has not the strength to embrace me, but stands at my side, smiling silently. When I can no longer bring forth tears, she slowly sits down next to me.

"Blima, is it really you?" she whispers. I look into the face I loved so well and see then that, yes, it is Ruschia, but not the Ruschia I had known. Not only because I can see the bones protruding from beneath her blouse, her round eyes sunken into a face covered with red blotches, but there is something gone from her essence. And I know, instinctively, that she will never be the same. I do not realize it yet, nor would I ever completely.

"What happened to you, Ruschia, those marks on your face and arms..?" She looks down at her arms and shrugs her shoulders.

"Typhus. It comes from the lice and fleas, and itches like anything."

"My poor sister-in-law! How did you ever get that?"

"Almost everyone here has this, or has something. Let me tell you, the diarrhea is worse." I cringe.

"How did this happen, Ruschia?" Again she shrugs her shoulders.

"It is the bodies. The crematoria are full, there are hundreds, perhaps thousands here. Haven't you smelled the stench?" I remember not being able to breathe. I do not smell it as much now. Have I so soon become accustomed to the stench of death?

I tell her I have learned to be a good worker on the machines, and ask if there are any in this place.

"Work?" she snorts, "we carry things from the kitchens, the men dig ditches, always too slowly, for the dead. But mostly we work to stay alive. We can do no more."

And what of Mama and Papa, Adele, and the rest? What of Victor and the girls? Ruschia makes a singular sweeping motion with one hand.

"Gone. The old ones had much hope from your letters, but they could see the time was short. Couple years later, Victor, you know they took from the bed. I had to pay someone off to get him to Klettindorf where he shipped for them in the warehouse. After that, I do not know."

"And the girls, Ruschia? Salusha and Chanusha, where are they?" Ruschia buries her face in her blotchy hands, but does not cry.

"Off the trains they pulled us. The dogs barking, the people running, there was such shouting. I had them each by the hand, and they didn't even know anything. They were pushed along with the other children. They were all crying. There was moaning, there was...Oh, God knows...I would have gone with them. I would have."

I picture Salusha's's clear white face, Chanusha's heart-shaped innocent mouth, the smile on it when I would hand her a special treat. And then I remember something else. I place my hand underneath my shirt, loosen the bindings, and hand her the pictures.

Ruschia spreads them out before her and looks at them as if she were seeing ghosts, and perhaps she is.

"You kept these...how?" I tell her of Gizella, the angel who saved me and our memories.

"If not for her, I would not be alive. So many are not... But, Ruschia, how do you come to be here?"

"Will, I suppose," she sighs, and proceeds to tell me of her work filling powder for guns in Auschwitz. She too was a good worker. She did not go to the gas.

"I was made to stand by the furnaces, so hot it was only a matter of time when each one of us would, well, need to be replaced. But I had a better plan. When my legs could stand no longer, I would bind them tightly so as to cut off the blood each night. Eventually, they had to take me to the infirmary. I think in this way, I was saved. For what, I am not sure."

"What do you think happened to the others, Ruschia?" I ask, "Do you think..?" She cuts me off.

"I do not think. And you should not think, either," she warns, then pointing to a woman hugging herself in a corner, "They are the ones who think. If you think, you go mad." Ruschia is right. I can no longer think about anyone but myself. Here. Breathing and alive.

Ruschia struggles to put one arm around my shoulders.

"We are all orphans," she says.

✡ ✡ ✡

A twelfth of a loaf of bread and a sip of water. Until there is none left.

Ruschia had been right; the business of staying alive is enough to keep us busy throughout the day. What lessons do you learn to stay alive in Bergen-Belsen? You learn to stay away from the kitchens because of the sadistic SS officer, Herta, who beats the girls with a wooden stick as they carry meager portions to the block. You learn to shrivel into yourself like an old woman when the doctor comes by looking for victims for his gynecological experiments. You learn to eat your food slowly and save your water so you don't get diarrhea. You learn not to panic over your own death when an epidemic breaks out and Kramer, the head of the camp, cuts off the food supply, yelling his credo, "If you don't eat, you don't shit!" You learn to push the hatred down into the depths of your soul when you hear that the SS has taken for themselves all but ten of the 150 kilograms of chocolate sent by the Red Cross for the young ones. You learn how to quickly snatch the socks off a man when the breath has left him. You learn not to cry out when you take your pot of urine outside and see rats eating the faces of the dead, while some bodies are still moving within the piles. You learn not to be appalled when you hear of the cannibalism, of men eating the hearts and livers of the dead. These are the lessons of war that you learn.

April 15, 1945. Ruschia is asleep in her spot below a window next to the men's barracks. She is awakened suddenly and looks out to see fires coming from all directions, and people running about, screaming. An Armageddon, she concludes. There has been no food now for six days, and the ground has already given up its supply of turnips. There have been rumors that this is the day the camp is to be evacuated, and since there is nowhere else to go, the talk is that they plan to line up and machine gun the remaining prisoners at 3 PM. But it seems too early yet. Well, she thinks, I can no longer walk, so if they want to shoot me, they'll have to do it here. She wakes up her sister, Sophie, who comes running to my barracks.

I follow Sophie outdoors, and at first think that I have indeed gone insane. I see fire trucks, and water being sprayed everywhere, but I see also something else. Potatoes on the ground. We run around grabbing as many as we can; Ruschia, who is too sick to walk, crawls on all fours. The sun comes out, bright and full, and right there in the bursting flames we cook the plump gifts from the earth.

A British general stands on top of a jeep and tells us we have been liberated. We sit down and eat our potatoes.

SECTION 2

THE NEW WORLD

FIRST

I am a Brooklyn girl.
Potsy on the heat cracked sidewalk
sweating now pink blue green pastels.
One long braid that smacks us on the back as
we run for a chocolate egg cream and
salty pretzel stick, a three o'clock treat.
Red and white plaid pleated mini-skirt so high now,
crossing our legs we are
on the verge of naughtiness.
Pouring our hopes into the lap of Desiderius,
clang the coins play on each other.
"Erasmus Hall, our hearts to thee with
fervent impulse turn."
Summertime birthday parties,
Jahns with the "kitchen sink" that you can't finish
with less than five–no, ten people.
Heap it on, boys!
We can handle it.
Just like we indulge in books,
as many as our skinny girl arms can hold
standing on the bus
across the street from the Grand.
The D line creaks finally to a stop.
We emerge past the smoking dankness
to the light of stars.
And Flatbush,
not the sun, we know
is the center of the Universe.

If you should see me sipping a white drambuie
at the Posh
and someone interrupts with a call for the Professor–
If you should see me there,
remember first
First I was a Brooklyn girl.

Betty

"Two Winston...Five Pell Mell...Three Lucky Strike...Right. And gimme five more Baby Ruth, one Red Hots, Six Good 'N Plenty... Two Sugar Babies...Yes. Okay, one more. Only one *Il Progresso*, one *Forward*, but I want three *El Diario*...Okay? Same price as last time, or–okay. Good." I can hear Chiel on the telephone with the distributor. When he hangs up, he makes a motion with the hand.

"Lusin gayen in drayit aran." Let him go to hell. Chiel has no patience with the businessmen, I think. But he does not want my help, and anyway, I wouldn't even know how to help with the books. But the *gelt*, the money, I can take from the customers. I do this *zaya git*, very, good. My business in the candy store is to stand behind the counter and give the children coming from lunch the penny candies. I wear a cobbler apron, and quickly I put the money in the pocket and take out the change. I do fast the *rachining*, the computing, in my head so I don't cheat nobody. They come in a group, and sometimes they are laughing and making fun of Chiel's hat, or trying to put the hand over the counter to take. But I watch them good, and most of them are very polite, anyway.

My hands go so fast, and pretty soon my pockets are filled up with coins and paper money that I give to Chiel. I think nobody is quick like I am, just like with the sewing. Already my hands are marked with the wrinkles and the veins coming up from the skin. At night I have to put them in warm water because the arthritis is coming. My feet too have the big corns, and bones growing from the side. I need a bigger shoe width now, or my feet feel like bundled in. Ruschia says to me, "Blima, stop going with the heels always." But if I wear the sneakers, I feel like I am going to fall on the face. Anyway, I like with the heels because I am a short one.

Chiel takes from me the money, and sits behind the fountain counting the change and writing in the book at the same time. Monty from the bookstore comes in to *kibbutz*, make talk, because it is slow now that the children are back in the school. He smiles and calls Chiel "Charlie," which is the name here in America. Me they call "Betty." I have no middle name, so it is Betty. But I think I like Blima better because it means "flower." I take a brush from the pocket and fix my hair while they are talking. I leave the *Daily News* now, because I have heard already about the President Jimmy Carter and the hostages in Iran. Sometimes, I cannot read so much because I worry about the cousins in Israel, especially the young one, Leon, who lost the leg in the war. Then the tears come to the eyes, and I have to sit down.

Why do I worry so much? Shirley is married, and she is a teacher *and* a writer. Sometimes she shows me what she writes for a newspaper, and I read what I can. But Chiel reads the whole thing about people who get awards, or problems with the community. She learned to type all by herself, and now she sends out the poems and the stories, but she says sometimes it is a waste. I don't know, I think they will take her. But she should not be so nervous. Thank God she is married and has a beautiful apartment on East 13th Street near Kings Highway, just a few blocks away from where we live. Arthur's parents are *Americana*, and his mother has the red nails and his father likes to show the rings. But I don't care. Arthur is a teacher also, and he takes Shirley to the school with the car. Besides, he is good to her, just like Chiel is to me.

Jackie is already in the Brooklyn College from where my daughter also graduated. He says he wants yeshiva school no more. He does not like the hat and the long black coat and the study. He thinks he wants to be a lawyer, and Chiel laughs. "You gonna' be a liar," he says. But Jackie is a good boy. He drives Chiel on Sunday morning before the light comes in the air, to get the bundles of newspapers into the store. Then Jackie lifts for him the bundles, and Chiel cuts the ropes. I say, "Jackie, you are too fat for this." And, in English, he answers, "Ma, leave me alone. And call me *Jack*, not Jackie!"

"Who is the *Jack*?" I answer. Anyway, from him I have not to worry, and not from Shirley, either. I tell Chiel all the time the *kinder* will be better than us. This is what we live for.

But from Chiel I have worry. He complains he has no luck.

"Luck?" I say, "You are the luckiest to come from your whole family the only one alive!" But I know what he means. I get some money from German reparations, but because he was in the camps only few months, he gets nothing. They don't care that he lost the whole family. Not even a brother. In another way, he has no luck with the business. First, he has the costume jewelry in Lakewood. But from this he cannot make a living, so he goes into the luncheonette on Sumner Avenue with Morris the *Gonif*, the thief! He robs from the register when Chiel is with the customers. You think the customers from the street are gonna' rob, and the *landsman* takes right from the eyes. So let him go, I say. He should have such *nachas*, success, as he has given us. I tell him then that I can make the money. Sometimes Mr. Silverstein calls me still for the sewing, but Chiel will not listen. He works at the uniform place and says he will look for a piece of business in the paper. So, we move again now to Flatbush for a launderette. Chiel loses the hearing from the extractors and the dryers, and I fold laundry and talk to the customers. But he doesn't like even when I talk to the women. I say, "Chiel, I am just being friendly. When the women say, 'Betty, how are you today?' I am not supposed to answer?" But Chiel wants me all the time just to talk to him. What a man!

Even we cannot buy our own house because Chiel is always afraid of owing money. Kalman has his own place in Borough

Park. He has many houses, even. But Chiel is afraid of chances, and I am even more afraid. So we know to put all the money in the bank where the interest is good.

When we close up the launderette and buy the candy store on Cortelyou Road, Chiel thinks maybe he will find the luck. I tell him, sure, he is a good *handler*, a real bargainer. Even today, he meets the people on the subway or the Lower East Side, and they kiss his hands for saving them in the war. Anyway, he has the hair on the arms, a sign of a rich man. One time, someone from the street emptied the bowels on a subway seat, and Chiel sat down. Anyone who sits in *dreck* has to be lucky.

Chiel is still a handsome man with his hair pushed back with the gel, and the white apron over the pants. He is making Monty, the Americana, *egg cream* with milk, seltzer, and chocolate syrup from the fountain. Shirley says Chiel is the best at this, and she comes in from Kings Highway with Arthur just to drink the egg cream and eat with a pretzel stick. Monty swallows down the egg cream with one hand and smokes the cigarette with the other one. I know Chiel would like a cigarette too, but he sees I am here. Like a child he is sneaking, Shirley tells me, even though he has the blood pressure and blackness in the lungs. But how much can I yell? Sometimes I think Chiel has had too many disappointments.

Always he is looking for another cousin maybe who survived the war. Just last week, he reads in the paper a person with the same name won the lottery. Chiel jumps up and kisses me. Then, he begins making the telephone calls.

"*Chielala Russak* from Lodz," he says into the telephone. But the people do not know him. They are not even from Poland.

So, what do you know, one day a few months ago, Chiel comes home from the candy store and takes from the pocket a handkerchief. And inside is a diamond.

"Have you ever seen in your life such a thing?" Chiel asks with a big smile. I look at the stone so big like an eye shining with colors like the blanket I used to have from my mother's home.

"Chiel, where you find this?" I say, taking the diamond with my two fingers.

"Saul from across the street, you know, the cleaner? He calls me in to see a friend who says I can have a good price!"

"Chiel, what you know about the diamond business?"

"Don't worry about it, Blima. I show it to Lester who worked once for a jeweler. He says it could be a treasure."

"I don't know," I answer him, touching my finger to the smooth glass, "How much you pay?"

"Five hundred dollars, cash only," Chiel says, taking from me the stone and wrapping it again in the handkerchief, "Tomorrow I will sell for ten times that much. Will be a good surprise for the *kinder.*" But tomorrow when he tries to sell on the East Side, they tell him he lost all the money. The diamond is not a diamond, just a fancy glass with colors. Chiel goes in the bedroom and cries for a whole week. But I tell him not to worry, that his luck will change. After all, he has the hairy arms.

Shirley

I never considered myself smart, maybe just lucky. Or intelligent, perhaps. But not smart like people who not only could memorize formulas, but also apply them to theoretical processes. Nor, in spite of getting a 92 on my report card in trigonometry, could I ever figure out if one man gets on a train and travels the same distance as the driver of an automobile who starts out earlier, which of the two would arrive first. I never even saw the necessity of figuring it out. Who cares, really? The same ignorance applied to directions when, after writing instructions down verbatim, I would still become befuddled by an arrow which wasn't quite straight, and find myself driving into a gas station in a town too far west as I began to hyperventilate.

At least I was intelligent. And so, at age fourteen when I was suddenly maturing both physically and socially, I learned to harness that intelligence and apply it to cover up for my lack of smartness. I had an Italian friend by the name of Maria. Maria was one in a series of best friends I would make as my family moved from town to town, a sort of touchstone. Maria, an only child of immigrants, whose father worked construction, lived two flights up in our small apartment building in Flatbush, and was preparing to attend Stella Maris Catholic School. Shortly after we met, I introduced her to *gefilte* fish and Bar Mitzvahs, and it was at her house that I learned of Saint Peter, had spaghetti with real tomato sauce, and ate my first rice ball.

After watching the movie, *West Side Story*, we practiced for a production which we would stage on the sidewalk in front of our four-story apartment building. I would play Riff, and she, of course, would be Maria. In spite of our best efforts leaping and rhapsodizing, the musical never materialized, but our friendship was sealed forever.

One afternoon, as we sat in Maria's kitchen splitting Oreos and licking off the cream, I noticed her stack of notebooks all neatly placed on a table in the vestibule.

"Can I look through your books for a sec'?" I asked, walking over to the neat pile which lay just below an oil painting of John F. Kennedy.

"Sure," she said, reaching for another Oreo, "but it's just a bunch of boring stuff." I picked up a spiral notebook and let my hand trace over the smooth eggshell blue surface where Maria had written her name neatly in glossy black ink. As I turned the page, I marveled at how each sheet was as finely and clearly detailed as the one before it. Headings were sharp and underlined, with asterisks and notations in red written in the margins. Her looseleafs were just as impressive, with dividers and tabs of every color of the rainbow separating each subject.

"Maria," I said, flipping the pages of her small assignment pad, "These could be textbooks, they are written so beautifully."

"No big deal," she murmured, running her fingers, their nails bitten to the quick, through the ink black hair which she always lamented as being too much like Brillo, "I am just well-organized." I removed and examined a diagram of the life cycle of a frog, done in green and red crayon.

"I could never do this," I sighed, "Every time I say I'm going to get organized, we end up moving, and it's all I can do to catch up at the new school." Maria took the sheet from my hand and inserted it back into her lab book.

"It's just that I don't like things being out of order," she said matter-of-factly, "I guess I'm just a neat freak. Besides, I hate losing the stuff." I nodded, returning to the kitchen.

"Anyway, it helps me on the tests," she continued. As Maria followed me inside, she unraveled the hiked-up waist of her salmon and teal plaid pleated skirt, something she always did just before her mother arrived home, that and rubbing the pink blush from her full cheeks. I considered what Maria told me. Organization. It wasn't that I was a bad student; in fact, since third grade when I read for the principal in my new school, I had always been placed in the "one" classes, "3-1," "4-1," the brightest of the bunch. But I was barely holding my head above water when it came to science, and especially math. Besides, I hadn't even made the seventh grade "SP."

"I don't know," I said, "I don't think I will ever be the student you are."

"Remember one thing," she said, hurriedly wiping the rose coloring off her lips as the door slammed in the hallway, "You are just as smart as anybody else."

And that was it. With those few words coming not from my parents, but a friend, Maria had changed my academic life forever. If I didn't believe I was smart, at least I could pretend it. Algebra still proved torturous, but with the help of a tutor, I managed an "82" on the Regents exam. After a while, though, my grades evolved into the 90's range, I began taking honors classes, and eventually I covered my bedroom walls with attendance and various honor certificates. Only I knew that I was faking the smartness. No one else even suspected.

My other secret weapon was of a more spiritual nature. Whenever the old fear of failing would crawl up my back and settle in the heart like a black water bug from the launderette, my father had a way of sensing. Putting his arm around me, he promised, "I will think about you." Then he would kiss my forehead and send me off to the test. In school, seeing the paper peppered with a blur of questions before me, I would remember the softness in his eyes, the customary scent of Aqua Velva in his collar, and calmly write my answers. It worked every time.

Although I still required Daddy's luck with even English and Spanish classes, I knew that I would usually be fine on my own. Books especially had become as familiar to me as the soothing warm bath water I would step into at the end of each day. I think there was nothing I anticipated more than opening a library book for the first time. I would scan the blurbs on the back of each book several times, and quickly review the list of other books written by the author, on the first inside page. At age eight, beginning with *The Secret of the Old Clock*, I began to hoard a collection of Nancy Drew books, imagining myself a daring detective as I sat with book and flashlight under the covers. The librarian in Flatbush became my best friend, and would often have a stack of new Beverly Cleary books waiting for me as I burst through the doors. *Little Women* stirred in me again a passion to become the writer that Jo was, against the odds. I too was the silent spirit who sat alongside the creative protagonist in *A Tree Grows in Brooklyn*. And, when I first opened *Jane Eyre*, I knew that I had found my fondest companion. Jane, shunned and quiet, yet bold and always the dreamer, would at last be rewarded with a life of love and happiness, the life she deserved. It was everything that a lonely child of survivors could hope for.

Blima

I am alive. In the midst of the chaos, confusion, the broiling anger, the dead–oh, so many dead–I know just one thing. I am alive.

How do I say it? It is as if I alone am standing in a hole with a bright full sun pouring into me, warm, secure. If I venture back from where I came, I too will be consumed by the fires, for how can I live whole with thoughts each day of my mother, my father, my sister, all my dearest friends? If I could escape the Nazi's fires, do I have the will left to escape my past? On the other hand, if I venture ahead, toward what is called the future, I see only a vast turbulent ocean which supplies no footing, and can only drown me. For now, I stand in this hole in this new light called freedom. And I am alive.

The guards are led away with rifles at their backs. They are forced to carry the naked bodies, two holding each man or woman by the ankles and wrists, and swing them into ditches as big as towns. I think that the act is a double sacrilege, a murder and the killer's touch upon a holy being, but there is no other way. There are so many.

Finally, the job is completed by men on trucks who scoop up the bodies like so much gravel and pour them into the ditch, arms and legs flailing, once men and women, now corpses falling upon each other. I cannot look, but like the proverbial moth drawn to the flame, I am compelled to record the sight with my own two eyes. My sister, Adele, could be in such a ditch, or Kalman even. But I cannot look outside my hole.

When the Red Cross comes with the food, we converge on it. Never, we think, have our eyes seen so much food–such beauty! We push into each other, competing for a place in the front where soup is being distributed. We have forgotten politeness, for our lessons learned in the *lager* say you eat or you die. But Ruschia holds me back.

"Slowly, Blima," she says, "A bit of bread and water only, for we will surely get sick from stomachs filled too soon." And, as always, she is right, for those who have the huge bowls of thick vegetable soup soon become ill, and the stench and moans again fill the camp.

We are all together now, Ruschia, Sophie, and I. And when we finally lift our heads, we find we are in, of all places, the military barracks, with white pillows under our heads, and soap with which to wash our hands. It is not *Judenseif*, as we fear, made from the bones of the dead, but American soap packaged with a name on the top. We have kerchiefs to warm our heads against the wind, and coats with buttons for the cold. We can talk to each other and say whatever we like. Mostly, we just say thank you a hundred thousand times to the British soldiers who have young, tanned, disbelieving faces. To each other, we say nothing.

When they march the guards, rifles at their back, I see Herta, and remember how she sliced Sophie's arm with the edge of a wooden stick, and how the blood spewing its redness erupted fast and red as if from a volcano. Gentle Sophie who drew pictures of elves as gifts for her young nieces. I see Erich, walking grim-faced into the truck, and I remember how he stepped on a boy's hand. The boy's crime was falling asleep on a space of floor on which the guard wanted to pass. When the boy cried out, Erich kicked him in the gut. We would kill the guards even with our bare hands, assured of God's pardon, if only we had the strength. We turn away instead.

Ruschia is sicker than we think, and there is a problem with her legs. The doctors from the Red Cross come and examine her, and they tell her there is no choice but to take her to Sweden for an operation. But she will not go.

"What if Victor comes for me?" she says. No one argues with her. She has already lost too much.

Some say it is a miracle that we survived. The British, our liberators, are kind, but they stand a little bit back too, as if we are not from the world. And truly, we think the same ourselves. When we walk, it is as if we are toddlers taking our first steps. When we speak, we are silent at first, for we have yet to learn the tongue of free men. When we drift to sleep, it is with the anticipation of rest, not the fear that haunts our souls even in our dreams. Although some, I sense, can never know true sleep. All of this the British, the Americans, and even the Russians now see. In Bergen-Belsen alone, they find 17,000, thousands succumbing daily, liberated for death. How can you hate a child just because he is a Jew, they ask. How can you destroy a people for their beliefs? How can one individual hate another so that he deals with him as less than a dog?

So, the miracle is that any survive at all, they say. But for me, the miracle is that we find each other.

A woman comes to the camp looking for her husband. She has a narrow face and disheveled brownish red hair; she wears a simple white button-down shift with little pink flowers on it, suitable for the summer months which we now endure. Already the numbers are off her forearm, but by the lost expression of her eyes and the tenseness in her brow, we can tell she is a *lager* woman.

"I have word that my Moishe is staying here," she says to anyone who will listen, "Moishe Abramowitz last from Birkenau, maybe you know him? A small man with thinning hair who is a carpenter by trade... Ahh," she adds, frustrated, "he should be here. What can one do without pictures? Moishe Abramowitz, a quiet man who has but one wife as family." A coterie of Jews gathers around the woman, as they do with other searchers, almost on a daily basis now.

"*Oy!*" exclaims one man suddenly, scratching his bald head. He is a stooped man who walks with a limp, and looks to be about sixty, though he is probably no more than forty years of age.

"Moishe– maybe I know such a man. Just last week, I think–" The woman grasps him by the collar of his plaid seersucker shirt and pulls him to her.

"Can it be you know my Moishela? Is he here, for sure? *Oy, Gott!*" The man bobs his head up and down, mutters something to himself, as the reflection of a smile shimmers across his face. He taps his head again.

"There is a Moishe who is, yes, a quiet man and...but a carpenter? I am not sure..." then, releasing himself from the woman, says, "Wait...Wait just a small minute." He walks away as quickly as one can with a limp, as the woman starts to pull at her own hair with anticipation. Before long, before even the man reappears, we see a short stocky man running toward us.

"Yetta!" he screams out, and before she can embrace him, the two begin to cry.

Many such reunions have taken place in the camps, and many disappointments as well. As for us, our family has grown to include Ruschia's grown niece and nephew, as well as two of our three male cousins, Froyim and Yankel. They are looking for their youngest brother, Lazar, for they have had word that he is alive. Everybody, it seems, is looking for someone.

Much later, as another night of wondering descends upon us, we invite Moishe and Yetta to a game of cards and begin to ask our questions, for time and curiosity have unlocked our mouths, and the words spill forth before we take the luxury of amenities.

"Have you seen my aunt, a big woman with short gray hair?"

"Do you know my brother, tall, blonde?"

"I have a sister. She was in Auschwitz...maybe..?"

The couple listens patiently, always touching each other, a hand on a shoulder or atop a head; watching only each other's eyes as they speak. They are reunited lovers, but also grieving parents.

"Perhaps you know my husband, Victor Weisstuch?" Ruschia asks tentatively. The man, Moishe, straightens up, and for the first time he turns his eyes away from his wife.

"Victor? Why, he and I were in the *lager* together. Buchenwald..." The breath escapes Ruschia's lips audibly, and before she has time to ask, Moishe exclaims, "Yes, yes, my *shvester*, my sister, the last time I saw Victor he was alive." They were together, he goes on to say, at Buchenwald's liberation in the Russian zone, and later stayed in the American camps. Victor had learned what had come to pass of Ruschia and their two little girls, and had small hope that any of them had survived the flames of Auschwitz. Only his one sister, Blima, who was taken away so early, did he have any hope of finding. Moishe confirmed too that Victor's cousin, Lazar, had been with him and was looking also for his brothers. Froyim and Yankel slap each other's backs in joy. To think, all three siblings, alive! But Ruschia looks down only at her still legs.

"How can I go to him," she says quietly, uttering more statement than question.

"He will come to you," I assure her.

Two days later, we receive more good news. We are surveying the new lists, just released by the Red Cross, names, age, birthplace of those found alive or, in some cases not yet dead. We eagerly scan the names, black on white, black on white, our eyes flicker like snapping camera shutters over each one. Adele? Miriam? And then our eyes set upon a bright ruby within dark clouds. Kalman Weisstuch.

"*Dine breetah laybt!*" Your brother is alive, Ruschia cries out, clasping my hand. I close my eyes, and for the first time in years let my youngest brother appear before me through the uncertain gauze of time. Kalman with his dark curly hair and laughing dimples. Kalman, his mother's favorite. But it could not be possible. He was so young, before Bar Mitzvah even. And yet, there on the paper is his name. Kalman Weisstuch. Alive.

Our second wave of good news overtakes us only weeks later as summer's heat begins to wane, and we learn to stretch our legs and arms with the push of each brisk morning's breeze. Another group of survivors arrives from Warsaw, a man with his two young girls whom he hid in the home of a blessed Christian family for the duration of the war. He had heard that his wife, a woman of thirty-three years named Ruthie, was staying here in the quarters with us. No one knows her, really. Perhaps she is one who had been taken to the hospital in Sweden, someone said. We have a hope for this, anyway. The man heaves a huge sigh, as if he has done this many times before, then, looking at the two tired girls by his side, asks if we do not mind if they rest here. Of course not, we answer, who could object, God forbid? The encounter, while disappointing for him, provides an air of brief exhilaration for us. That night, we sit again outdoors drinking glasses of tea with apples, watching a half moon sail forward in the gray darkness. The man tells us that he too knew Victor and that, in fact, my brother and a cousin were already on their way to this very place. Ruschia and I look at each other through dropped lids, not wishing to impede on the man's personal misery. But our eyes, though shielded, are smiling.

Betty

Jackie is so stubborn. He has ideas. He wants to go now to Israel with his friend Ira, but first he goes to Egypt to ride a camel, and then Jordan to walk across the bridge. What for he wants to go to these places? He says, "Ma, don't be so nervous." Okay, maybe I am a nervous one, but I have a right.

The bell rings loud in this apartment. Shirley and her husband, Arthur, stand at the door with a white box in the hand. It is seven-layer-cake from the kosher bakery, says Shirley. What for we need the *nosh*, I say, grabbing her around the neck with a kiss.

"Hey, I would have bought the poppy seed sweet rolls you like, Ma, but they were out. Anyway, Jack likes these. And, now that he is skinny, it's okay."

"I heard that," says Jackie, coming out of his bedroom down the hall, "Does that mean you won't be force feeding me like you did with that package of Oreo cookies?"

"No, not this time," Shirley laughs, "but that was about ten years ago when you were around a hundred pounds fatter...Hey, remember the four bialys with butter and orange juice you would have every Sunday morning while watching cartoons?"

"That was orange *soda*," Jackie corrects, "Ah...those were good times!"

"Where is the good times?" Chiel walks in, gives Shirley a kiss, and shakes Arthur's hand. The children look at each other under the eyes. Chiel cannot hear and all the time he thinks we have secrets. That is why he likes me not to talk to the women even. I tell him to wear a hearing aid. But he is too ashamed.

I put out the goulash and applesauce on the table. Shirley tells me to mash hers, so I mash with a fork, pour the Coca Cola for everybody, and we sit down. Then I run in the kitchen for napkins. Always I am forgetting something.

"I saw the article in the paper today," says Chiel, taking another bite from the meat.

"That's my own column, Daddy. It's called 'Breathing Room,'" answers Shirley, smiling at her father. Chiel is the most proud of her. He tells her all the time to write a book of the life, of what we went through. So all the time he is telling the stories. He is not like the other fathers who want only for the girls to stay home and have babies. She has time, Chiel says, let her write.

After we finish the seven-layer cake, and I package up some grapes for Shirley to take back home, we go into the bedroom. The whole family, except for Arthur who likes the ball game on the television, goes inside. Chiel changes to the slippers and puts the shoes neat under the bed. He is a neat man, always with the tie and the hat to match. Shirley opens up the perfume bottles on the dresser and sniffs them. Jackie lies down on the bed, with the hands behind his head. When we talk of something important, it is always in the bedroom. Don't ask me why.

"Look, Jackie, why you have to go someplace so far? You know how afraid I am for you," I say. Jackie lifts himself up on the elbow.

"Ma, you are afraid of everything...I will be perfectly fine."

"Jackie, you know how nervous—"

"Well, stop being so nervous. You look at a starving baby from Biafra on TV, or see an earthquake, or whatever, and you go hysterical. Ma, you have got to calm down!" Jackie is right. I am too much nervous. I watch Shirley at the dresser, and I see she looks at the picture of me with my sisters, Ruschia's children. Adele is laughing still.

"Is it totally necessary that you go to Egypt and Jordan too?" asks my daughter, turning now to Jackie. He gives her the sour face. With the mustache now and the early gray hair, he looks like a man of forty, not the twenty-one that he is.

"Give me a break, please," he just says tiredly. Before I can object, he interrupts, "The mistake I made is telling you at all, Ma. I should have just said that I'm going upstate for three weeks, and you wouldn't say boo." I feel the blood coming to my face again.

"No secrets!" I scream, and Jackie gives me the look like I am crazy. Everybody always keeps the secret from me. When Marcus was so sick and Victor gave him the kidney, I knew about it two weeks later. When Froyim's daughter from Toronto had the cancer and died–*oy, Gott*–it was a month later that I knew. When Chiel's cousin had the breakdown, oh, I could tell anyway, I first found out after she came from the hospital. Even when his Tante Sifra,–a ninety-five-year-old, they shouldn't die younger–was put in the home, Chiel first tells me on the bus when we are going to visit her. I thought I should know, I said to him, after all, she brought us to this country. But all I hear is I am too emotional. Maybe they are right. Besides, I have my secrets too. I never told Chiel about Smulke.

"And when you go away, I will drive the car to the store." All of a sudden, we hear from Chiel. Jackie gets up from the bed and puts his arm around Chiel.

"The bus will take you there just as well," he says, laughing.

"What is the big deal," Chiel objects, "Only a few blocks down Coney Island Avenue I have to go, and I am a good driver." Shirley, Jackie, and I look at each other with smiling eyes. Chiel is not such a good driver. He gets the tickets, and one time when we lived in Lakewood, he even put the car into a telephone pole. Thank God, he was not hurt, but the car was a ruin. Since Kalman gave to Jackie the car, he drives Chiel in the mornings on Sundays to bring in and unbundle the papers. He drives him to the bank and where he has to go, but still Chiel thinks he is a driver.

Jackie is driving everyday, anyway, and has good practice. He drives for a congressman. Yes, a congressman! He takes him to the meetings and all the engagements, and in the summer he works in Washington as an intern. One time even I met this congressman and his wife. Jackie tells him that Chiel and I are survivors from the war, and they jump up and shake our hands like we are movie stars. The congressman even writes for Chiel a letter trying to get money for reparations. When Jackie tells him we vote in every election since we are citizens, the congressman says, "That's terrific!" What is so terrific, Chiel answers, it is our right. The congressman nods and shakes our hands again. This is the truth, I think, we do vote in every election. I read the papers, but still I ask Shirley and Jackie who to vote for. Chiel asks nobody, and when he votes, it is a secret. Such a funny man!

Jackie and Chiel are Indian wrestling on the dresser. They say they will settle about the car in this way. They have been doing this since the wrestling they were watching on TV. I think better they would like to be wrestling on the floor like Bruno San Martino and Haystack Calhoun. But Shirley says that was a fake, anyway, even if I still believe it was real. Sometimes, I went in the kitchen to hide my eyes from it.

Jackie wins the fight, putting down Chiel's arm, but then they go again, and he lets Chiel win.

"This is a moot point, because Brian is borrowing the car, anyway," Jackie finally announces, walking away.

"What is the *moot*?" I ask.

"Irrelevant, not important."

"Here's my wedding gown!" says Shirley. She is in the closet. "I'm glad to see you didn't give this away, Ma. Remember when you gave away my white rabbit fur jacket with the round fur buttons to the neighbor in Lakewood?"

"It was too small for you," I answer. I walk to the closet and touch the lace at the cuff and high neck. After only four years in the plastic, already it is getting yellow.

"Don't worry about me. I will call you everyday, like I always do when I'm away," says Jackie, reminding me about my worry.

"Jackie, but–"

"Why don't you two get a dog to keep you company?"

Chiel and I open the eyes and start to laugh.

"Okay, instead of a son, we will have a dog," I say, scratching and shaking my head at his foolishness.

"Hey, Daddy, remember that time we had the dog, in Flatbush?" asks Shirley, falling backwards on the bed, giggling.

"How can I forget this? It was when we had the launderette, and you dragged me to every store until you found a black and white dog, and–"

"And it had diarrhea all over the apartment!" says Shirley, laughing all over again.

"Well, then, a cat? They catch mice, Ma, and you'd like that," smiles Jackie, leaning against the dresser. Shirley is hysterical with laughing now.

"Don't get me started on that, Jack! Wasn't that alley cat we had for a week black and white too? It used to jump at us and we had to stand on the bed to get away from it. And then, when the cat pounced on Daddy's head when he was on the toilet? Well, that was the end of the cat!" We all start again, laughing, as Chiel stands with the quiet smile. I wipe the tears from the corners of my eyes.

"I had a cat once," I say, "Her name was Masha. What a smart cat!"

"I remember you telling me about her, Ma," answers Shirley, "So, seriously, a cat might not be a bad idea."

"No more cats," Chiel says, quietly, but firmly. And that is the end of that.

We decide to let Jackie go on his vacation. He will not listen, anyway. He reminds us that soon he will be living by himself in Manhattan and going to law school. What have I to complain, anyway? My son the lawyer, and my daughter the writer and editor. It is what we live for.

Blima

Victor arrives a day before Rosh Hashanah, and Lazar with him. How do I have words to express such a joy? Ruschia's and my happiness is matched only by that of Victor himself who, having lost half his stomach and gained two dark circles under his eyes, beams nonetheless. When he embraces me and stares relentlessly into my face, I feel it is good to see again eyes which match my own. After a silence which is richer than words, he describes how he worked from the first light until the shroud of night, bolting Nazi rifles together or carrying boxes beyond one hill to the next. He tells us too how he would stand tall and puff out his chest on each selection when they would place the stick under his chin. He then asks how it is possible that we are here, so Ruschia narrates the subterfuge she conceived in binding her legs, and I tell him of my angel, Gizella.

"When we are all together, I will find her and thank her," I say.

"Oh, *shvester*, I fear we *are* all together, Mama, *Tata*, all of them in the house were taken at the same time. Only the *Tata* came back once to the house, but then, the SS took him out again like a kitten from its milk. And, *oy*, you know the story...Our parents, *mine Gott*, I am sure went to the fires, and what use had the swine of the younger ones? Miriam, no doubt, went with the children, in her foolish stubbornness." He turns as he hears Ruschia murmuring under her breath, "Maybe it was not stubbornness, but because she is a mother, as I once was..."

Victor kisses Ruschia's forehead and cheeks.

"You could not, my dear one, and even if you could, it would leave you in the same place as Miriam...No, it was for you to live," he says, adding, "But Efraim, Adele, Brandl, and Kalman, they had no luck..." I open my mouth to speak when the image of our family sitting in the parlor, *Tata* with his newspaper, Mama sewing, and the rest talking, playing games, at once normal and precious, flashes like a camera shot before my eyes.

Victor leans over and gives my arm a tight squeeze.

"I am sorry for you, Blimala. Adele who was your constant companion, and your own twin, Efraim...Do you remember how he protected you?...Ah, even your Smulke, always so headstrong, I hear he was shot trying to escape on a death march in the forest....," he lowers his voice, "All, wiped away with one hand."

I can do nothing but look down at my feet, warmed now by white anklets and simple loafers. If I gaze backwards, I tell myself, I will surely be consumed by the fires of the past, so I must stand here beneath the sun. Stand here with the remnants of my family, my one beloved brother...Oh, what was I thinking just a moment ago? What was I about to say when...And then it comes to me.

"Victor, our brother, Kalman, is alive!"

Victor's eyes open incredulously. He breathes out the words, "Blima, it cannot be...he was too young." But Ruschia confirms my words, telling Victor about the list and how she noticed only a few days ago that Kalman Weisstuch from Dombrowe was on it. Victor shakes his head, disbelieving, but then, strangely, he begins to sob like a small child. Ruschia, Sophie, and I cannot bear the sight of a man crying, especially a man such as Victor, and soon we are all crying. I am not sure if we are crying about Kalman or the ones we have lost, but the release of tears so long forbidden, and releasing them all of us together in this way, revives us like a sudden spring rain. We cry for a very, very long time, and when we are done, Victor determines to look for his brother as soon as the holiday is over.

And such a holiday it is! Never has there been a New Year such as this, nor I suspect will there ever be. We put on the best of our charity clothes, and the men gather together in a tent which we use for a synagogue. By a miracle, one of many, someone is able to secure a Torah, and as it is carried outdoors, we tap our *siddurim*, our prayer books, against the Holy Scrolls as tears fill our eyes. From afar, we women prepare fish and set tables with *challah* and even some wine as we watch the men, each bent and swaying, head covered by a *tallit;* it is not the prayer shawl received at the Bar Mitzvah, but a new one signifying a new chance, a renewal of life. The prayers go up to God in a series of moans and tears, enough, they plea, to pierce heaven itself. Some of the older men and women keel over, struck by the raw emotion of the day. But not I, for since the day I left my home, I have had not one fainting spell. God has blessed me with a newfound strength, and this is just one of the things which I thank Him for on this day. I tend to the weak with soft words and a steady hand, and dole out pieces of apples and honey to the few young ones who wait for the treats, shuffling their feet impatiently.

At Kol Nidre, that most beautiful service on the night before Yom Kippur, our paeans are sung with a passion which would rival the voices of angels. Oh, and when I look up, I can see the clouds parting slowly in the purple sky, and as surely as I know there is a God, I can hear Him listening with each murmur of the wind. The next day, our leather shoes and belts removed as required by Law, and, *siddurim* in hand, we stand once more before God. And although one day is not enough for our multitude of prayers, we stand close, women on one side, men on the other, and, with our fists pounding our chests, say aloud our public, our most private yearnings. *Forgive us, Oh Lord, for eating of the* traife, *the unkosher, for our blasphemy, for our traitorous ways against our brethren and our enemies, for the foulness of mouth, our stiff-neckedness, our pride...Oh, Lord, forgive, forgive..."* And, for the first time in my life, I say *Yizkor,* the

prayer for the dead, the *zichronam livrachah* of blessed memory....
"*God, remember the soul of my beloved, and bind them with the blessed souls
of Abraham, Jacob, Isaac, Sarah, Rachel, Rebecca, Leah...*" We thank
Him too for the multitude of blessings bestowed upon us, and the
possibility of *geschenkte yahren*, the extra years which surely will flow
from life. As the darkness paints its first stars against the sky, we
leave our tent with voices hoarse and spirits filled with conviction.

Outside, Victor, Ruschia, Sophie, the cousins, and I kiss each
other, but none of us makes a move back to quarters, for our stomachs do not call to us in hunger. Instead, we are content to stand
and watch the Jews all around us, walking home as free men who
have just completed a Yom Kippur fast on the soil of their enemies.

Shirley

Holidays at home were a private affair. Whenever I gazed at a Norman Rockwell painting with dad carving the turkey as children, mom, and extended clan proudly looked on, the scene seemed as foreign to me as a vintage photograph from Siberia. Until I married, except for the occasional Thanksgiving, when we would join our aunts, uncles, and cousins, we celebrated each occasion with the immediate family. The four of us. My friends asked if I missed having grandparents, and a large extended family, but I said no. How could I miss what I never had? I admit, though, wondering what my father's sister, the one he said I resembled, really looked like. And my maternal grandmother who, Aunt Ruschia once revealed, was a lot like my own mother. Yes, I would have liked to have met her, if only once. But for the most part, I was content with just the four of us. Who needed to be squeezed in between cigar-smoking cousins and cheek-pinching great-aunts? We created our own traditions.

Yom Kippurs Daddy would wrap himself in the old white and dark blue woven *tallis*, the prayer shawl, put on the white sneakers which he wore only once a year, and he and my brother would walk the ten blocks or so to the synagogue. There, the two would spend all day in prayer, emerging only for a noon break to walk the ten blocks home where they would rest on the couch until it was time for evening services. Mommy and I would remain at home, except for some years when we would get dressed in our finest suits and meet them in synagogue just in time to hear the exalted notes of the *shofar,* signaling the New Year. But most of the time, I would be home wearing a button-down shirt and dungarees waiting simply for the sound of the key turning in the lock. As the girl, I was the only one in the family who never really had to go to *shul,* but sometimes Mommy decided to say Yizkor, the prayer for the dead, at home. And so, we would remain, she with her *Forward* newspaper, and I with my novel, reading together.

At nightfall after Yom Kippur, the holiest day when we fasted, it was the same every year. My mother would proclaim the words, which I already knew by heart, in my ear. "*Zolsta usgibatin a guta yuah.*" I hope you receive your prayer for a good year, I would also proudly announce, kissing Daddy and my brother as they walked through the front door. Ceremonially, Daddy and Jack returned our kisses, Daddy even giving my mother an extra hug. Then, after wishing each other a good New Year and, as my mother would remind, especially a *healthy* one, Daddy would carefully fold and place his *tallis* in the bag. My mother was already running to get extra napkins and bottles of soda as Daddy took his place at the head of the table. And then, the feast would begin.

Daddy and I would immediately devour the bits of herring in cream sauce, savoring the long white slices of onion as we dipped chunks of *challah* into the cream. Then the eggs, soft-boiled for Daddy and scrambled for the rest of us, french toast sweating with thick maple syrup, scallion and vegetable cheeses, tuna fish with chopped onion, the way only my mother could make it. I was on my last bite of tuna wedged between the folds of a slice of rye, when my mother would come running again, this time with a heaping plate of her gefilte fish, a dish she had labored over two nights earlier.

"I can't eat anymore, Ma!" I laughed, holding my stomach. It was tradition for my mother to serve breakfast, lunch, and dinner in rapid succession for Yom Kippur's "break fast." No one, not

Arthur's family nor any of my friends, ever did this. It is not a Jewish thing. But it was my mother's.

"Don't be such a child, it is excellent. Taste it," she persisted, taking my fork and feeding me a piece of the fish. I knew, in spite of my objections, that I would eat the fish, and then willingly have another. I knew too well my mother's reasoning for all the food. The beginning of the New Year is the time to thank God and celebrate our abundance. But for her it was also a time to remember when one rotten potato was all she had to sustain her for three days.

Barely ten minutes later, we were dipping our spoons into chicken soup in which meat-filled dumplings called *kreplach,* bobbed invitingly. Boiled chicken, brisket, fried potatoes, and applesauce followed. But by that time, all I could hold was a tea-spoonful of the applesauce, and I pushed my plate away, heading for the bathroom. When I returned, I'd find Daddy meticulously cutting a piece of his brisket "top of the rib" as Mommy placed a platter of *ruggelech* along with sliced honey and sponge cake on the table. I grabbed one of the chocolate *ruggelech* and ran for my room where I could finally finish my homework, all writing having been forbidden for the day. But as I opened my science textbook, I would hear my mother's melodic appeal ring down the hallway.

"Shoiley, *please.* You ate so little!"

Pesach, Passover, was also a time when the bonds of our family strengthened. But they were often tested as well. In the week prior to our celebration of liberation from our Egyptian masters, the house would undergo an amazing and rapid transformation. Mommy would wash all the floors on her hands and knees, poking with rags even into the corners of the kitchen. The vacuum would protest loudly as she dragged it across the large Oriental rug in the living room and the plush beige carpets in the bedrooms. Each knick knack would be lovingly wiped and polished, each table caressed with ammonia or oils. And when each item in the household was scrubbed clean so that it was rejuvenated to its original glow, Daddy would climb onto a kitchen chair and reach back onto the highest cabinet shelf in the kitchen to retrieve the special *Pesach* dairy dishes to be used for the eight days of celebration. The set of dishes used for meat were easier to attain, having rested in the living room armoire throughout the year. Since we had only one stove, Mommy would wrap sheets of aluminum foil around each of the burners before meticulously scouring the pantry for any food item which was prohibited. Then, shortly before the advent of the holiday, Daddy and Jack would search for stray crumbs with candle and feather. And finally, we were ready for the Seder.

My most profound memory of our two annual nights of Seders is of Daddy and my brother fighting. Daddy would open up the paperback *Pesach siddur* with the Maxwell House advertisement on the cover, put on his reading glasses, and begin the Hebrew recanting. His face was cast downward in concentration as he read the words in rapid-fire order. His eyes half-closed, index finger moving along the page, he became absorbed in prayer, his own spirit oblivious to the rest of us. He would get no further than that first page before my brother, the yeshiva student, would interrupt.

"You are going much too fast...You're not pronouncing that word right...You're skipping that whole section!" Daddy would look up slowly and squint at his only son.

"I have been doing this for thirty years before you were born! You think you know everything? Not yet, you don't!" And then he would straighten himself in his chair, search the spot in the book with his index finger, put the finger to his mouth, wet it, turn the page, and begin again. But, once more, just like the moving hands of a steady clock, my brother would interrupt. "You're not doing it right at all!" And so went the annual test of wills to which we had become accustomed. My brother trying to assert his right to give more meaning to the occasion, and my father desperately trying to hold on to his paternal, and dominant, role. My mother, for the most part, remained silent during these confrontations, except for occasionally inquiring the page number as she dipped and licked her pinky finger during the reciting of the plagues. And when it came time to taste the horseradish representing the bitterness of our lives when we were enslaved, Mommy iterated the same cautionary phrase. "Better to taste the bitter from God than the sweetness from the nobles," she would say in Yiddish, as Daddy handed us the little matzo sandwiches. Bitter like the arguments in this family, I thought. Not understanding Hebrew, I would just sit back passively, sipping wine and tasting matzo at the appropriate times. Frustrated for many years by my brother and father's stubbornness and arguing, I soon became amused and even began to look forward to their exchanges.

As I pushed my chair back from the dining room table, I felt terribly ignorant. Of course, I could read the words in English which were on the opposing side of every page, yet I couldn't help but feel a void. It was as if I was walking down a road and a swift spring breeze full of jasmine, lilac, and rose had brushed past me. I could sense it barely, but could never totally be enveloped in its wind, not really. So looking at my family, my mother still humming the "*Dayanu*" to herself as she brushed crumbs off the table, my father lingering over his last glass of tea, my brother looking again for a word inside the prayer book, I did the only thing I could. I went into my room and prayed. I didn't pray for new clothes, or a boyfriend, or straight A's. I just prayed that everything would remain the same.

Betty

Shirley takes a piece of the chopped meat with the hand.

"Mmm...This is so good!" she says.

"You think more garlic?" I ask, shaking more powder into the chopped meat and egg mixture. She closes the eyes and smiles.

"You can never have too much garlic!" I wrap the raw hamburger in wax paper and put it in the refrigerator. Then I wash good the hands in hot water, and wipe them on the apron.

"I'll be ready in a minute!" I say, running into the bedroom to change. Shirley wants us to come this year to her synagogue by the house they own in Staten Island. I don't know even if Chiel will go, he likes all the time to be for the holidays at home. But Shirley insists. How can I say no? Already we are in the last year of the '70s, and my Shirley is married for almost six years, over a year already she is in Staten Island. Now she also insists to take me for a new outfit. I tell her I have a whole closet filled with outfits I don't wear, but she answers they are a hundred years old already. So, I should throw out?

I put on the stockings and the white dress with the orange polka dots, fix myself just with the lipstick, and go out. She will take me with the car to Kings Plaza, and, I don't know, maybe I can find something on sale.

Chiel likes to go with me too always to buy like I am a *pritza*, some princess. But today, he goes with Jackie to buy a television set on the Lower East Side. He says he will make him a good deal so he has for the new apartment. This makes me happy. Since Chiel gives up the store, he has too much time. Always he looks in the paper just for a little job, like to open up a *shul* or something. If he doesn't look, he walks down Kings Highway. One time, Shirley sees him there because she is out to lunch from the high school where she works. She tells me he smokes the cigarette, and when he sees her, he quickly throws on the sidewalk, like a child. I cannot be his *shamus*, his guardian, everyday, I tell him. This is a bad habit he picked up from the store.

Chiel cannot sit still. Now he is retired so he *shleps* me on the vacations. For me, I can be happy at home, but he is a man with *spelkas*, needles all the time. Even when we had the store, he was running to the country, to the cousins in Canada with Shirley. Somebody has to watch the store, so I stay. Even Chiel goes to Israel by himself, and *oy vay*, he is so mad when nobody is there at the airport to meet him. Everybody, he says, has the family meet the person coming from the plane. Shirley and Jackie say they did not know the time, and they are crying. But he is still mad and talks to nobody for days. Such a *shtila maruk*, a silent stone that man is. Anyway, now I go with him to Israel, to a spa in Italy, to Miami hotels many, many times. We even go to Germany to see the rich cousins. But to Poland I will not go. There is nothing for me there.

Shirley parks the car and we walk into Macys. She walks in front like an expert, and I follow. Right away she goes to the fancy section.

"How about this one, Ma?" she says, pulling out a light blue one, a sweater with a matching skirt.

"No, I answer. I don't like with the raglan sleeve," I answer, pushing away like it is fire.

"Oh, Ma, how about this one then? It has the polka dots that you love...And it looks like it's silk." She runs the hand on the dress like it is one of her dolls from home. Then, she takes it out and holds it in front of me. The ladies with the shopping bags are pushing, and all over there is too much perfume.

"Here," she says, "let me take your bag." I look at myself with the dress in front in the long mirror. I am too fat. I am too short. The dress will need fixing. Okay, so I find the price tag in the sleeve, and I see $49.99.

"Shoiley, who spends like this? Give me one with the sale price." Shirley shrugs the shoulders like I am the crazy one. Then, she starts to look for her size. I think she has no patience with me, but I think she is the one with a problem.

A skinny woman with curly black hair who wears a mohair sweater of many colors makes the motion to me. I go over and say hello to the little girl she is holding by the hand.

"Excuse me," says the skinny lady, "but do you think this jacket or this one looks better on me?"

"Try on," I say, taking the brown one from her while she puts on the navy.

The little girl is showing me her lollypop, but I say no, thank you. You eat it, it looks so good!

"What do you think?" says the skinny one, standing in front of the mirror, looking at herself with crossed eyebrows. I go to her and pull down the back more under the hips. Then I look in the mirror with crossed eyebrows too.

"I think maybe too low the shoulders, and too much fabric here," I answer, pulling from under the bust. "Try on the other one." I give her the jacket, and put on the hanger the one she tried.

"This color I think is much better for you. Goes better with the eyes, same color as your daughter." The lady smiles and turns herself in front of the mirror.

"Only to fix a little the cuffs, and–"

"Ma, there you are!" Shirley comes up behind me with maybe five outfits on the arm.

"Oh, sorry," explains the lady, "your mother was just helping me decide here. And I think she *has* helped." Shirley gives her a polite smile, saying, "That's my mother, she always likes to be of assistance. No problem."

"Well, thank you so much," says the lady, taking the jacket in one hand and the little one in the other, "It was a pleasure meeting you."

"Likewise," I say. The little girl waves me goodbye with the lollypop.

"Ma, what is it with you? You seem to attract people like bees to honey. Especially kids." Shirley is trying on a pink shift with a lace collar.

"Now you know why the *Tata* is so jealous all the time. It is not my fault,"

I say, pulling down on the hem. Another one I will have to fix.

"Who said it's your fault? I wish I could be like that. They all seem to like you."

"Well, I don't know why."

Shirley tries on all the dresses and makes some faces, saying she is too fat. I don't think so, and I tell her this. She asks if I am sure. I'm sure, I'm sure, I say. Then she pulls out two sweater dresses, both in medium.

"Look what I found, Ma! We could both be twins," she announces, showing me first the price tag. Big sale. Not too bad.

"Okay," I say, "I try on." Shirley helps me pull off the white dress with the orange polka dots so my beauty parlor setting does not get messed up. She sees my old brassiere which I sewed and fixed with safety pins, and gives me a look. Why should I throw away when I can fix, I think. But I decide to maybe buy a new one next week.

I see myself in the black sweater dress with the aqua, purple, and violet stripes on the sleeves. I bend down to look at the hemline, and Shirley tells me no, I am making it look longer.

"Really nice," she says, straightening the shoulder pads, "You have such good posture...Now, let me try this one." Shirley looks beautiful, much better than me.

"You buy," I say to her.

"We both buy," she answers, "just like twins." I take off the dress with her help, and tell her I will think about it.

We walk a little bit through Macys, and Shirley sprays the perfume on herself and then on me.

"Phew!" I say, "What a stink. Smells just like Mrs. Blum, the landlord's wife."

"How is Mrs. Blum, anyway?" says my daughter, her nose this time in a lotion.

"Oh, she complains about everything," I tell her, letting her try on me a cream for hands, "But I forgot to tell you! The landlord, the Mr. Blum, comes yesterday to the door for the rent. *Tata* was in the bank, and I tell him we left a check for him under the door. I was so scared! I think maybe the landlord comes to arrest us." Shirley pats me on the arm and puts her head next to mine.

"Don't be ridiculous. I told you that a landlord can't arrest anyone. You shouldn't be so frightened of anyone in authority. Even if you did forget the rent, he can't hurt you."

I don't know what this "authority" means, but still I tell her that the wife took the check from the door. It was his mistake, not ours, thank God.

Shirley takes me to the shelves where there are all kinds of shoes, some in boxes, others on the floor. She pulls out the high heels and tells me to try on.

"Wait, wait, wait," I say, looking at the straps and poking on the leather of each one. Then I see a shoe, a brown sandal with wide leather straps and a two-inch cork on the bottom. I put on the right one and am pushing down the corn on one toe and winding the strap around the sticking out bone.

"Put on the other one," Shirley suggests. I do it, and look in the small mirror on the floor. "What you think?" I ask her. She says, "Perfect." She shows me the price that they are on sale because it is end of season. So I look in the mirror again, and say okay. Ma, she says, I can always get you to buy shoes, if nothing else. I tell her not to worry, that one day she will get all the shoes.

"Don't talk like that," she says.

We wait at the register, Shirley holding the two black sweater dresses and another one for herself, and I am standing with the shoes. I take out the money from my bag, and tell her I will pay.

"I know," she tells me, "Put your money away until we get there." The line is long, and Shirley begins to tell me about a dream. She is running and running into a meadow where there are white daisies and a big sun shining like a new mirror. The daisies start to grow till her knees then the waist and even up to the head. She keeps running but cannot smell now the daisies that cover her eyes like bandages. Her legs trip in the long stems and she falls. She is no more in the meadow, but she falls off a cliff. Then she wakes up.

"What does that mean, Ma? What would Tante Mima say about that one?" I close my eyes and try to remember what Tante Mima, the interpreter of dreams, would have to say.

"Oh, the flowers are bringing you so many good things," I inform her, "and falling off a cliff is you will fall into more luck." My daughter laughs out loud and shakes her head, "You say *every* dream will bring something good! Even when Daddy had that dream about snakes when Jack was in Israel, you said that was happiness twisting around us."

"Well, Tanta Mima before the war always said the snakes are for good," I argue.

"As I recall, when Jack came back from Israel he told us he was hospitalized in Jerusalem with food poisoning. How good was that? Maybe the snakes represented IV lines, not happiness!" I shrug my shoulders.

"It was happiness it wasn't worse," I sigh.

Shirley puts the clothes on the counter and takes from me the shoes. I look on the register and check the numbers. She tells me the total and I count out the paper money and the dimes and pennies because I don't like the credit cards. I have one, but I do not use. After all, money is money.

Shirley takes from the counter the bags, and we walk out of the store. She says she does not really need so many new dresses now, but she will wear them soon, anyway. I don't know why she needs even one, but she wants it, so it is okay.

All of a sudden, she asks me about Tante Mima again. She wants to know what is the meaning of the water that like magic turns blue. I tell her, I do not know, if only I could look in Tante Mima's special book. Don't worry about it, Shirley answers, she has an idea. I ask her then what the dream means.

"I'm going to have a baby," she says.

Shirley

In some ways, a house is like a living soul. Empty, it is sterile, devoid of personality or identity. But when people occupy it, the house fills with promise, frenetic busyness of lights and refrigerators plugged in, currents afresh, furniture settled, footprints etched in and out and in and out the door. And when a child, a newborn, enters that house, the promise blossoms like abundant fruit. It is a soul fulfilled.

This was the feeling which surged through me on the day of my firstborn's *brit*, the ceremony of circumcision incumbent upon the fathers of all males of the Jewish faith. I looked at myself in the wall-to-wall mirror of the living room. I was proud to be fitting so soon into the white polyester skirt suit hemmed by my mother. The hot pink silk shirt appropriately reflected the blush of happiness placed there the day my new son, Howie, was born.

Among all the fears I had growing up, two of the greatest were never getting married and never having a child of my own. These were fears born of a child's insecurity and fostered in the home of my parents where, like a rag doll, I was constantly supported and held aloft. I never paused to consider my own mettle which was propelling me socially and academically from a shy skinny girl whose pale face became dusty with the breath of books to the self-assured and poised woman I would become. At least that's the way others saw me.

When I first met Arthur, a blind date introduced by a friend at Brooklyn College, I described him as being "pleasant." Pleasant!

But I knew in my heart, if not my mind, that we would be together for life. Our interests were divergent to the extreme, proving the old axiom "opposites attract" true. He was a jock, a self-confessed basketball freak, who was manager of the team at Long Island University. From the beginning, he knew too. No flash, just a quiet pool of knowing.

I never voiced my fear about not being able to have a child of my own, but waited until we turned twenty-eight, bought the house, had the time and expectations held by many young married couples. And, mercifully, I became pregnant as soon as intent became action. The water had turned blue. From the first exciting quiver within me, I knew I was having a son. It seemed everyone else did too, especially my mother. "You are high and out," she would observe, patting my protruding belly, "that is a boy because girls are lower and round." Then she would add quickly, "What matter? As long as it's healthy." Like my mother, I felt confident that I too would deliver via Caesarian section. Even the doctor had his doubts about a more natural delivery, noting my small hands and thumb, which were some sort of indicators. Arthur and I exuberantly dove into Lamaze classes, and we even agreed to have a Wagner College student majoring in nursing assist with the birth. "I doubt that your help will be necessary," I told her, "I'll probably be a section."

As it turned out, she never did get the chance to help me, not because I was a "section," but because I delivered three weeks early while she was on spring break. My water broke on the morning of April 5, 1980, just a day after the nursery had been wallpapered. It was during the Passover holiday, and we had visited friends living in Brooklyn only the night before. My girlfriend's rubbery "Kosher for Passover" chocolate cake fueled a series of caustic remarks which seemed to propel both gales of laughter and the baby. "I can't be having the baby today," I objected in the car on the way to the hospital, "It just doesn't seem possible." Arthur just smiled at me and whistled along with a Kenny Loggins tune on the radio. We arrived at seven in the morning, and eleven hours and sixteen minutes later, Howard Allan was born. No Caesarian section, no medication. I called for my mother once only. But in the end, I was proud that for once I was as strong as she.

"Thanks for letting me make my dinner engagement," the doctor said, shaking my hand. Howie, my child, was squirming, squealing, platinum-haired, and instantly perfect. He was wrapped like a present in a pink blanket because there were so many boys born that week that no more blues were left. At 5 lbs., 2 1/2 oz., he was automatically named "peanut" and "little chicken" by all of the nurses. When we brought him home, there was a giant blue stuffed rabbit in his room, purchased by the new father. Rabbits were in particular abundance then, Easter being the Sunday after my child's birth.

I bent to help my parents who were both squatting in a closet in the nursery, scooping up papers and books to make room for their new grandson's necessities. Stooping, I was relieved to feel the last of my stitches dissolve. We picked up most of the mess, and I finally succeeded in urging my mother to join us downstairs once the bell signaled company arriving.

Like a wondrous glass mosaic, my colleagues from Madison High School joined my new neighbors from Carlyle Green, who joined my companions from college, who joined Arthur's old friends, parents, his brother and daughter, who joined my family. When I kissed my aunts and uncles, I could see their eyes shining.

"Are you happy?" my father kept asking me as I hugged friends and scurried to place paper plates on the dining room table. I looked at his face, afraid still to acknowledge the wrinkles appearing more frequently under his eyes. And I knew he was remembering too the last time we were together at a *brit*, a *brit* performed in the hospital for my brother.

"Yes, Daddy, I'm happy," I said. He reached down and squeezed the top of my kneecap, knowing he could always get me to squirm. I smiled, nevertheless. In fact, on that day, it was difficult not to.

My mother stood near the stove nervously wiping some crumbs off the burner. Too nervous still to touch the newborn, she was keeping her emotions in check.

"The house looks *zaya shein*, very nice," she whispered in my ear. I pressed her hand between my own. Mommy had always wanted a house of her own, and was almost convinced she would have one. One afternoon, when I was only six and we were walking along the boardwalk at Asbury Park, we stopped at a mechanical fortune teller wearing a turban, dropped in a quarter, and watched the lights pop as the prophet's arms moved the cards. One came out of the slot reading: "Someday you will own a beautiful house." Mommy smiled and placed the card in her wallet. For her, the prediction was never fulfilled. But it was for me, and to her it was just the same.

I waited downstairs along with the other women as the *mohel* and all the men went up to the nursery for the circumcision. My father, the "zandek," had the honor of holding the baby during the procedure. Marcie, a friend I had known and kept since we sat next to each other in tenth grade gym class, was to be the godmother. And my brother, slender now, with black hair threaded with gray and looping over his eyebrows, the godfather.

We women huddled nervously together, and when the baby cried, so did my mother, as she dug her fingers into my arm. Shortly afterwards, we heard the shouts of "Mazel Tov!" and we bounded upstairs to find my son contentedly sucking on a wad of cotton dipped in wine. Arthur's brother already had the camera poised, and had begun clicking.

In one photograph, I am standing holding my new son, my husband is next to me, my mother and father alongside on the right, my in-laws to the left. I remember posing for the picture and knowing that, for the first time, the sweet grape scent of wine had begun to replace the sting of ashes. Finally, I had given back, a gift to my parents, a redemption. It was the best day of my life. And I was not to have another like it for many years.

Blima

Victor leaves to find Kalman, but returns alone after only a few days. He is distraught, and believes now he has lost his youngest brother a second time. He relates how he met a man on the train to Munich. The man's words, he tells us, were as sour as his face.

"He knew Kalman from a work camp when they were together in the salt mines," Victor says, "There was a selection and Kalman with his own brother were taken to Dachau. And there, the brother tells him, he witnessed Kalman selected for the gas."

"But the list!" I scream, "The list tells us that Kalman lives!"

"*Oy, shvester,*" answers my brother, exhausted, "the one thing worse than despair is hope followed by disappointment. We must find our happiness in each other."

But it is Ruschia who will not let the matter rest.

"No, Victor, you must continue to look. You know how quick young Kalman always was. Perhaps...perhaps..."she looks for the words in the air, "he jumped from one line to the other, or ran down a road unobserved. You must go back. Cousin Lazar is not back yet, so perhaps he has already found him. But this time, I will go with you, if you can wait just a few days."

And in those days, Ruschia is sufficiently recovered to walk, although the doctors caution that an operation will still be necessary. She sets out with her embattled husband, who admits that if it weren't for her he would not have the strength for the trip, as growing discouragements weigh heavily on him. I remain behind to cook and care for the others, but already I am planning my mission to find my savior.

And five days later, when they return, Victor tells it to me this way:

"We were just off the train, walking into the city of Munich, you know how it is, everyone seemed to be running to work here and there, like ourselves, looking for family. People, some dressed in the finest garbs as if there had never been a war, others in flimsy jackets, confused, and it is these whom I approached. I repeated the name of my brother until it came from my mouth without thinking. I must have looked frantic, like a *meshuganah*, a madman, I don't know.

"Finally, a tall man with graying hair came up to me and placed his hand on my shoulder. 'Don't look so disturbed, my friend,' this kind man said, 'We all have our sorrows, but you must remain strong, and not get your expectations too high.' Then, looking into my face, he thought he recognized me, but after we talked awhile, we realized that we had been in different lagers, and this was not possible. I told him my name which he said sounded somewhat familiar, but how? Then, suddenly, as if a bell had summoned him, the man stood erect and said he had just met a boy of the same name, and was talking to him as they came out of the station not five minutes ago. 'Why,' I exclaimed, 'that is my brother!' Without replying, the man pointed to the crowd of people a few feet ahead. Already I was running, screaming his name, and when I saw the curly dark hair turning around, and the dimpled face of a boy much taller but skinnier, *oy shvester,* it *was* a miracle!"

Not only was our Kalman alive, but he was well, too, and had been staying in a Displaced Persons camp outside of Munich. Our cousin Lazar had arrived there only days earlier. The two would be on their way in less than one week when, finally, two brothers and their sister would be reunited.

I cannot recall having been happier, and I now understand what I never did before. Before the war, with my family of seven siblings in all, I was content, and I could have been so for the rest of my life. But when the fabric of contentment has been ripped apart in such a way, and when one experiences the gaping hole that is loss only to find again something of what you had before, that is true happiness. When Kalman comes in, we three fall upon each other, locking together in a steel embrace, links in a chain of family. And in my tear-muddled brain, when I see Adele with her cocked hat and fur muff chiding me imperiously, my dead Mama telling me to hold still as she adjusts the hem of my skirt...my Mama who knew me better than any being on this earth...I gaze into the faces of my dear brothers and know that in them is my past and my future. When I see Kalman, his face so serious, with a maturity too precocious, I know there is a purpose to my having been saved. And now, more than ever, I am glad that I was.

✵ ✵ ✵

We continue our lives in Hohne-Belsen, just outside of the main camp, for many are still ill, and others like ourselves have not the strength or inclination to venture forth. Kalman returns to his home outside Munich, but visits often, returning with copies of *Unzer Veg* (*Our Way*), an official newspaper produced by the Central Committee of the Liberated Jews in Bavaria. We spend our days looking through the lists of survivors and reading the testimonies of other Jews from the camps and the ghettos who had undergone atrocities even we could not imagine. Kalman also often ventures into the center of the camp to listen to the words of Josef Rosensaft, a political leader who had been a businessman in the Polish town of Bedzin. Kalman agrees with much of what he says about the need to re-establish ourselves, but utterly rejects the harmony of shared leadership with the German-born Norbert

Wolheim. What he most likes to listen to are the Zionists who lambaste the Brits for limiting the number of Jews who enter Palestine. He tells us that in July he even marched with other Dps to Munich Burgerbraukeller, where Hitler rose to power, to sing *Hatikvah* and say the *kaddish* prayer for the dead. But not all of us are swept along by this political contagion to establish a Jewish State, and when we beg our teen-aged brother to join one of the camp's soccer teams as he had in the old life or continue his studies in one of the many small *yeshivot* sprouting everywhere like flowers, he points to the barbed wire which still surrounds the camp and asks us if we still feel ourselves to be free men.

"It is no different," he says, "throughout the cities in Germany where the citizens, without guns or dogs, curse and spit on us as we walk the streets just the same!" When he returns to Munich, Kalman does afford himself recreation in the form of theatrical productions like *Kiddush Hashem* (*Martyrdom*) performed by the Munich Jewish Theater Group. But in this we do not join him, preferring to plan our immediate future instead.

I have but one thought, and that is to find my Gizella. Cousin Lazar tells me to be patient, for he has some contacts with some German Catholics whom he too had befriended in the camps. Finally, my patience is rewarded when I receive a note from someone who knows of a woman in Munchberg, a woman who once lived with Gizella before the war. Victor accompanies me on the train. As I watch the countryside fly past me like a foggy dream, I recall the last time I boarded the train, and the icy fear which gripped my heart like a vise. I am confused and do not know what I will say to Gizella once I set my eyes upon her, but I know that I will never leave her again. Of that, I am quite sure.

✳ ✳ ✳

Etta Danhaus's apartment reflects the fastidiousness of one who is accustomed to doing things her own way. Shades resembling white doilies are hung primly over sparkling windows which let in the raucous sounds of the city streets below. Hot tea is served from a polished silver tea set placed on a round table covered by a white cotton tablecloth trimmed with purple fringe. On the wall over the table hangs a large simple wooden cross flanked by pictures of the German countryside. I can see already how Gizella would have fit well into this place, so ordered, so neat, so far removed from the insane chaos of Grunberg.

"I trust you have not had an unpleasant journey here," says Frau Danhaus, bending slowly to pour the tea into little cups of china. The frail woman of about eighty, has an appearance which matches that of her home. Her hair, a pure white, is loosely piled in the back of her head, and fastened with an onyx comb. She wears no makeup except for two lines of pink rouge painted in streaks on her cheekbones. She is attired in a tangerine-colored suit with huge round buttons, and as she pours, I can smell the scent of cheap German cologne. But I am at once humbled that she considers my visit an occasion for formality. Overall, Frau Danhaus reminds me of a small sparrow, so quick are her movements. Even her voice has a chirping quality.

I assure her that my journey was most pleasant, and I confide that for many months since the war has ended, I have been driven by the desire to see my old friend. Etta eases herself into the chair opposite me.

"Ah, such tragedy. And, for what, my child, for what?" She takes a slow sip of her tea before adding a cube of sugar.

"You say you know Gizella from the factory, yes?" I nod, leaving my tea to cool before tasting it.

"Well, then, you know Gizella was a remarkable person from a remarkable family. Such a tragedy, yes..."

I strain to understand the heavy German accent which in most mouths is close enough for my home-spoken Yiddish, but not always.

"I really know nothing of her family," I reply.

"Ah, so sad," she says, stirring her tea slowly. With each clink of the spoon against the cup, I feel my nerves rising with impatience.

"*Bitte*, please..." I try, "I just come to find out where she is. Perhaps you can accommodate me?" Frau Danhaus shakes her head briskly from side to side and bites her lip.

"Of course, well, our poor Gizella was all alone in this world, and she was a boarder here, in this very apartment. Small, but it suited her needs. You see, I was more than her landlady, really. And she paid me what she could for, as you know, she was a brilliant finisher, and when she worked in a factory for ladies' dresses, she actually was paid quite a handsome sum. Even before, I knew her parents, God bless their souls, I knew them well. Her father and I grew up on this very street, only four houses away. And her mother, so tiny, little mouth, little feet, as tiny as her husband was tall, as Gizella herself would become." The old woman begins to lose herself in reverie.

"Almost comical it looked when the parents walked down the street together. Ah, but her mother, Marta, was the very breath of kindness who did not know even one bad word...did you know Gizella's mother's father was a Jew?" She goes on, stopping not to look at my face which turns at that moment white.

"I think that is why Gizella had such a feeling for the Jewish people, you see, knowing that in her blood there was Jew, too...Of her husband, Klaus, I do not know, but certainly he was a tolerant man, not like some of the other Germans."

"What?...Do you mean to say that Gizella was married?"

Frau Danhaus closes her eyes and nods. "But, sure, if only for a short time. And then, of course, the tragedy..."

"The war, I see."

She dismisses my words with a wave, puts down her cup, and stares into my eyes.

"But...did you not know?" she continues, "I was home right here when I could hear the screams even from down the street. I could not even move, for I had broken my ankle only a week earlier, and I could only sit home holding my head as the sirens came closer. This was in 1933, before the problems of the Jews, and sirens were not heard each day. So you see, it was unusual. Only many hours later when Gizella came running to my house like a wild woman did I realize that the foul odor coming through my window contained the ashes of my friends, her parents, and her husband. They say it was probably her father smoking in the bed which caused the fire...ah, but what does it matter now?" The old woman rubs her eyebrows as if to wipe the picture from her memory. She inhales before resuming, "If Gizella had not already left for her work, Klaus and her father worked at night in a bakery, then she too would have been gone."

"And I as well," I murmur to myself, but I don't think Frau Danhaus hears.

"Such the pity for this orphan," she sighs, "that I had no choice but to take her in. I would have done it even without her giving me money. I would have done it for her dear parents...So here we were, the two of us, and she so depressed over her losses that she miscarried the baby inside of her. She had not been what she once was, and when the war came, she left without a word. But in a way, I thought it would do her good, you know, to busy her hands, even if it was for those godless swine."

"But, excuse me, Frau Danhaus, have you seen her since the war? Has she returned since, or have you had any word?" I press.

"Ah, no, my dear. Her friend who had known her in the work camp said she left one day towards the end of the war, you know, and she left with the SS, but never returned. There were rumors, oh, Jesus forgive me for repeating them, that she was helping a

Jewess, and was found out and shot for the deed. But, please, these are only rumors, and it is just as likely that she has left her homeland for good. I tell you, I wouldn't be at all surprised....But, my dear, are you upset? I really did not mean to upset you with this gossip. My dear?" Frau Danhaus, noticing me put my hands in front of my eyes, lowers her cup and bends toward me.

Glancing at my watch, I quickly jump up from the chair.

"Thank you so much for the tea, but I am sure my brother is already downstairs pacing the street with worry," I say, removing a piece of paper from my purse and handing it to her, "I ask only one more favor. Here is my name and where you may contact me should Gizella reappear. Tell her Blima is looking for her... Her daughter, Blima."

Frau Danhaus stands, gazing at me quizzically, as I rush out the door and down the stairs. The lobby door slams behind me, and I hear a tinkling of bells as they signal the end of yet another chapter in my life.

Betty

Chiel had a dream. He was dreaming that he was swimming for a long time, and his body was getting so tired. He tried to come out from the water, but his legs could not move him. When he looked down, he could not see his feet. That is because he was swimming in raw meat.

Tante Mima would say that is a bad sign. To dream of raw meat is to be weighted by one's flesh, down to the earth. Chiel asks me about the dream, but I just tell him not to worry because it is nonsense, and he cannot even swim. I tell him too I wish I had Tante's book, but it is now in another world. But, I think anyway he knows the dream is not good.

We are planning still another trip to Miami Beach. This time, we will buy even more presents for our new grandson. I think they make even a size T-shirt for such young babies that say, "Beach Baby" or something like that. I think I will buy him something in red because that keeps off the *biza punim*, the angry faces, or the Evil Eye. We say *kineina hora* that nothing bad should befall him. Already he has about ten pairs of the red baby socks.

As for me, Chiel has bought a new lilac jacket and some shifts for the warm weather. I still have plenty in the closet, but he insists. For himself, he goes today to buy the walking shoes, some brown loafers with a cross stitching on the top. Chiel likes to walk all over, on the Lower East Side, down Kings Highway, he does not care. Sometimes now, I go with him so he does not smoke. But sometimes I stay home, where I am just as happy. He says one day he will walk down the avenue holding his grandson by the hand. That will be his proudest day, he says.

Chiel has just shown me his new shoes, which he bought for a good price on the Highway. We go inside for a little lunch of herring and challah, so *batampt*, delicious, and then the sun is shining each day this summer so we sit on the benches. Here on Ocean Parkway is a big highway, but a little street on both sides, one goes right, one left. And on these little streets are all kinds of people walking, the yeshivah *boochas*, the students, the Hassidic women with the baby carriages, the Russians pushing old ones in the wheelchairs. So much to see, so we walk a little bit under the trees that have the big green leaves now so the sun does not come on you too much, and sometimes we walk all the way down to Avenue U even. When we get tired, we sit on the benches. All the time the women come to me to say, "nice day" and I say "delightful," and smile to them. But then Chiel pulls me quick away and wants to know why I talk so much. I cannot be impolite! Anyway, I am just glad no men are coming up to me.

So we are sitting on the bench by ourselves, and Chiel puts the hand to the back of the head. *"Voos es de mayer?"* What is the matter, I ask him. Ooh, just a bad headache, he says. Never does Chiel have headaches, so I tell him maybe we should go inside, away from the sun. He listens, and we go back in the house so he can take a nap and I can sew for Shirley the new pants. When he wakes up from the couch, after maybe a couple hours, I ask if the headache is away. He says, yes, he feels much better, but his arm and leg on the left side are still sleeping. I slap him on the arm a few times, and he laughs.

We have a supper of some boiled chicken from the soup, a few noodles, and even some carrots I throw in. Chiel takes the glass for some soda, but he cannot hold it.

"Chiel, what is wrong with you?" I ask him, putting down my own glass.

"I don't know," he says, rubbing his arm, then seeing my worry, he adds, "It will be okay. Sometimes happens like this. I will rub it out." But then he gets up from the table and starts to walk to the bedroom, and he is walking *azofa shika*, like he is a drinking man. And then he almost falls, but saves himself by holding against the wall.

"Chiel, what is going on with you?" I scream.

"I will be okay," he yells back, but I can see already in his eyes little points of nervousness, like little shaking stars in the sky. When I help him walk to the bed, I grab his arm. When I look down, I see my hand is shaking.

I move quick the two valises with the clothes which he has already started packing even though we are not leaving for another week. Chiel starts to object, he never likes for me to move things when he is there. But he lets me this time. He knows I am iron when I want to be.

I make for him the bed, and he lies down. I have seen nervousness in him before, but never the fear which the points in his eyes have now become. He is asking me with his eyes to do something, but I don't know what. Chiel has always done everything.

"Just lie down and sleep now, Chiel," I tell him, fixing the pillow under his head, and pushing up the blanket to his chin. He gives me the weak smile.

"I should call the doctor," I suggest. No, he nods, all will be fine. But maybe a glass of water? I bring to him the glass, but already he is asleep. It is only 7 o'clock.

I do not call the doctor, because I have promised Chiel I would not. I do not call Shirley because I do not want her to worry for nothing. I do not call Jackie because he is in Washington, D.C. working for the congressman. So because I cannot even sit now to read the paper or watch the television, I walk through all the rooms. I go to kitchen to dining room to living room to hall, to Jackie's room to my bedroom where Chiel still sleeps. Then to

Jackie's room, to hall to living room to dining room, to kitchen again. I have just one thought. Let my Chiel be fine.

I have done this maybe twenty times till when I am in the kitchen, I hear a loud noise from the bedroom. I run inside and I see Chiel on the floor next to the bed.

"I went to get up, and my whole side is not working, Blima! Help me, please."

I pull him, using all my strength, back to the bed, and then I call Shirley.

"Hello?"

"Oh, Shirley, I am sorry to call you, I know you have the company, but–"

"Ma, it's okay. What's wrong?"

"Oy, the *Tata ut gefallen*. Daddy has fallen from the bed."

"Is he all right? Has he hurt himself?"

"No, no hurt. But in the afternoon, he had a bad headache, and when we came home later, he was walking like a drunk one. Now his whole side he cannot feel. Shirley, he fell from the bed!"

"Listen, Ma, you have to call the doctor. Just call Dr. Ornstein, and try not to be nervous. I'll be waiting by the phone for you to call me back. Do it!" I put down the phone and look quick for the doctor's number. Right away he says to give Chiel an aspirin, it may be a stroke. Stroke? What will I do if my Chiel had a stroke? I give him the aspirin, and I watch him like the doctor says to do. If he gets worse, I must call him again. Soon, Chiel goes to sleep. I don't know how he can, and I know already *I* will be up all night. I telephone Shirley back.

"Just try to stay calm," she tells me, "I am sure Daddy will be all right."

"Stay calm," she repeats. But I cannot stay calm. I put down a comforter on the floor next to him in case he falls again. Then I put on the nightgown, get into bed, and look at Chiel sleeping. Try to stay calm, Shirley said. But I don't know what to do. I don't know what to do.

Shirley

When I got off the phone with my mother, I knew that I had just received the call I had been dreading all my life. That quiet smooth fabric which had surrounded me like a childhood blanket had begun to fray, and I panicked suddenly as I could feel my world, my sense of stability and calm, unraveling.

Daddy had had a stroke. Early the morning after my mother first called, I summoned the ambulance. It seems he had fallen out of bed twice in the middle of the night, and my mother was beside herself. The aspirin hadn't worked, and now we began to rely on prayers. The doctors at the local hospital confirmed the diagnosis. Daddy had become paralyzed on one side; even his mouth began to droop. Fortunately, the stroke had not affected his speech, and we were told that he could be rehabilitated with therapy. When I saw him that morning, I felt something inside of me, inside of my heart, opening like a tiny bud. Yes, I had hope. He smiled with half of his mouth, patted my hand, and told me he would be fine. When I looked into his eyes, I could see they were still like my own, hazel, deep pools filled with an unknown sadness. He was there, he was still my father.

My brother quickly returned from Washington, D.C., and promptly had my father transferred to the NYU Medical Center, and a bright airy room with a view of the Hudson that belied the morose silence within. In the beginning, with my Uncle Kalman and Uncle Victor beside her, my mother would sit in a chair and cry into her hands as my father slept. I knew why she cried. While my world had begun to unravel, for her the tight coil of despair which always sat within had only begun to tighten.

The calamity taught me many things, not the least of which was an appreciation for my one sibling. The moment Jack returned to Brooklyn, he claimed that burden, the burden of supporting our parents, from me. He spoke with the doctors when I could not, he asked the questions which fear made mute in my own mouth. For me, these tasks became even more difficult as Daddy's optimism too quickly began to fade.

"*Miz shtarben*, we all must die," he would sigh as he struggled to put his arm through a sleeve or lift a spoon to his mouth. At the Rusk Institute for Rehabilitation, he quarreled with the therapists and endured the indignities of having to relearn what he first learned in his Lodz home as a toddler. And I learned to drive my mother to Manhattan and to go through the motions of caring for my three-month-old without ever really hearing his cries or looking into his questioning blue eyes. But it was my son who would prove to be an even greater blessing than we knew in my father's, albeit temporary, recovery.

Of the three more years my father would live, the first was a year of adjustment. At least once a week, I would travel into Brooklyn with my son so I could work as a substitute teacher in the high school from which I was on a child care leave. For six hours, I would leave Howie with my parents, lightening my mother's load and diverting my father's attention. It gave them both something to look forward to.

My father would watch as my mother diapered, fed Howie, and put on the orthopedic shoes with the bar between them used to straighten his feet. He would laugh when Howie stubbornly reached for his cane. Perhaps that stubbornness was one of the reasons he loved the child so much, he reminded him of himself. And the first time Howie let go of the coffee table and took off, my father screamed in shock, "*Blima, de kind gite!*" The baby walks!

Even when Howie learned to say his first words, words that *Zayde* couldn't hear, my father would smile and nod his head just the same. And there was always the kiss on Howie's forehead from *Zayde* whenever we arrived and when we left. On the phone, the first question, "How is the baby?" And my reply, "How are *you*?" "Okay, goodbye," he'd answer, not hearing again. Then I would hang up, take Howie into the nursery, and show him the small turtle bench Daddy had fashioned out of wood for him when he was at the Rusk. We all proclaimed it a masterpiece, Daddy thought it was silly, and Howie...well, he took it with him when he left for college.

Always Daddy's main concern was for the family. "I worry about everybody" was his constant remark, after waiting impatiently for my phone call as I sat in traffic on the Verrazano, or arrived at their apartment five minutes later than expected. But on a few occasions, he had cause to worry more than usual.

One morning, I was turning the corner, about to leave Howie with my parents before driving the few blocks to work. My mother, always waiting outside a half hour before I was to arrive, was already standing on the corner when she saw me, and tried to beat the car back to the apartment building. I saw her go down even before I spied a parking spot. Just as quickly, she retrieved herself and, holding her nose, waved at me as if nothing had happened. We spent the rest of the morning in the emergency room where she received first aid for a broken nose. Another time, after my mother had begun sleeping in Jack's old room because of my father's restlessness, she received a black eye. She had run into a door as my father summoned her with the banging of his cane against the floor. I didn't want to deal with my mother being hurt; I didn't even want to hear about it. The polyp on her ovary, the time she cut herself under the arm while shaving, the back problems she would have only a few years later. Was I the child or the parent? I could never reconcile the conflict, and I yearned to be that skinny girl again in my mother's bed.

If the first year of my father's illness was a time of adjustment, the second could only be termed crazy. At first, he was on an upswing in his treatment. A therapist was seeing him weekly. Each day, the steps he took increased a little bit more. I would watch as he slowly made his way down Ocean Parkway, the street with the benches. As he leaned against his cane, I remembered the time only two years before when I was pregnant, and we had gone to the grocery store together. Returning, as he opened the door to the lobby for me, he said suddenly, "Remember, Shirley. Always remember you had a father." I just shook my head from side to side, dismissing the thought. He was always the sentimental one. But then, as I watched his slumping figure disappear down the block, his head propped erect, the hat with the feather in place, I did remember. I remembered.

How long do people endure after a stroke? Two, three years? We would devour stories in the paper. There was the guy down the block who had one eight years ago. And so, we would hope again. Maybe my father wasn't doing as well as that guy, maybe he'd have a bad day when he would blame us all. After all, we had been fore-warned by the doctors. Good days and bad days. Sure, some people died a couple of years after a stroke. But not my father. After all, he was a survivor. He would live forever.

If my mother was his partner before the illness, she became as essential to his life as every breath God still bequeathed him. Whenever she left the apartment to go to the bank or an eye doctor appointment, he would stand at the window leaning on his cane until she returned. Once, she had to take the subway into Queens, meet my Aunt Ruschia there, to see a doctor. I came to the apartment to care for Daddy, but when my aunt called to inquire why my mother hadn't arrived yet, my father, pulling the old blue cardigan tighter around his body, began to tremble. It was less than ten minutes later when my aunt called to say my mother, having missed a connection, was now with her. I saw my father sag into his chair, and pity for this man, once so proud, sailed over me like a giant wave.

☆ ☆ ☆

He was exercising and suddenly he couldn't breathe. My mother called, and I insisted she phone a doctor. He advised my father to get to a hospital. It was the first of several such visits which wore the family and frightened my father until, of course, he was sapped of stamina. Once, he had to spend a few days in a hospital in Queens. Treating him for water in his lungs, the doctors feared heart failure. My mother stayed at our house and, frankly, I thought she felt relieved. The burden of caring for him, worrying about diet, medication, clothing, even physical support, was removed, if only temporarily. He was under good care, and she had only to visit him.

One afternoon at the hospital, I was greeted with a sight which I shall never forget. There was my father, sitting by a window. The familiar smile was there too, spreading gradually as we appeared, to lighten his face. The sun shone, one burst of warmth pouring over the straight gray hairs on his head. He asked about everyone. An IV in his arm, he implored us to take a walk with him. My mother and I exchanged surprised glances. I ran into the corridor, but his request was refused, it was too soon. This disappointed him, but I was happy, no, thrilled. Perhaps there *was* reason to hope.

As it turned out, the feeling was to be short-lived, for the next time I saw him, he was the old man again. On the day of his homecoming, we had forgotten to bring his clothes, so my Uncle Victor ran to his own apartment for a plaid jacket which proved to be oversized. This was my father on that summer's day, dragging the recalcitrant foot along as my brother held up the side of his pants. No smile on his face, only a steady stare in his eyes as he approached the car, like death itself, waiting outside. And so began the third year, the year of despair.

There were more emergency trips to the hospital. His breathing was labored, he couldn't swallow, he hiccupped, he became incontinent and no longer cared. That was the worst of all–his zest for life had gone. Once, when my mother had gone on an errand, my father soiled himself and asked me to clean him. "I will never forget this," he told me, sobbing as I removed his pants. It was the least I could do, I told him. If only I could have done more.

My mother cried daily, cried all the tears she could not during the war years, until exhausted, relieved. Despite the daily, hourly strain, she protested, "Let him live, if only for a picture." But even I began to wonder if she was right. My father, who slept now more than he remained awake, had begun seeing social workers and mental therapists. Depression. Well, he insisted, didn't he have a right?

On May 14, 1983, I gave birth to my second son, Brad. At the *brit*, as his new grandson was placed into the arms which could no longer hold a child, my father cried. "Two boys...Who will help Shirley with the babies?" he kept repeating. I assured him that we would be fine, yet I couldn't help but recall Howie's *brit*. Who will help my father, I wondered.

Less than a week before he died, we attended the wedding of my cousin Shaindee, Kalman's daughter. And again, my mind flipped back the years to the time just after his stroke when we were guests at Shaindee's brother, Joey's, wedding. How proud and handsome Daddy had looked then, even with his cane! But now, sitting in his wheelchair shriveled and swallowed by the same tuxedo, cummerbund askew, he appeared pathetic and old. I wondered if we had done the right thing in forcing him to go to the wedding at all. As we sat at the table during the reception, I could feel the eyes of the family on my father who ignored the pickles and challah, reaching only for a cube of sugar which he stored in his mouth for the duration. Pulling up to the building on Ocean Parkway, Arthur then carried my father in his arms back into the apartment.

Five days later, on a Monday morning, the phone rang. My mother was screaming. She had slept through the night, and when she went to check on Daddy, he wasn't moving. He wasn't even breathing. I phoned my brother who had already called an ambulance. But I knew it was too late. I knew.

On the last day, when my father of nearly seventy-three years went into the earth, I couldn't cry. The memories, quick flashes, fought each other in my head until I had to close my eyes. When I opened them, I saw each man, my brother, my husband, uncles, shoveling earth over the plain wooden casket. I wondered how many of the more than one hundred present at his funeral really knew him as we three, my mother, brother, and I.

The summer wind blew, the graveyard workers looked at their watches, the rabbi spoke, a leaf fell. Just another day. Just another old man being buried. As I lowered my veiled head into the backseat of the limo, I no longer worried about the tears. I had only one wish for a moment longer with Daddy so that I could tell him. It was something we all knew during his lifetime, but he himself never could realize. And yet none of us could tell him he wasn't alone.

Blima

We are like Gypsies now, moving from one town to the next. We establish roots nowhere, though, knowing that our place can never be among the Germans. Besides, we are yet fearful to separate, and find a certain peace of mind in the security of each other.

Ruschia, Victor, and I are together now wherever we go. Victor has found a little business for himself, selling silverware and such, and already Ruschia has had the operation on her legs. I keep up the homes as best I can, and try not to think too much about the 30,000 who have died out of the 58,000 liberated from Bergen-Belsen. If I think too much about it, the war will never end, and I want it to end now. So if I am not yet happy, I would say that I am content.

My brother and sister-in-law want me to marry. I am not so sure. It is not that I miss Smulke so much, and going back is impossible, anyway. But I am not sure if I can make the small talk or even reinvent myself as someone's sweetheart. But they assure me that this will not be necessary as, of course, any Jewish boy will also have his difficulties. I agree, finally, because I know that I have been burden enough to my dear brother and sister-in-law. After all, I can't stay with them forever.

Cousin Lazar is staying in Munich now, and has met somebody suitable for me. His name is Chiel, and he is from the Lodz Ghetto. I do not know much about him, except that he is all alone. But, many of us are now. He is to arrive for the weekend, with cousin Lazar and his own cousin and his wife as chaperones.

Ruschia is well enough now to help me prepare. She teaches me how to make her tasty chicken soup, with the trick of putting in a spoonful of sugar for extra taste. We travel the few miles to the kosher butcher for his finest cut of brisket, and cook it in a brown gravy with many onions, lastly adding thick slices of carrots and potatoes. I am even able to find a bakery which is not quite as good as Tante Rachel's, but has the black bread which I so love. Ruschia has now also gone to the trouble of making a honey cake, and it is not even the New Year! Hours before the arrival, she bobs my hair in the front and curls it just so it covers my eyebrow, then she makes me wear her coral lipstick and a touch of rouge on my cheeks. Finally, she gives me my belted blue dress on which she has sewn a big letter "B" for Blima. I am a little worried. I hope she does not want to get rid of me too fast.

They arrive at 4 pm on Friday, just before the *Shabbat*. When Chiel comes in, I notice two things about him immediately. First, he is short. Of course, he is a few inches taller than I, almost everyone is. But he does not have the commanding stature of Smulke, who would pick me up by my elbows to give me a kiss. The second thing I notice about him is his hair, which is thick, soft, and very dark. This is unusual, especially for a man of thirty-seven; most men I know have but a few strings of hair, if any, which cover balding heads. I wonder what it is like to put my fingers in such hair.

Everyone is appropriately silent during our meal, their eyes running from Chiel to me as we try to manage conversation. Chiel overly praises the meal, as I avert my eyes.

"Such a sweet soup!" "The brisket so *ba tampte*, so tasty!" "May I have another piece of that wonderful bread?" "I am so stuffed... maybe just another glass of tea?"

Finally, we push back our chairs, and Chiel asks if I would like to take a walk outside in the yard. I agree, and he holds the back screen door open for me as we go outside. The May air is brisk, and I wrap my cardigan sweater around my shoulders as he helps adjust the collar and then quickly returns his hands to his pockets.

"Look at that moon," he says, pointing beyond the branches of an oak tree. The moon is unusually round and luminous as puffs of clouds sail slowly past its face.

"Mmm...quite lovely," I answer, but I can feel the blush rising up my face as I look back and see Ruschia, Victor, Lazar, and Chiel's two fat cousins sitting outside cutting pieces of apple into their tea. They seem involved in conversation, but when I turn, I feel their smirks at my back.

"I am by nature not a talker."

I come back to the moment. "Oh, well, how much can one talk anyway?" I say, looking down at my fingernails as Chiel rests against the oak tree.

"May I ask of your story?" I know exactly what he means. Every survivor has a story to tell, and some release it more willingly than others.

"Well, of course, as you know it is not so easy," I answer, still looking at my fingernails. I realize that I have never told the entire story to anyone other than family; I never really had to. I begin slowly, but once I hear the sound of my own voice, I am surprised at how fast the words come. I tell him of my life working in the bakery, my sisters and how one had won a beauty contest, my twin brother, my *Tata* and Mama, whom I never saw again after the Nazis took me from the street as she screamed and screamed my name. I tell him about how I learned to sew and how quick my hands became with the needle. I tell him about my angel, Gizella, who saved me from starvation. I tell him about the exportation to Bergen-Belsen, and meeting Ruschia who was sick with typhus, and the tears when we remembered her two little girls. I tell him everything, but I do not tell him about Smulke. Not yet.

I feel his eyes, large and hazel, are upon me the whole time I speak. But when I ask to hear of his story, he looks down on the ground and unclasps his hands. His white pants and shirt float momentarily in the breeze and shimmer in the moonlight.

"My parents owned a fruit store, and my brother Aron and I worked there with them," he says, his eyes never leaving the ground, "There were also three sisters, one with two young children, one just married, and the youngest, just a girl, sweet and quiet, with a long sad face. My *Tata, beshulim,* may he rest in peace, died before the war. He went to bed one night and simply left the world, like a king he died in his own bed. He was fortunate..." At this point, Chiel exhales and places his hands on his head as if to coax the memories.

"So in the ghetto, you know, it was not so good. They closed us down almost immediately. Rumkowski was not so good for us, and the *ressorts*, the factories, you know were really labor camps. I too learned the machines, but I learned to be a smuggler of sorts, helping people find hiding places during the exportations, getting them necessaries, like lamps and radios. Ah, they were all afraid of the *Schupo* patrolling the fence, but I managed. There is a good thing about being small and quick."

He flashes me a smile then, a warm smile. As I again survey his short wiry frame, I can understand why Lazar calls him a hero.

"As I say, then, I managed. For me, the watery soup with the sausage made from the horses, was enough...." Then, dropping his composure, he lifts his arms to the sky, exclaiming, "God, only you know, dear God, our sufferings!" We are quiet then, both of us, before he resumes.

"So this is how it went. And in the end, they came for everybody, for Aushwitz, you know. Well, the SS took one look at me, I was much thinner than I am now, and they pointed to the left. And just like that, they shoved me to the line for death. Sure, I knew when I saw all the sick ones, some of the older ones too. But the SS did not know Chiel Russak so well, and so while they were busy barking orders, I ran for the right side. No one saw, and I guess I was a little bit lucky. They tell me all together 74,000 left for Aushwitz, and not many returned. I suppose I was lucky." Here, he pauses, looks over to the back porch, then takes my hand and motions for me to sit, right there on the grass by the tree.

"It was only after the liberation that I found out they had all been gassed. My Mama, my brother who was my best friend, my sisters, even Dvora who could not bear to leave her little ones. Only Shani, the youngest of twenty-two years, survived. I heard she was sent to a hospital in Paris, but when I got there she had already died of food poisoning...Ah, that's how life goes, I suppose." I notice then how calmly and evenly he relates the story, but I guess it is the same for most of us. We learn to disengage ourselves. It is another story in another life. Chiel goes on, "It was then that I realized that I was all alone, except for a few cousins like Avrum and his wife, Bela, over there," he motions by lifting his eyebrows and giving me a half smile.

"When I returned from Paris, I was sick myself, quite swollen myself with the face, you wouldn't recognize me," he chuckles, then turns serious, "I found our old apartment, would you believe. Things all over the place, old toasters and blankets, most of it ransacked. I was looking for some pictures of the family; I had none, not one,"

I interrupt, "I have pictures. I will show you later...But, oh I am sorry, please continue." And I was sorry, almost immediately when I learned the rest.

"I searched for hours and found but one picture...Would you like to see it?" I nod, and Chiel reaches into his pocket and removes a wallet, showing me a photograph. It is a studio picture of a handsome young boy, about twenty, with intense eyes which stare straight into the camera. He has a neatly combed head of thick black hair. It is a photograph of Chiel.

"Isn't that something?" he smiles, poking the photo as if to make it jump, "the only photograph I could find was one of myself."

We stare at the picture for many minutes before he puts it away, and we walk back toward the house, unaware that we are still hand in hand.

Many hours later when the *Shabbat* candles have already gone out, Ruschia, in her nightgown, comes into the parlor where I am sitting in an armchair alone.

"So...?" she says, raising an eyebrow.

"I think he will do," I say.

Betty

I cry a million tears. On the little night table next to the bed are the marks from the cane banging against it. Chiel was trying to signal me at night, but for the first time in many months, I slept. Why did I sleep? The children tell me not to blame myself, that it would have happened anyway. I suppose so. When I looked at his face that morning, I could see a smile. He died just like he wanted to, in his own bed like his father. Like a king.

I do not think I can stop crying for Chiel, for my parents, for all I have lost. In my mind, I see a film of my husband smiling like the first time I saw him in the other country. On his tombstone, the children write that he is a survivor who helped others to survive. *"He gave us strength, spirit, and infinite smiles."* I think the smile will never come to my own face, but it does. After a week, I tell Shirley I cannot stay with her anymore. I need to go to my home, the last home I will have, the one where I also will die. My daughter tells me I am strong, but I don't think so. I do what I have to do, what choice do I have? My daughter tells me I have great faith. Well, how can I not? I believe because I have to believe. What else is there? These things I know, but day to day it is not so easy.

This is my day: I wake up very early and wake up my son who now is Jack, not Jackie. Since the accident, he wants I should call him at his apartment to make sure he is not late for work to his law firm in Manhattan. Then I call Shirley to ask if Howie is on the bus for school, and to talk to Brad if he is willing. "How are you, Bubbe?" he asks me. He is only three, but he is so smart. When he was born, his eyes were round and dark, and I told Shirley he had all the answers to the world in them. Today, the answers spill from his mouth like precious jewels. I get such pleasure from him! I get pleasure from them both. Then Shirley asks about my plans for the day, and sometimes she talks to me in Yiddish. She knows this makes me laugh because her Yiddish is so broken now. Just the same, I like it.

I make myself a little Cream of Wheat and drink a glass of orange juice. Then I go down Avenue P to the butcher or for some grapes at the Associated. I do this a few times a day because I am forgetting something even when I take the wagon. Always I see someone I know, and if it is nice outside, we walk together. Hannah in the building is like a mother to me. She is over ninety herself, and buys me pieces of flounder from Brighton to make sure I eat. When she comes over, I must talk loudly because she cannot hear. One time, her granddaughter took me and the other women to Queens to a party for Hannah's birthday. They even gave me pictures. Sometimes, I see Edna who is also older than me, and very, very skinny with shiny coral lipstick on the lips. Edna wants I should go to functions at night in the city, but this is not for me. At night I just close the door, I answer her. But in the daytime she convinces me to join Hadassah, and always one time a week we walk there for meetings and luncheons. One time, we had a discussion about the Holocaust, with a speaker who was a survivor and a book writer. I mentioned to Edna that I too am a survivor, and soon the women wearing the hats and the pearls at our table had all kinds of questions. I tell them about my parents, my brother and sisters, even about Gizella, and they say, "Betty, you must go up and speak! You need to tell everyone your story!" But I refuse because of my English, and I am too ashamed.

I never knew so many friendly people were in the building! Besides Hannah and Edna, there are the young Hassids with the baby carriages. The little children always wave to me, and one little boy with the *payut*, the hairlocks, even comes at 4 o'clock to my house to watch cartoons. When Chiel was alive, he never allowed me to talk to everyone like I do now. The dead deserve the truth, I am afraid.

After lunch, I sit with the paper or watch a little television. Shirley calls me at 9 o'clock every night and asks me if I have checked the locks and the gas, which always I have. Sometimes, she tells me about a program, a *Candid Camera*, or a show about animals or Israel on Channel 13. Sometimes I enjoy a movie with Barbra Streisand or even Elizabeth Taylor, who was so beautiful. Or I listen to the Jewish songs on the cassettes which Jack has bought for me. Many times Jack must come from the city to fix the cable or the stereo, or sometimes the alarms on the windows. He comes over one time a week anyway to do the bills which Chiel always used to do. Chiel also wrote always the New Year's cards until he became sick, but I have stopped this altogether. Only I still have to sign the checks, and my hand shakes so much that I am ashamed and afraid that the check will not be good. Jack tells me not to worry about that. If there is a problem with the money, and especially a lease or something with the landlord, Jack handles. I am too afraid.

Every week for one night I go to Shirley's house so she can sub-stitute teach in a school in Staten Island. Arthur comes from work where he teaches in Williamsburg, and he picks me up. But when I go in the car, I am always forgetting something like the chicken soup I am bringing, or the chow mein, or to check the locks again. Arthur says nothing, but I think he is mad at me when I want to go back after he has started driving. When I go to Shirley's, always there is laundry waiting for me to fold. She knows I can do this good because of my work in the launderette, and she is too busy for it, anyway. So I sit and watch *Sally* on the TV and fold, and sometimes Howie comes to me to show me how well he reads. And Brad always likes to get for me the spools of thread and sit next to me when I hem the pants. After the supper, I wash all the dishes and then sit with Shirley to watch TV. I thank Brad for letting me sleep in his room when he goes to the room with his brother. The next day, Shirley goes to the work and I take care of Brad and play matching card games and dominoes with him. In the afternoon, Shirley makes me shop with her. I never need anything, and usually she buys too many clothes. When we go to the grocery, she lets me pick out the best fruit, and we talk about her friends, the children, things like that. The next morning, Arthur takes me home, even though Shirley always tells me to stay. What for, I say, I have my home in Brooklyn, and I am busy enough inside the house. My friends tell me I can work in a bakery on Avenue P if I want. I have the experience from Tante Rachel, I know, but I do not need to go back in time. Not when my daughter needs me.

Sometimes, I go on trips by myself. I don't plan too long in advance because I have learned from Chiel and our plans for Miami never to plan anything, but the children take care and I go. I have been to Israel with Hadassah, and I did not know anybody when I was going. But the people were friendly, even the guide in Jerusalem, a young girl who was a soldier and told me I remind her of her own mother. People always tell me things like that, a mother, a sister, a daughter. I don't understand how I can be all those things to so many people. When I went to Miami by myself, I met a Jewish man, a jeweler, who wanted me for a wife. He used to sit next to me near the pool, and tell me how I looked like his wife who died the year before. "Blima," he said, "we will be a good match." But I looked at him like he is the crazy one. I do not need to come into a family with five daughters that have the knives in their eyes. I do not need to take care of a sick one again. But I do not tell him this. I just tell him I do not want to talk about it, that we should be enjoying the sun instead.

It is in Miami that I see Clara again. She is staying in another hotel, and I see her walking down Collins Avenue, just like that. She recognizes me first.

"Blima? Blima Weisstuch from Grunberg, is it you?" she screams, and all the people are looking on her. I fall on her and begin to cry.

"Clara. Coming back from the dead? Am I dreaming?" I say. She tells me no, I am not in a dream. She tells me I am looking just the same, and then I laugh. To think that Clara is living in the Queens as long as I am in Brooklyn, and that she has two daughters, a grown grandson, and no longer a husband, an *Americana* she married after the war. I tell her about my years after the war, and at night she comes back to my hotel and we spend the whole time talking. When she leaves, we make plans to see one another. Then I lie down on the bed and cry for a long time.

Many months later, I cry like that again. But this time it is not from sad memories, but from joy. Shirley has had another son. His name is Chiel Laybash. But we call him Charlie.

Shirley

Imagine this. You are standing in the basement of an apartment building or maybe a launderette. Suddenly, a giant black water bug falls on your shoulder. Frantically, you begin screaming and trying to shake the slimy thing off. But before your mind can comprehend the fear, you look down and pouring in waves across the floor are insects, water bugs and cockroaches, beetles and spiders, striped, squishy, shiny, and dripping. As they begin to attack, making their way in coils up your leg, a strange thing happens. You forget all about the water bug on your shoulder.

That's the way it was when my brother had his accident. It was less than a year after Daddy's stroke, two years before his death. If I had known the insects were coming, I would never have answered the phone.

Quincy Me. was on the tube when it rang.

"Hello, Shirley? It's Heather." It took me a few seconds to recognize the voice as my brother's girlfriend, someone who had declined numerous invitations to our home, someone whom we had yet to meet.

"Heather...Hi! How are you?"

"I'm fine," she returned abruptly, "but...are you sitting down?" I've always hated those words, "Are you sitting down?" because of the ominous weight they carried. I've hated them more since that conversation with Heather. I thought immediately of Daddy.

"Yes. I'm sitting." (I wasn't.)

"There's been a little accident. You see, Jack and I were riding our bikes along the underpass near Houston Street, and this dog came running in front of him. Jack stopped short. Well, he fell, hit his head, I guess it was pretty hard. But he got up, said he was okay, and then, bam, had a seizure. A police car brought us to St. Vincent's, and Jack's been sort of in and out ever since. Anyway, he's admitted for observation only. I'm sure he'll be okay...Shirley, has he ever had a seizure before?"

I could feel the strands unraveling again, but was able to muster, "N-No, he never has, but...Did you call my mother?" I hoped she had not.

"Yea. She didn't really understand, and told me to call you."

"Should we come?" It was already past ten, and the baby was sleeping. How serious was this?

"No. No, I'm here now. I'm sure it'll be fine. He'll probably call in the morning."

"Are you sure?"

"Yes. Don't worry." As soon as I hung up the phone, it rang again. This time, it was my mother, hysterical. I did my best to calm her down. It had been less than a year since my father's stroke, and the burns were still raw. As I went into the living room to tell Arthur, I comforted myself with Heather's words, "It'll be fine." They settled softly around my mind like thread trying to patch the fear.

In the morning, I was awakened once again by the phone ringing. It seemed that Jack hadn't quite come out of it yet, and the doctors needed family permission to inject a dye. We made a hasty drive to my in-laws who would watch our son, and arrived at St. Vincent's. I had always hated the smell of hospitals, a sterile blend of medicine, alcohol, and illness. I hated it even more that morning, as I felt the nausea creep up my throat. We scanned the corridors. 14B. Two beds were occupied, one by a portly older man who was sitting up blowing his nose. In the other bed, was a large, muscular man with a mustache, someone apparently in pretty bad shape. He turned his head from side to side, as if in a fitful dream. I walked out, stumbling into Heather outside.

"Jack's not in there," I said, "Where is he?"

"There he is," she answered, pointing to the man in the bed. Jack, I thought, my alarm becoming real. That's not Jack?

My brother, my friends, and I are getting ready for Halloween. What a pest! Maybe my friends don't mind his tagging along, but I sure do. I adjust my black witch's hat and look behind. He is, as usual, still there. Someone suggests that it would be cute to dress up the kid as a little girl. So we find an old skirt of mine, tie a pink scarf around his head, and march down Lenox Road. He looks oddly cute as a six-year-old girl, with his round apple cheeks and dark bangs. I laugh, and then we all do, even Jackie. The next Halloween, he would reject the silly outfit, preferring to go simply as himself. That was the year he got more treats than anybody.

Jack was mumbling something. Water. He seemed thirsty, yet couldn't lift his head, or even drink. My Uncle Kalman, already at work in the boarding house in Manhattan, and some of Jack's friends, arrived. I left the room, not knowing what I should do. I just wanted to get out of there. Heather and Hal, a good friend of Jack's, mentioned that they requested the special neurosurgeon, not the resident on call. For a minute, I thought their choice extravagant, then immediately berated myself for being penny-pinching at my brother's expense. This wasn't like buying a shirt or taking a trip to the Caribbean, but...I stopped thinking.

The doctor, a tall, ruddy-complexioned man, was of Indian descent. His calm, matter-of-fact demeanor became a foil to my own rising hysteria. Dr. Asani was explaining the need for a placing a shunt in my brother's brain. Although the device carried little risk, it would be best to place him in intensive care. How many needles would be used to prick his skin? I wanted to tell them that he was afraid of needles, that they made him faint. I wanted to tell them how when he was six, he would lead Dr. Hasbrauer, needle in hand, in a chase around the dining room table. I wanted to tell them how he would barricade himself in my parents' bedroom as the exasperated German-Jewish family doctor pleaded, "Yah, Jackie, come be a man now!" I wanted to tell them, but instead, I watched, tears slowly building behind my eyes, as attendants hurriedly wheeled Jack into the elevator.

My parents wanted to know why they hadn't heard from him. Since my father had become ill, Jack had made a point of calling the Brooklyn apartment on a daily basis. He had, in fact, been the catalyst for finding a hospital for my father and later obtaining accommodations for his rehabilitation at Rusk. My brother, in times of stress, was the pin which held us all together. Now with the accident, the responsibility had fallen to me. I knew, I just knew, that I wasn't up to it. Pointedly leaving out the words "intensive care," I quietly explained to my mother that Jack's head had been injured and he was receiving attention. My mother, fearing the answers, asked no questions.

It was early morning when we arrived at the hospital the next day. Heather was seated on a small couch in the lobby, the sun from a nearby window drawing a distinct line across her brow as she read.

"Shirley!" she called, suddenly noticing me, "Come look at this poem, it reminds me so much of Jack." I glanced at the poem, but could only see a mirage of grays on the page. I decided then that I didn't like Heather, with her clipped hair, flowing skirts, and scuffed sandals. My brother in intensive care, and she was reading poems.

Jack's doctor emerged from an office. It seems, he announced, a subdural hemotoma had developed, and it was best to operate. I looked up at the doctor, my face contorted into a mask of anguish which he did not acknowledge as he rushed toward the operating room.

"You're a fat pig, Jackie! A fat pig!" I am yelling at the ten-year-old who had just downed half a bag of newly-bought Oreo cookies. Using the force of my body to pin him to the carpet, I begin cramming the rest of the cookies, one by one, into the pudgy boy's mouth. Our parents are out shopping and wouldn't be back for some time.

"You're a fat pig, a fat pig!" I shout, one arm pressing into his chest as the other worked the cookie bag. He spits a mouthful of chocolate crumbs and cream into my face, and we roll, wrestling across the living room floor.

As an uncustomary heat of a mid-May afternoon attacked my brain like bee stings, I realized why the expression "broken hearted" was used. Indeed, I felt as if my heart was exploding within my chest. My Uncle Kalman and Aunt Naomi offered the solace of their car which was parked across the street from the hospital, and I accepted its privacy when all I really wanted to do was escape. To run, to flee, get out, get out, get out...

Someone, one of Jack's friends, had managed to get me a bottle of valium from his physician father. I downed the pill mechanically. After two hours, or three, or four, I don't remember how many, we were called back into the hospital. The neurosurgeon, still clothed in green scrubs, walked towards us. As he approached, I could see the hygienic mask dangling under his chin, beads of perspiration flying off his forehead. When he stopped before me, I felt as if I had taken one step out of reality, and I saw colors swirling overhead.

"The operation was successful," he said, adding, "but he's not out of the woods yet." I found myself collapsing to the floor as Heather, arms open, lifted me, laughing.

My father had just concluded one of his angry tirades. This time, he accused my mother of leading on a cousin of hers. The sounds of our parents' arguing split the air as if it were glass, sending splinters shattering upon us. I tell Jackie not to worry. Daddy burns fast and cools slow, I reason, wondering if that would really be the case this time. When I hear my mother in the next room crying, I begin to cry too. I can't bear the thought of my parents being separated. Jackie is standing next to me, and when I look into his eyes finally, I see a fear matching my own. We fall into each other's arms.

They said that Jack was semi-comatose, which meant that he was moving and babbling, but not yet aware of what was going on around him. His close friends, many I hadn't even known of, kept a quiet vigil outside his room and took turns standing, speaking to him at his side. I was to find out, days later, that they had each donated blood for him just in case Jack needed a transfusion. I said a silent thanks for them as I prayed for my brother. He slept quietly whenever any of his friends, even Heather, visited him in intensive care. But when I entered the room, he fidgeted, tried to sit up, pull out the respirator.

I remember encountering a young doctor, a clean-shaven Dr. Kildare type in the hall after he had just checked on my brother.

"How is he?" I implored, really meaning when will he come out of it, when will he be my brother again? The doctor, probably a first year resident, merely relayed his current state, a condition already obvious to me. I gulped. Jack had been on the verge of graduation from Benjamin Cordozo Law School when the accident occurred, about to study for the New York Bar Exam–the toughest in the nation. I asked one of two questions that came to my mind, the easier one.

"Can you tell me, doctor, will he ever become a lawyer?" Sun streamed down the open corridor as the baby-faced intern looked into my eyes and opened his hands so that the palms faced me.

"We just don't know."

We are all on the queen-sized bed in my parents' bedroom. The family is having one of our serious "discussions." Jack wants to accompany a friend to Israel, Egypt, and Jordan. Israel is fine, we reason, but a Jewish college boy in Arab lands?

"Listen, it's my graduation trip. Hundreds have done it before me. I'll simply be crossing into Israel on foot through Jordan. Most of my time will be in Israel, anyway," insists Jack. My parents and I defend our stance, but Jack, always the attorney, parries back, arguing, cajoling in the process. He promises to wear a headdress, start eating ham, and bounce away on a camel–sholom aleichem! Our fears melt into inexplicable laughter, and we let him go.

The private nurse noticed that there was something wrong with my brother's eyes, and the doctor determined it was water seeping into his brain from the operation. Jack needed another operation. I received the news over the phone just as I was folding laundry in the bedroom, but I couldn't bring myself to go to the hospital. I had been cutting a tenuous path those last few days. At home, I was unable to tell my parents the full truth, why they hadn't heard from their beloved son in over a week. In the hospital, I would sit by my brother's side just to watch him squirm with the respirator plunged into his throat. This last phone call was more than I could take, and I threw myself down on the bed, hysterical.

The operation went well, though the prognosis was still uncertain. Days Jack spent in the darkened sterile room, and yet I, his sister, could no longer bear to see him. His friends said they understood, but in their eyes I saw the blades of condemnation. Could they ever understand how each time I saw him, I saw myself lying there, helpless? I was the one struggling to get that device out of my mouth. I was bound to the bed. I was crying helplessly inside with no one to hear. My brother and I, my parents– survivors all.

Some days later, after struggling with the device and finally having it removed, Jack said a word, a name, and soon began to call all the nurses by that same name. Shirley.

We are walking down a Bensonhurst Street in mid-July. It is so hot that the air seems to be shimmering in waves across the storefronts before us.

"What would Mommy and Daddy think of us now?" asks Jack. I smile, agreeing that they would be happy. A daughter, the editor of a local newspaper, and a son completing his first year of law school.

"I think they would be pretty proud of us," I say. Jack agrees, and we head into the luncheonette.

My brother resembled one of those individuals in old magazines of Holocaust survivors after the liberation. It was the first day my parents were to see him since the accident. He had been speaking for awhile, and the doctors admitted finally he was "out of the woods." I was making regular visits to the hospital now, some two weeks after the accident. When Arthur and I arrived home, Jack would even begin calling us from the hospital. I couldn't wait to get home.

Daddy could always sense things better than my mother could. Years earlier, when he and Mommy had walked into a "surprise" twenty-fifth anniversary party, my mother was flabbergasted and crying; it took her several minutes to compose herself. But my father just winked at me and smiled as a silver party hat was placed atop his head. He had known all along. In the same way, he realized the severity of my brother's condition, and when I visited their home, he would often pause, lay down his soup spoon, and raise his hands in the air, imploring, "God, take me instead!"

Three weeks after the accident, my mother walked two steps ahead of my father as he made his way, cane in hand, toward Jack's hospital room. I watched as Daddy kissed Heather and asked her if she planned on marrying his son. She smiled only.

Jack was sitting in an upholstered chair next to the window. His head was shaven, but the definitive dark mustache remained in place. His skin clung tenuously to a now skeletal frame, but he smiled, thick-lipped, as he saw my parents enter the room.

"Where do you live?" he said, trying to focus his still-jumbled brain.

"Jack," said my mother, her voice trembling, "You know where I live." Then, she took my brother's hands and we, all four of us, began to cry.

There was more, much more. The seizures and innumerable bruises, the speech therapy, the tracheal reconstruction after his having ripped the respirator repeatedly from his throat, the incessant phone calls when he made me listen as he tried to recite the Pledge of Allegiance, again and again. All tattoos upon the heart. Jack became an attorney, and then a judge, and a husband, and a father. Until finally, I had begun to let go. But still, in some ways, I never could.

Betty

I am forgetting things. Last night, I forgot to light the *Shabbos* candles. I thought it was Tuesday. Today, again, I forgot to call Shirley at 9 o'clock. Good thing she calls to remind me to take the medicine.

Everyone says it is hard to get old. I never complain, though. I remind them, "Look at the *mentrika*, the birth certificate." Then they nod and smile to me, and we sit on the benches until a little wind comes from the trees or it is 6 o'clock and we go in for supper.

Jack never invites me for supper. I am not complaining, of course. He has Emily and the baby, another Charlie, God bless him, so Jack does not have time for his mother. I am just glad Jack is healthy, and no one should know what I have lived through with his accident. But, thank God, he is even a judge now, and I know he is very busy. Since this accident, he and Shirley talk on the telephone everyday. I know this because when I ask him about it, he says, "Ma, what are you talking about?" And then I laugh because he knows just what I am talking about.

Every morning, I wait for the mailman. This is easy because the mailboxes are just outside my door. The mailman, I forget his name, knows me already and always he leaves the check from Germany compensation under the door so I can right away take it to the bank. When I check the statement that comes in the mail, I see all the time I am missing the interest. I call up Jack and ask him about this, and he tells me, "Oh, Ma, don't be ridiculous!" Many nights in the week I cannot sleep in the bed because I am wondering why my children want to take from me the money. The night before Chiel died, he cried to me that we have no money in the house, how will I live? I told him not to worry, but I did not expect this. I would give my children all the money and they will surely have it one day, anyway. Only they have to ask.

Jack comes to the apartment with Shirley, and they take out all the statements and put them like a black and white tablecloth over the dining room table. Even Kalman comes and tells me, "Calm down, Blima, you are making yourself a nervous wreck!" I put on Chiel's old glasses, and they show me the numbers. There, there is your interest, they say. But I know better. After all, I am not stupid.

How can I stop from talking to my children? I telephone Jack, and always he answers me with the low voice, and I know he is keeping secrets. I wanted only for him to be happy, to marry a Jewish girl, and to make a home. So when he met Emily from an ad in the New York Magazine, I think, fine, he is settled. But now, he and his wife have secrets from me. She looks to me and then to him, and she laughs. I do not understand why she is laughing at me. Even at the wedding, after I walked holding onto my son's arm, people at the table were starting to talk about me. But Shirley had put the coral on my lips, and I was wearing the hot pink silk top with the black skirt that I did not even need to sew myself. And I spent three hours sitting in the beauty parlor, and even wrapping my hair to hold all night. So there was no reason for them to laugh.

To think, Kalman's mother-in-law ignored me completely. So, I politely asked her, "Mrs. Hershman, how are you feeling today?" Still, no answer. Kalman tells me that she is over ninety, her mind is from the old age. But I look at her eyes, and I can tell she does not like me.

Emily makes Jack happy, so it is okay if they have secrets. Sometimes, Shirley and I talk about her, and I say what a nice new black coat Emily has, or how she gave me an expensive present of a silk scarf. Emily talks with her mother too, and of this I have no objection. When Jack brings me to her parents' apartment, which is also in Brooklyn, Emily and her mother jump into each other's arms and begin giggling like teenagers. The *Americana* mother pats Emily's stomach which is just in the fourth month, and whispers in her daughter's ear. I am still standing in the hall, and I wonder what she says about me. Does she not like my hair, or does she make fun of the way I talk like a *greenhorn*? Then she takes from me the coat and pocketbook and puts them in the bedroom.

When we sit down, Jack helps his father-in-law from the sofa to the chair. He has a worse stroke than Chiel, and he cannot talk so good. When I see him moving slowly the foot, and with the deep breaths, I feel like I have to cry. But I am happy he has such a good son-in-law like my Jack.

The meal is a good vegetable soup and turkey with potatoes. I compliment the mother, and she says to me, "Have some more, Betty, please!" Then we have the tea, not too hot, and the marble cake, and the cookies I brought from the bakery. I drink only the tea, because I do not want to have the heartburn all night. I smile to the whole family, and let them kiss me when I leave from the door. I tell them we have only good things to look forward to, and just a healthy baby is what we need.

But when I come to the house and put on the nightgown, I remember what I saw on the table. The bones from the turkey, sticks on top of each other in the middle of the table, even when we were drinking the tea. And then, in the bed, I feel like I have a bone sticking in my throat. Such an insult to company, to leave dead bones on the table, Tante Mima would say. Worse, when I go up from the bed to check the money from my bag, I know why Emily and her mother were laughing. But I say nothing to nobody because I am too ashamed. Just another night I cannot sleep.

But the baby is my joy. I tell my friends I have all kings and no princesses in the family. Such a blessing, they say. This child, Charlie Number Two we call him because Shirley has a Charlie also, has the same first and last name as my Chiel. Jack keeps asking me, "Ma, what do you think?" "Good, good," I say, and laugh into Charlie Number Two's eyes that are big and blue like the ocean, like mine. What can I say? I know he is everything, my mother, my father, my sisters and brother. For me, my grandsons are everything. Each the same, like fingers of one hand, each as necessary.

So then why, I ask myself, do my children want to make fun of me? I have only love for them all, and yet Emily puts the garbage on the counter. Jack says this is so the baby will not walk over and take the food from the garbage. And I am glad Tante Mima is no longer alive to see this insult on company.

But it is not just Jack and Emily, but Shirley's family as well. No longer do her children kiss me when I walk in the door. They say, "Hello, Bubbe!" and only if I ask them will they give me the top of the head to kiss. Sometimes, Howie who already wears half the pants at age fifteen, comes up quiet behind me when I am folding the clothes, and makes me laugh when I turn around and see him. Brad, only a year from Bar Mitzvah, so kind, always asks how I am feeling and sits next to me to help me thread the needles which I can no longer see to do. And Charlie comes home from elementary school, drinks his milk, and right away goes to the cabinet to get the dominoes to play with me. Sometimes, I am tired or have no patience, but always I play. So, one can only wonder why the children take from me the five dollars from the purse when I am sleeping. I smile and wink to Shirley to let her know I know the secret. I do not want to tell, but she forces me.

"How can you say that, Ma? Why would they do that? They love you," she is screaming with the tears down her face. I look at my daughter whose mind is filled with the same letters, the same music as my own. I say only, "Yes, oh, they love me very much." Then I walk into Brad's bedroom where I sleep, and very calm close the door. But my whole body is shaking.

✳ ✳ ✳

Not more than a month later, the phone calls begin. Once a day at least, sometimes when my eyes are just closing, it rings just like a Nazi siren, and I jump. The man says he makes a wrong number. But right away, I recognize the voice. It is Emily's cousin, the one I met at the wedding, and I am sure he is doing this because of the landlord. I call Shirley five, six times each night.

"Take your medicine, Ma," she tells me, "the blue one." But I cannot take my medicine because the landlord has come in and stolen it from my purse.

"Look again," Shirley tells me in a voice too loud. An hour later, I find the medicine back in my purse. But now, just for spite, I will not take it.

"Please, Ma, won't you?" my daughter pleads on the phone. But I will not. I just want to be left alone.

Shirley

My mother loved to say a certain word, and whenever I heard her say it, I loved it too. The word was "delightful." She had heard it from the *Americana* when they described a spring day or luncheon with their daughters. So she tried it a few times, letting it roll off her tongue, stretching the long "i" and raising the melody of her voice an octave higher. She would tell me about a walk along Ocean Parkway with the neighbors and say, "It was so de*light*ful!" Soon, she tried it out on the neighbors themselves, and when they would nod their heads and smile on the benches, my mother would sit back, contented.

That is how my mother mastered and finally claimed the word as her own. For me, "delightful" meant my mother had finally conquered her past, her travails in the Holocaust, the pain of my father's illness and death, the trauma of my brother's accident. Indeed, my mother *was* iron, and she could live and enjoy the day, just like anyone else. Only with the knowledge that she could, at last, live her life was I able to finally live my own. Ultimately, when things were good, my mother came to define "delightful."

But the word soon became lost in the jumble of threads in her mind, and I began to hear it less and less. Since my Uncle Victor's death from cancer, an event which I revealed to her one day as she folded laundry on my sofa at home, and which caused her eyes to become slits as she sobbed open-mouthed, it seemed that a part of her also had become lost. At first, I blamed a hearing problem caused by nearly a decade of working in the launderette next to the pounding mammoth dryers. When we complimented the chicken soup which she brought in jars to our home in New Jersey, she thought we were insulting her. Hearing aids didn't help much. When she grew angry over being stood up by a friend for a walk to a Hadassah meeting, I reasoned that my mother's poor English was the cause of the confusion. But there were other incidents which couldn't be explained so easily. Mornings she began to search frantically for a bathroom in my familiar, but multi-roomed, house. Never having driven a car, she still would walk automatically over to the driver's side of my van before being corrected. Once inside, she couldn't manage the seat belt until I reached over and helped fasten her in. Merchants were constantly trying to cheat her out of change. She also insisted that one of her closest friends, Edna, was ignoring her and, along with Emily's cousin, the two were calling her on the phone and hanging up. She became terrified of the building's landlord, who wasn't a landlord at all, but just a building superintendent in charge of rental collection. She called me at 9, 10, midnight, petrified of the mice she saw scurrying between her feet as she sat watching the news. At these times, I calmly reminded her to take her medication, go into her bedroom, and shut the door. She did as I requested, but sometimes, still, the phone would ring in the middle of the night.

Once, she tested the fabric of my mind even further. After a frosty silence and biting sarcastic responses of "Nothing is the matter, nothing at all," she opened up, accusing my young sons of robbing her of five dollars while she slept at my house. Brad, only fourteen, had been sitting next to her threading a needle, which he dropped immediately and stared at me, wide-eyed. I told him to go outside. But as he ran out, I thought I heard a whimper.

I reasoned, ranted, became hysterical as blood surged to my head, and tears slashed my face. But she remained implacable, sitting with one hand on a pair of Charlie's jeans. Another hand, shaking, held a spool of thread. She demanded to go home. When

I told her she would have to wait until the next morning when Arthur went to work, without a word, she marched upstairs and closed the door to Brad's room. Except for trips to the bathroom, she didn't come out at all that afternoon or evening. She didn't even eat dinner or the apple she had brought along. There was just one thing she wanted to know. Why was everyone doing this to her?

The following afternoon, I called her apartment as soon as I got home from my job teaching at the college. When she answered the phone she was calm, repentant.

"I ate some Cream of Wheat this morning then I went to the butcher and bought a pullet. Do you need any grapes?"

"That would be nice, Ma, but you'd better wait because you're not due to come over for another week." I purposely didn't mention her accusation, but suddenly, she brought it up.

"I found the money."

"You—what?"

"I found the money in an apron pocket at home."

"You never brought it with you?"

"No. I thought I did, but it was in another apron at home."

"But you thought the kids had stolen it from you..."

"Shoiley, I'm sorry," she hesitated, "I'm not myself."

I felt I had to reprimand her so she wouldn't make these outlandish accusations again, but the words which came were not what I intended.

"It's fine, Ma. Next time, just don't think the worst."

"Shoiley?"

"Yes, Ma."

"Don't be mad at me."

"I'm not mad at you, Ma. I could never be."

"Shoiley, can I ask you something?"

"Sure."

"Can you come over for a little while?"

"Oh, Ma...You know I don't live around the corner. I'm in New Jersey and you're in Brooklyn, well over an hour by car."

"Yes. I forgot. I'm sorry."

"Go have something to eat, Ma. I'll call you later."

"Okay, I will...Shoiley?"

"Yes, Ma."

"You're the only one, the only one."

"I know...I love you too."

"Goodbye."

"Bye."

I hung up the phone. Sometimes, I would call right back on some pretense of having her pick up plums or anything, the way a mother rushes back into a nursery to make sure her child is still breathing. Sometimes, I waited. But the conversation stayed with me until our next conversation that evening. Always on the verge of tears, I thought again of that expression, "a broken heart," and how apt it was for the pain which seared through my chest. I became like the apple my mother always loved to eat. She was within me, the core, and all the rest like peel simply spinning away. Conversations with friends, dinner parties, meetings at work, projects with my children–all spinning away. But forever, forever, my mother remained at the core.

✿ ✿ ✿

We were all sitting in an Italian restaurant, Arthur, the boys, my mother. This is normal, I thought, this is good, as I watched my mother pinch Charlie's cheek, unfold her napkin and place it neatly in her lap. It was the day after she had gotten lost on her way to a Hadassah meeting held in a synagogue only a few long blocks from her home. A trip she had made maybe twenty to thirty times before. She had started home with her friend, Hannah, when she suddenly realized she had forgotten her jacket and returned to retrieve it herself. Hannah went home alone, and my mother walked the block back to the synagogue only to find a wardrobe full of empty hangers. Had she forgotten to bring it, or had somebody taken it? At least she had her change purse in her bag.

As she walked with a purposeful stride, the street names gradually became unrecognizable, the storefronts, a jumbled blur. She didn't dare ask anyone for directions because they might grab her up right there off the street and she would never see her home or family again. So my mother did the only thing she could. She huddled against a streetlamp and cried.

"The girl was so kind!" she explained to me later that day. A young Yeshiva girl, a girl who resembled me, she said, asked if she could help. Then the student walked with her, the two linking arms, all the way to Ocean Parkway.

"Some people are so friendly!" she exclaimed, and I could hear the relief in her voice.

"The fish is very delicious," she said, biting into the salmon and pasta primavera dish I had ordered for her. I sipped my white wine, letting the security of my surrounding family seep warmly into me.

"Why are those people looking at me?" I heard her say, a bit too loudly, as she pointed her fork in the direction of a nearby table. Two teenagers, a boy and a girl, were laughing and deep in conversation.

"They're not talking about you, Ma."

"Well, they were looking at me. Everybody in the restaurant is looking at me. Do I have a mark on my dress?"

"Ma, they're not," I tried, then, "Did you hear that Charlie made the honor roll?"

I succeeded in diverting her attention long enough so that she could finish half her meal. The conversations at my own table sailed over me like a fine mist. The secure feeling I had felt only a moment ago was again lost.

I was not scheduled to teach any classes the next day so I drove my mother home with two empty soup jars and half of her salmon and pasta primavera dish. Reminding her to take her medicine and lock the door, I left for the hour's drive back home. I recalled her warm good-bye hug as I settled into the driver's seat, and prayed that the sunny day coming up would be another "delightful" one.

But it wasn't. As always, when I called, I could tell by the tone of her voice, the very first words, that the day had not turned out as either of us expected.

"Hello!" she barked, "I'm very busy and I can't talk to you."

"Ma! What's wrong?"

"Nothing. Nothing is wrong."

"Please, Ma, tell me."

"Nothing. It's just that I won't be able to sleep again all night because of what my own children have done to me."

"Please...just tell me."

Click. I tried again, and the line was busy. I tried again and there was no answer. The hamburgers I had on the grill burned, and I was late to pick up Howie from tennis. No matter. I was like a woman possessed. Finally, about a half hour later, she picked up. After much wrangling, I was able to determine the source of her anger. When I used the bathroom, she accused, I had taken a roll of toilet paper with me.

"Why, why would I do that, Ma?" I screamed, exasperated.

"I don't know why!" she screamed back, "I would have given it to you."

"Calm down, Ma, think clearly," I tried to restore balance to my voice, "Did you eat the fish and pasta you brought home?"

"No!" she snapped, "I threw it out."

"Why? I thought you liked it."

"It wasn't what I ordered. You gave me the children's meals that they left over, and they kept mine...There, now you know the truth!"

Eventually, I apologized for the food, the toilet paper, for everything. She calmed down. That security, if only for a moment, settled warmly over me again. At precisely 9 o'clock that evening she called, crying.

"Don't be mad at me, Shoiley, please!"

"I'm not mad, Ma, I could never be."

"Please, you're the only one, the only one."

We both found ourselves yet again crying into the phone. So the cycle began once more, the accusations, hysterics, my apologies, her self-recriminations.

When I put down the receiver, I immediately picked it up again, placing a call to the one person I knew would understand.

"She's flying again," sighed Jack, a term he had coined for Mommy's episodes of paranoia, "Way, way off into the clouds." His voice was steady, monotone, and for the hundredth time since his accident, I was glad to have my brother around.

"You have to take these things in stride, Shirley," he continued, "She hangs up on me everyday. She thinks Emily and I are stealing her money."

"She hangs up because you don't apologize."

"You can if you want to, but Emily is my wife, and I won't have her wrongly accused."

"But she doesn't understand," I implored, "Remember when she was desperate to have the apartment painted to take care of her mice problem? Then, at the last minute she changed her mind. That apartment hasn't been painted in over twenty years! Is that logical?"

"Look," responded my brother, defeated, "she's got dementia, and possibly Alzheimer's. You heard what the doctor said. Soon the five pills she takes everyday, the Aricept, the estrogen, they won't even work anymore. She's flying now, and we have to accept that. It will only get worse...Seriously, maybe you should see a therapist to help you deal."

"Really? So I can have my insides gutted like a fish, blood and all?"

I cut the conversation short. I grew weary of his platitudes, his euphemisms, his pessimism, and most of all, his despair. I would not, could not, believe that my mother was a victim of a disease no one could even prove she had for certain. After all, my mother was a survivor, my strength, my comfort. Imagining a world in which she was not a part was–well–unimaginable. And something I knew I could never accept.

Betty

"Ma, where were you?" Shirley is screaming at me. I tell her I just went out for a walk, so what is to be mad? So she tells me the time is 8 o'clock in the morning, and it is too early for walks. But when one does not sleep a whole night, 8 o'clock is just as good as 3 in the afternoon. What's the big deal?

"I told you last night I had a conference to attend today so I would call you in the morning, and not at 3 o'clock as usual."

"Okay, you told me, you told me."

"Look, I'm on my lunch break now. It's just that when you didn't answer the phone, I thought you were sleeping or couldn't hear it ring, or–I didn't know what to think! I couldn't concentrate all morning."

"No one's going to kidnap me."

"Okay, just the next time you go out, will you please let me know beforehand?"

"Okay, okay."

"I'm doing a presentation now, so I've got to go. I'm just glad you're all right."

"Okay. Bye."

"Talk to you later."

I go inside the bedroom to make my bed. The time again is flashing on the clock radio, and I will have to call Jack to come fix it. Good thing I have a watch. Soon, Nadia, the old Russian woman who helps me, will be here. This time I will be ready and not sleeping like on Thursday when she called Shirley from the pizza place.

Again, Shirley yells at me to go open the door. I cannot help it if I was sleeping. I am up all the night, anyway.

Nadia is maybe ten years older than me, and I think already I am almost eighty. I can walk better than Nadia, too. She huffs and perspires when she walks because her heart is not so good. But I accept her because she cooks for me a little potato soup and chicken, she gives me the medicine, and is some company for talking. The old people in the building are dying all around, anyway.

Nadia knocks on the door and she says to me we will go outside. I put the change purse in the light jacket Shirley made for me a present, and we go. But again when we are out the lobby doors I think I did not lock the apartment, so we go back and I check it. Good thing we were not around the corner yet. Outside, we see the Hassidic women with the kerchiefs on their heads. They say, "How are you, Betty?" and I forget they know my name. The children of no more than five years come running to me, and when I smile and wave at them, they hide behind their mothers. They are just like Sammy, Jack's little one who is a *kveksilver*, a firefly, he runs back and forth so fast. Not even three years yet, he grows up so soon. I wish I can see him again. Maybe Jack will bring him tonight. We continue our walk, go back home, and soon Nadia leaves, complaining that her feet are hurting her.

When Shirley calls at 5 o'clock, she asks about my day. I say it was delightful. Then I ask her about the presentation, and she is happy I remembered. She tries to use her Yiddish, which is so broken now that I have to laugh.

"Shoiley, you're the best!" I tell her, and I really mean it.

"No, *you* are, Ma," she answers me, and then hangs up the phone.

Then, I sit down at the kitchen table to suck the bones from the chicken we had for lunch. I wrap up half a slice of rye bread in wax paper and place it in the bottom of the refrigerator. Tomorrow I will have to go to the butcher again, I think, when I see there is no more meat in the freezer which soon will need defrosting. Then, I make myself some tea with apple, and hope that my hand will not shake too much when I bring the glass into the living room.

I press the remote control to watch the news, but soon I must get up again because all of a sudden I hear the siren from the tea kettle. Shirley would be mad if she knew I did not hear it. Before I am able to sit again, there is the siren from the front door. I look through the keyhole and see it is the landlord with the muscles and the dark blue shirt.

"Mrs. Russak, you had a problem?"

I open quick the door and show him the leaking under the kitchen sink, which comes every week from the religious neighbors upstairs who do their laundry at home instead of in the basement like everyone else.

The landlord does not want to hear explanations, but goes down on the knees and begins emptying the cabinet under the sink. Soon the Brillo, Joy, aluminum, wax paper, and Ajax are on the linoleum right in the middle of my kitchen. They are all sopping wet from the leak, and soon there is a flood on the floor, too.

He bends into the cabinet, takes from his pocket a tool, and turns it a few times. Then, he raises himself up and holds up the tool in the air.

"All fixed!" he says. But I point to the floor.

"Can you clean up, please, for me the floor?" I ask. The landlord looks down at the Brillo and Ajax sitting in the dirty water. He makes an unhappy face. No patience. He says he will bring something to clean, and goes to the door.

"Be right back," he says.

I cannot look at the floor, so I sit with the tea in the living room and watch the news. But then something funny happens. The people saying the news start to look at me like I have a mark on my dress. They can see me, and the lady with the blonde hair smiles to the man with the red tie and makes a joke. Then they begin to laugh at me. I get up and walk to the window. But their eyes follow me, and soon they begin to whisper to each other. So I walk away from the room altogether. But when I go in the kitchen again I see still the mess from the flood, and the landlord is not coming back.

I call up Shirley because I feel the landlord will not come back, but leave me here with all my things on the floor so that I will be thrown out. It is not Shirley who answers the phone, but Arthur.

"Can I speak to Shoiley, please?" I ask.

"She's outside walking with her friends. Can she call you back?"

I don't know if Shirley is outside walking or she knows it is me and will not come to the phone. I remember one time during *Pesach* when I was making the *matzo brie* for her family, she made believe that she went to the work when I know she was really upstairs watching the television in her bedroom the whole day. She even came from the garage with the books in her hand, but she couldn't fool me. Now she will not come to the phone, so I must explain to Arthur.

"The landlord came to fix the sink, and everything is on the floor. I don't know if he will come back, and I cannot leave it like this. What do I do?" Arthur tells me to take it easy, and that Shirley will call me back as soon as she gets in.

But when I hang up, later it is five minutes or ten, and Shirley still does not call back. I stand still in the puddle on the floor and am afraid to go back into the living room because of the eyes following me on the TV. And that is when I hear it. The sirens coming down Ocean Parkway.

I run right away into my bedroom and close the door tight. Now I know I must never go to the door when the landlord comes because he will take me away and I will never see my family again. Soon, I cannot hear the sirens, but I know it is a trick. I wait for the loud knock on the door.

Instead, after a half hour or two hours, I hear the siren coming from the telephone next to my bed. I go in the bed and hide, covering up my ears. But the sirens will not stop. Ten, twenty, fifty times it rings. Until finally, finally there is quiet and I listen for the footsteps.

When I look out from the covers, I see him standing next to the bed. When I look closer, I realize it is not the landlord at all, but someone I didn't expect.

"You must come, Blima," says Ruschia, reaching out her hand.

"I expected the landlord, I expected the Devil," I cry, "But not you!"

"You must come," Ruschia repeats. But I just hide my head in the covers again.

Soon the siren starts again from the phone, ten, twenty, a hundred times.

"Stop! Leave me alone!" I scream. When it stops, I hear finally the lock, and the guard outside my bedroom says, "Betty, it's your friend, Edna...Your daughter was concerned so I came down and used the key she left me...The television is so loud, maybe you didn't hear the phone?"

"Go away from here!" I cry and run to the door to stand against it with my whole body.

"Are you okay?" asks the guard, and I know again it is a trick.

I hide until the footsteps go away and my head stops hurting. In a little while, Jack comes to my door with a pizza. We sit together, and I tell him the whole story from my life as I enjoy the slice with some Coke. When Shirley calls on the phone, she asks, "How are you, Mommy?"

I tell her I'm fine. Why shouldn't I be?

Shirley

After Mommy shut herself in the bedroom, Jack and I were determined to get her live-in care. We braced ourselves for an argument saturated with the usual tears and sarcastic insults. To our amazement, however, she agreed almost meekly to our suggestion, simply conceding, "It gets lonely in the nighttime."

We contacted the same agency which had provided us with Nadia and was known for its stock of Russian immigrants, many of whom spoke Yiddish. After work, I found myself weaving rapidly through the traffic on the Staten Island Expressway and the Verrazano Bridge to Brooklyn, where I interviewed a disparate group of quiet, outspoken, immaculate, and haughty women for the job. And with each one, I never forgot to mention the fact that my mother was a Holocaust survivor. It served as notice, I believed, to "handle with care." Each of the prospective employees opened her eyes wide at this, and nodded knowingly.

A big-boned woman with artificially black hair who only lived a few blocks away from my mother's apartment, assured me, "I will take care of your mother just like my own." But, despite her good intentions, the married woman couldn't stay there nights. Another, a fragile ivory-skinned woman of about forty, nodded in assent to each one of my questions, speaking only to apologize for her poor English. She indicated that not only could she live in, but her grown son also could be available on a moment's notice, if need be.

Afraid that she just wasn't assertive enough to handle my mother, I rejected her too. But there was one more woman who arrived only an hour later that same day. She was the one we settled on.

Ivana was a tall, slender woman who radiated the unique combination of self-assurance and humility. Her blonde hair was twisted back in a prim ponytail, and when I offered her a seat, she sat straight-backed, knees together, and listened as if I were a teacher and she the student. She was a widow in her thirties with a teen-aged son who lived with her mother back in the Ukraine. Ivana hoped to earn enough money to bring them both here to the United States. She boasted of her culinary skills, her pierogies and blintzes, her green thumb, her affinity for cleanliness. My mother sat smiling, unable to hear any of this, but when Ivana remarked that she was only half Jewish, my mother suddenly blurted out, "My savior in the war was not a Jew, but she was my angel." I reached over to pat my mother's wrinkled hand, which had steadied itself for the moment.

"So, what do you think, Ma?" I asked.

"She's okay," she said, and turned again to Ivana.

"Did you know that Shoiley is a college professor and a writer, and my son, Jack, is a judge?"

Ivana moved into Jack's old room that night. As promised, my mother was well-fed and her apartment sparkling and immaculate. Her new caretaker would gather twigs as she walked with my mother, and then spray them with white paint and place them in vases around the house. She called my mother "Mrs. Betty," decorated her cheeks with rose and her eyelids with sky blue, and squirted "L'Air du Temps" on her neck. Mommy, in turn, raved over Ivana's "gourmet" dishes, leaned into her as they walked along the Parkway, and sat back on a playground bench and observed as Ivana rode the swings back and forth. Occasionally, she would accuse her of keeping the change when she gave her money to buy peaches or celery, and a tearful Ivana would telephone me in bewilderment. But these accusations grew less frequent and became easily forgotten.

Gone too were the frightening episodes like the time during *Pesach* when my mother accused me of hiding upstairs when I had actually spent the day at work. While she spent less time in my house, on the days my mother did visit there was an aura of calmness about her, none of the agitation which had accompanied her every action. Sometimes, etched across her face, there was even a trace of the old joy. All this I attributed to Ivana. Once, my mother even confided to me that Ivana had become, in fact, a living angel just like her Gizella.

For me, Ivana was a lithe sparrow who came to bear the burden so long sunk into my heart and carry it off into the trees along the Parkway. When I fueled my car over the Verrazano, it was without the weight which had begun to consume every fiber left in my spirit. There had always been the questions. Would she answer the door? Would she be angry and sarcastic because of a perceived theft of bread or toilet paper? Now, I let the cooling winds carry me to the double glass doors of the lobby, and when I rang her bell, it was no longer with dread, but with a sense of anticipation.

One summer afternoon, I walked into my mother's apartment and saw something I hadn't expected at all. Ivana was at the sink, and my mother sat by the kitchen window, wearing a pink flowered shift and a welcome smile. I bent down to kiss her as the sun washed her face in a happy yellow light. It was as if the rays had lifted the colorless shadow which had settled stubbornly over her those past few years. Cleansed now, she was recognizable again as my mother.

"How are you, Shoiley?" she sang, greeting me as if I had just returned from a long journey. From my bag, I removed recent photographs of the boys, and spread them out before her.

"Pictures..." she murmured to herself, placed her hand on her chest, and looked up, smiling. "I have pictures too."

"Yes, Ma, you have plenty. But see, these are new ones of the boys." She closed her eyes briefly as if lost in a puzzle, but when she opened them, began to marvel at how Howie, seventeen, looked suddenly like a man. She gushed over Brad's warm knowing smile and was stunned by the invincibility of Charlie who would soon be going to sleep away camp. I reminded her that the year was already 1997, and again she exclaimed how time flies. She questioned me about their exploits, commented on how busy Arthur was with his coaching, and worried that I was working too hard in my graduate courses. I, in turn, polished her nails in a shiny lilac color and massaged her thin-skinned hands with one of my lotions. I lit lavender-scented candles, a therapy one of the magazines said might restore peace to her mind. For the first time in many months, I did not want to rush home. Only when I bent down to kiss her good-bye did an echo of her broken self return.

"Next time, don't forget to bring the black bread from Tante Rachel's bakery," she whispered, smiling. I squeezed her arm.

"Tante died over fifty years ago, before I was born. Don't you remember?" I said, kissing her cheek.

"Oh, yes, I forgot!" she exclaimed, putting her hand to her forehead.

As I drove home, my thoughts were mingled with both joy and worry as I recalled the one perfect day when I had seen my father sitting up in his hospital bed. It was then that I determined to do something I had been planning for many months. I knew, instinctively, that it had to be done soon.

✻ ✻ ✻

I sat back in the faded gold velvet seat of an old wooden chair, and listened as my eighty-year-old mother spilled out the story of her life. Except for her shaking hand and trembling voice, she looked pretty, even younger wearing the black sweater dress we had bought together years ago.

I was careful to remain out of sight, as required, to prevent her from gesturing to me. I was especially vigilant not to move in my chair, as any errant squeak might be caught by highly sensitive microphones. But at times during the two and a half hour session, when I heard a sudden catch in her voice, it was difficult for me to sit still. When she sobbed, it was especially difficult.

Only weeks earlier, the Shoah Foundation had contacted her to confirm that she did indeed have an appointment for an interview. The Shoah Foundation, launched in 1994 by the director, Steven Spielberg, was in the process of compiling a living record of the experiences of survivors of the Holocaust. Those who agreed to narrate stories of their imprisonment, battle, seclusion, or experimentation were being documented, and thus far, over 25,000 had been videotaped in twenty-five different countries. Expediency was a priority, for the survivors were elderly, and their stories had to be told. My brother and I realized it was imperative that they refute the protestations of those deluded individuals who still said the Holocaust never occurred, and to ensure that the world never ever repeat the mistakes of the past. But as far as my mother was concerned, hers was a story to be retold as a living testimony for her grandchildren.

As I sat listening to her tell the tales I had heard from childhood, I thought of my father, who had left us only thirteen years earlier. He had always been the loquacious one, anecdotes of Poland rolling off his tongue with an easy fluidity to anyone who would listen. I knew them all by heart. He had been in the Lodz Ghetto, and he alone survived of a family of seven. He had survived by his own audacity and cleverness when he stealthily ran from the line destined for the gas chambers to the workers' line. Yet here was my mother in her living room telling her story, a locked box imprisoned within her heart until only recently when spurred either by time or loneliness, she assailed every neighbor with the experience.

My Uncle Kalman was against the interview from the start. Why, he asked, should we dredge up the past?

"Your mother is not an outspoken woman; she is too emotional and besides," he admonished, "she won't sleep for weeks." Nevertheless, my brother and I persisted in our determination that this was the right thing to do. And so, the interview was scheduled.

"Higher" was the first word my mother said once the camera began rolling. I bit my lip.

"Higher...speak higher."

"What is your full name?"

I relaxed as she began to recount the fragments of familiar tales. Growing up in a family of eight, including a protective twin brother (a whole "head" taller than she), working with her aunt in a bakery, going to school. And the girls, she the eldest, then Miriam, Adele, and Brandl. My mother stated that she was the first to be taken–and here she breaks down–right off the street. She recalled her own mother running after her, calling her name. The Gestapo, two of them, held the older woman back, and my mother never saw her again. Then there were the four years in Grunberg, a labor camp where she learned to sew soldiers' uniforms. It was in Grunberg that she met the "angel," Gizella.

My mother spent at least ten minutes speaking of the German woman who informed her that she would be her daughter, and begged her not to cry, assuring that no harm would come to her. And none did. While my mother witnessed the harsh rebukes suffered by the other girls, she alone had Gizella to protect her. She smiled, recalling the sweetness of the hard rolls the woman stuffed into her bosom, to be consumed later in a toilet stall. Months spent in Bergen-Belsen, and then liberation. She would search for months, but she never saw Gizella again.

My mother was luckier than most of her family of eight; she and two brothers, one older, the other younger, survived. But the twin brother, her protector, was gone, and so were the sisters, parents, nieces. Gone like millions, countless others. Later in the tale, my mother suddenly giggled like a sixteen-year-old as she told of meeting my father, a quiet, resourceful little man, the sole survivor of his own family She narrated her journey by ship to America, and the happy, giddy feeling of sea sickness. She found work as a seamstress, had two children, and learned to live again. Her story, half in English, half Yiddish, was disjointed, rambling, as she paused intermittently to stab at the air with her fingers, seeking the words. Still, she told it all– all– as the Shoah camera rolled.

Only when I brought the old photographs in from her dresser did I begin to understand the depth of her confusion. The photo of Hitler on a jeep which was taken by her younger sister, Brandl, she recognized immediately. But then I pointed to the black and white one of her, her sisters, and the children, all taken before the war. She identified Adele as Ruschia, and one of the youngsters as me. She looked at another photograph taken of my father in Germany, and identified him as her brother, Froyim. Each time we corrected her, she would put her hand to her forehead and apologize for forgetting. She asked why there were no recent pictures of her parents. I reminded her that they had died in the war, and she stared at me incredulous, as if hearing the news for the first time. The interviewer and videographer were patient, but I doubted that the tape would be of much use as a complete account of her experiences. Yet I knew too that for us, for our children, these hours would always be a legacy.

There was a moment just before the family surrounded her at the end of the tape. My husband, brother, sister-in-law, and our five boys, her grandsons, waited in the dining room. The interview was over, and we all rushed inside.

"How did I do?" she asked, her translucent, heart-shaped face smiling up at me. The rose-colored blush I had brushed on her cheeks hours before was slightly streaked.

"Fine, Ma, you did just fine," I answered, kissing that cheek. Suddenly, though, my uncle's warnings come flooding into my head. I pushed down the fears, and with the gratitude and love of a child, embraced my mother.

As I sat next to Arthur on the drive home, I replayed each reel of her narration, her terrors, again and again in my head until I grew dizzy. In a strange way, her story comforted me, for it served to block my fears of the future. To this, I closed my ears just as she had closed hers to the sound of Nazi boots marching closer and closer.

Betty

Ivana has deserted me. She went out to the store in the morning, and never came back. So, I am mad at Ruschia because all night when we were talking in the bed she did not tell me that Ivana would leave. I will never forgive her for that.

Jack came from the work to say hello. He wears a raincoat over a dark gray suit, and his navy blue tie with little white dots on it. Almost like the polka dot dress I have. His hair is all gray now, even though he is not even fifteen, and when he puts the bag of groceries down on the table, I think he is mad at me.

"What's the matter, Jack?" I ask.

"Nothing is wrong. I came to meet the new woman who will take care of you. And I brought you these groceries."

"Groceries?" I laugh, "You know I have a full refrigerator. Besides, I have no more money left in the bank. How did you pay for it?"

Jack ignores me, opens up the refrigerator, and makes a face. He squeezes the strawberry ice cream into the freezer which no one has bothered to defrost, then bends down and puts the milk and purple grapes in the refrigerator.

"Where is Ivana?" I ask, walking up behind him. He stands up, closes the refrigerator door, and helps me into a chair.

"Ivana had to go back to Russia, Ma. We talked about that a few weeks ago."

"But she was only here a week!" I protest. Jack puts down his head and talks slowly.

"She lived here for over a year, Ma, a *year*. Anyway, someone new will be here to take care of you. You won't be alone."

"Will Ivana be back in a few minutes?"

"No, Ma...It'll be all right."

The new Ivana comes in a little while. She is tall like my Ivana, but her skin is the color of coffee, and she talks too fast.

"You are a nice lady," she says to me. She tells me she is a grandma too, and she is already in the sixties, even older than me. Then, I look for Jack, and he has gone away. Probably with Ruschia, I think. The new Ivana takes me by the arm, and we go outside. We sit on the benches and I link my arm inside hers. I look at my shaking fingers; I see the polish peeling already from my nails. When Shirley comes over, I will tell her to fix them, and I also will tell her to ask the doctor why I am shaking so much. Even my head, now. And why are my eyes so dry? So cloudy and dry.

When we walk back into the house, Ivana lights the *Shabbos* candles and asks me if she is doing it the right way. I don't know, I say. Is it Friday already? She makes for me the chicken, but with too much spice, and I push away the plate. I am too fat, anyway, I think.

I am up all night and it is so quiet that I must run into Jack's room to see if my Ivana is there. But the coffee-colored lady is now snoring in the bed, and from the wall the big pink swirly picture which Ivana brought me maybe five years ago, is gone too. Then, I must go to the bathroom so I quick run out. But I see someone has moved the bathroom because there is only a sink and a stove there now. I yell to Ruschia, "Why did you move the bathroom?" The new Ivana comes running in with her thick dull hair all right and left, and takes me by the hand to the toilet.

On some days, other Ivana's come. Shirley calls them the flowers, but I do not see them wearing tulips or anything like that. They are all coffee-colored, light and dark, and speak like they have marbles in the mouth. One is fat and takes me on the bus.

She wears a big gold Jewish star around her neck that she says was a present from a friend. I don't believe her, though.

Another one has thick braids all over the head like I used to make for Shirley. She tries to teach me her language, but I am too old to learn it. I know three languages already, and I am even forgetting those. One more Ivana is an old Nazi who squeezes my wrist and slams the apartment door on my hand when we are going out. I scream on the phone to Shirley to save me from this camp, and she says no more will the Ivana come. But the next day, again and again, she is there. I shake my fist to her and will not let her touch me. "I am iron," I say. I don't care even if she cries.

One Ivana is even smaller than me, and a grandmother too, and a nurse. She tells me her flower name, and I say it is pretty. But soon I forget the name. Shirley comes that afternoon with the dog, and she tells me to pet her. But my hand is shaking too much, and soon I fall asleep on Shirley's shoulder.

When I wake up, the toilet is in the middle of the living room. I use it, and little flower Ivana helps me to the couch. I see the Parkway from the window. It is a cloudy day, but then the gray cloud lifts and I can see Ruschia in the alley waving good-bye. I turn to Ivana again.

"Why am I this way? I don't want to be like this." She shrugs her shoulders and comes over to hug me.

"Only God knows the answers. We can only do the best we can." Her bracelets jingle as she walks back into the kitchen.

That night, I chase the shadows dancing across the bedroom walls. One lands on my reflection in the dresser mirror. I try to capture it from the face of the old woman with no teeth and sunken cheeks, but soon it falls on the floor. I try to pick it up, but this time it does not move.

"Zalman!" I cry, "Why did I drop you? Get up!" But my baby brother does not hear me, he is so stubborn.

"Mama, *Tata*, please help me!" I hear my voice saying. But Mama and *Tata* won't come anymore. I rush to the bed, leaving Zalman on the floor.

Wiping the tears from my eyes, I watch all of the shadows on the ceiling dancing together, playing games with me.

"Please don't punish me. I do not know why I was left alone.... Please do not punish," I whisper to them.

"I'm sorry. I'm sorry I could not save you." Then, I turn into my pillow, my body still heaving and sobbing and shaking until, at last, I am fast asleep.

Shirley

Suddenly, she clutched my wrist and said, "I love you." I nodded, meeting her eyes briefly. We both felt uneasy, embarrassed by such verbal expressions of affection. Even though there was no need, I gradually understood her desire to say the words, again and again.

On the last day she visited my home, I brought her to the doctor to have ear wax removed. She was always seeing a doctor for something, as frequently as every week. Only a day earlier we were at her ophthalmologist's office in Brooklyn. The beginning of cataracts, he said, but why put her through an operation now? The dryness was a side effect of the medication. So was the itching of her hands. Ironic, I thought, how my mother usually loathed going to doctors for tests. She never even had a mammogram. Yet now, each day she would telephone, pleading with me to take her to a doctor or a hospital.

I retrieved her from Brooklyn, giving her new caretaker the day off. While she lacked the compassion and efficiency of Ivana, Jasmine admired and cared for my mother as best she could. When I visited the apartment, she would sometimes take me aside and, crying into a tissue, complain that my mother accused her of hateful things. Making her way from the living room couch to the bathroom, she would shake her fist at Jasmine and call her a Nazi swine. I tried to explain my mother's confusion. She no longer had a steady caretaker, and while Jasmine was usually there during the week, a merry-go-round of aides entered the apartment on weekends, sprouting like either flowers or weeds in a desert. One

Saturday afternoon, a brusque woman who had neither patience nor wit grabbed my mother so tightly by the wrist that she left marks on her skin. My mother also received a black and blue mark across her hand when the unheeding woman closed the apartment door too abruptly. That was on the Fourth of July, and when I telephoned her on my way to Atlantic City, she pleaded with me, crying to come and rescue her. I thought it was all in her mind, closed my eyes, and proceeded with a tug at the heart, on my trip. When my brother called her, later that day from a boat on the Hudson, she reacted in the same way. It's in her mind, we told ourselves. Was her mind now her reality, or had a sliver of reality somehow wound its way into her mind? Now, she couldn't even trust Jasmine. I prayed that she could still trust us.

Something within me was glad to have my mother to myself again, but also fearful. I was listening to the news on the car radio when, suddenly, she raised her finger in the air.

"Oh, do you hear her?"

"Hear what, Ma?"

She smiled. "Ruschia is talking to me. Don't say you don't hear her." I switched to music, and finally turned the radio off altogether.

With Ivana gone, there were no longer any jars of chicken soup. My mother had given up hemming clothes, and looked forward only to sitting on my living room sofa. When I placed a laundry basket of clean clothes before her, hoping she might want to feel useful, she picked up one of Howie's T-shirts, folded it haphazardly, and let it fall back in the basket. She had no strength, she confessed, and, still sitting, fell quickly asleep.

The morning after our appointment, I had to wake her at 6 am in order for her to be ready for Arthur to drive her back to Brooklyn. She had always been up at dawn's first light, but lately she could sleep till almost 11am, another disturbing sign of her decline. I nudged her gently on the arm until, finally, she lifted her head and turned to me, perplexed. Later, when I checked on her again, she was asleep once more, but this time awakened immediately. She asked me who the stranger was at her bed earlier. When I insisted that I was the one who had awakened her, she became agitated, so I just let the whole thing go. I implored her to move quickly so that I could get her down the stairs in time. Was it so long ago that she was cajoling me to get up for school, feeding me Cream of Wheat as I pulled the covers to my chin, evading the icy dawn? It was many minutes before I got her to her feet. I moved her breasts inside the cups and snapped on the old bra with the visible stitches. She had misplaced the newer one. I left her in the bathroom, but soon heard a thud as she slipped on the cold ceramic tile. Checking her, I breathed a sigh of relief. She had grabbed onto the side of the bathtub and gone down slowly, her buttocks absorbing most of the fall.

On Sunday, Arthur and I brought the children to visit her. As my sons hugged her, I could see not a glint of recognition behind her hazy blue eyes. She was asleep more than awake, and dozed off as I began polishing her nails. She wanted to rest in bed, and as she slept, Arthur and the boys sat down on the couch to watch the Yankee game. I sat at the kitchen table, barely sipping the glass of Coke in front of me. Howie was to begin Georgetown University in two weeks, and I grew suddenly desperate for one last gift from his Bubbe. She had to recognize her beloved grandchildren. She just had too.

My mother, holding tightly onto the metal walker, slowly entered the dining room. I called my children inside. I pushed my Howie, muscular, blonde-haired, and as tall as his father, in front of her.

"Ma, Howie is going to Georgetown soon. He wants to be a lawyer, do you believe it? What do you think of that? What do you think of him?"

She looked up at him, still standing, through half-closed eyelids, and said, "Wonderful."

Then, I grabbed my youngest, Charlie, the child named after my father.

"Charlie just got back from sleep away camp. He earned a swimming medal. What do you think, Ma?"

Her voice was thick as she gazed into his face. "Very brave," she said.

And then Brad walked in front of me and placed his hand on her arm.

"And Brad, Ma, what do you think of Brad?"

"The best," she whispered, her eyes steady on his round young face.

I grasped her to me, and kissed her. "Thank you, Mommy, thank you." On this day, the last day they saw her, she had given my sons her final gift.

✡ ✡ ✡

I had come to her house with a sheet of paper in my hands. She was sitting, awake, on the plastic-covered gold couch in the living room. When I came into the room, she smiled. I knew then that the time was right.

I gave Jasmine a grocery list, and told her to take her time. Before leaving, she placed a bowl of green grapes on the coffee table in front of us. Again, I hoped that this one would stay, at least for awhile. In spite of her protestations, my mother often would look up at her as a child does to her mother, and on the benches she somtimes would place her own hand upon the aide's. But I feared the constant change could only hamper her condition. These ladies from the islands were in all shapes, ages, and sizes, and wore boldly colored skirts of tangerine and royal blue, and big round strings of beads which clanked as they walked. I referred to these ladies as the "flowers," for almost each one had a name like "Daisy" or "Violet." "Rose" was even my own middle name. And, of course, my mother, Blima, was the center of us all.

With Jasmine gone, I retrieved my own list. I quietly explained that I wanted to tell her how much I loved her, I needed to tell her. So, with the buzz of tires along the Parkway and an orange sun streaming between the blinds of the living room window, I took my mother's hand and read. My voice grew hoarse, but I did not cry. When I was done, she looked into my eyes and smiled again.

"Very nice," she said.

Betty

I dream all the time. I cannot help it. The ghosts swim in my head, and I rush to catch them because in my dreams I am strong again. I would call out to them if I remembered their names, but I do not. Besides, my breath has anchored my vocal chords and my tongue is now turned to stone. But if I could speak, I would say, "Forgive me, Mama and *Tata*. Forgive me, please."

When did day become night? When did the light shift to darkness? I remember a young girl made of iron who once pushed the light with all her power into the black abyss ahead. But her candle is going out now, and she has lost the power she once had to fuel the sun. From the inside out, her essence falls away like ash and is lifted by wind into the sea.

I used to be able to walk. No, I ran all the time. I always ran to something, never away. But now I cannot even remember what I was running toward. I ran through the forest and ate leaves. I ran through the streets looking for people never found. I ran down the Parkway and fell once. But I picked myself up with my hand to my nose and kept running. Now, when I fall I have not the strength to recover myself. I let the wind and flowers lift me to my stubborn feet. When I rise, I say I am sorry. I am sorry, sorry. Forgive me, please.

A woman comes in and shows me how to bend my legs. I thought I knew this, but maybe I didn't. She gives me a metal piece and tells me to put my hands on it. I move one foot in front of the other, and like magic we are on the Parkway. I see Chiel wearing his hat sitting on the bench waiting for me. Or perhaps it is my brother. A memory, like a feather floating in my head, tells me that when Chiel and I were in the store together they said we looked more like brother and sister than husband and wife. Short, hands moving, a foreign sadness behind the eyes. Chiel on the bench does not look at me as I and my metal edge toward him. But I think he is mad since he does not recognize me.

"Don't be mad at me, Chiel. I am sorry that I could not help you, but my strength is gone. Please forgive me," I cry. But the words are stuck like paste in my head, and I cannot say them.

I am so tired so we stop to rest. I look up at the tall woman sitting next to me. This is not easy because the sun is in my dry eyes and the rays sting like a thousand angry bees. The lady's yellow hair is wound tightly in a bun that looks like a rose, and her smile is secret but pleasant. Of course, I recognize her.

"Thank you so much for everything, Gizella. I've been meaning to tell you that."

"You need to walk some more. Let's go," she answers, putting my hand on the metal as we continue on the Parkway. I tell her I was iron once, but now the iron has jumped outside of me and all I can do is hold on. The tall lady looks down to the concrete, still smiling.

My legs betray me. Always I had such beautiful legs, but now their beauty is useless. I sit all day in a chair with a flat hard seat. It is Chiel's old rolling chair, but Chiel was a king, and this is no throne. When the hurt in my behind becomes more than I can bear, I let myself go like a rag doll. But they bind me with belts and strips of cloth. Even when I scream, they push me down. I hate the Germans.

Food will keep us strong. I ate dirty apple peels once and thought they were a treasure. I have not even the strength now to suck the meat from the bones. So many bones. Bones piled one on top of the other, sunken cheeks, matted hair falling over their eyes. Their mouths were open like tiny beaks waiting for the worm. Why did I survive?

The flowers put food in my mouth, strawberry pudding and applesauce. I can hear the metal spoon clack against my dentures. I see hazel eyes, deep mournful eyes looking down into mine. Just like the son I once had. Once, he forgot to speak too, but Chiel saved him. I could not, yet I never told him I was sorry. It was Chiel who gave his life for his son's. So now there are two Chiel's. Double good luck. This man with the graying beard like my son comes everyday. He brings packages and carries me to the bed and talks with the flowers. "Ma, Ma," he says, "I love you." How lucky his mother is to have a son like that.

I had a daughter once too, or did I just imagine this? Chiel had a sister who was my daughter. She died of food poisoning a long time ago. In the war. Her face was pale and thin, and she wore her chestnut hair in a long braid. She was my best friend.

There is a voice from very far away. I can walk to it. My thumb shakes, making tapping noises on the metal in front of me. That is how I know I am awake. The voice tells me to look, look out the window. Do I know these men? I look up. They are so tall and strong and handsome. Of course, I recognize them! They are my English soldiers. The first, the tallest, comes from the town and has genius over his eyes. The second one coming to the camp is muscles and laughter and hides behind the tall one. The last knows me the best. In his eyes rests all the knowledge of the world, and his heart sits like a medal upon his smile. I know, of course, that these soldiers have come to save me. I wish I had the words to thank them for helping me cross the sea. They are wonderful, very brave, the best. With them, I will have my freedom. With them, I will have my future.

Finally, the flowers put me on the bed. The sheet is white and cold and clean. There is also one sheet over the lower part of my body, and it touches me softly like a baby's hand. Someone has put Vaseline on my behind so I do not feel so much the burning. The door is closed, and the quiet settles around me like a furry cat. Even Ruschia has stopped whispering in my ear. I told her that later when I have finished in the bakery, Adele and I will help her and Victor with the children. We will feed them and put them to bed, not to worry. Only now I must work.

When I wake up, I see a face next to mine. I can feel her breath against my mouth, like tiny dewdrops. Her eyes are like my eyes, her lips, my lips. But still I do not know who she is. Only my heart knows her well, but it does not reveal the secret to me. She is speaking to me in a language I once knew. I see in her face the clouds on a humid day that shiver and become water. The water rises and covers her face, covers mine, submerging us both. I wish I could save her, but there is too much water, too much. Then, very slowly, I see the face quiver and turn gray black until it too becomes a wave and floats away. I try, but I can't remember. Maybe–maybe she is my mother.

Shirley

My mother cannot speak. She cannot walk. She cannot feed herself. She cannot use a bathroom. She can't even laugh or smile. I accept that she is gone. But I still can't accept that she is leaving me.

It does not help that Jack and I argue all the time. He visits the apartment almost daily, bringing groceries, diapers, ointments. He hires the aides, brings them food from the take-out, and accompanies my mother on most of her doctor's appointments. Futile now, since she is completely off all medication. He pays all of my mother's bills and constantly seems to be waiting on hold for doctors, accountants, lawyers. His mother-in-law is critically ill and in the hospital, and when he is not there or at my mother's apartment, or at work, he is watching Charlie and Sam. He says that I do not spend enough time with Mommy. He wants to place her in a nursing home and does not care that she will lose her life savings. It is her money, he says.

I love my brother, but I cannot abide him. He simply does not understand. I do not tell him this, but I've always viewed him as the guardian of her body in a crisis. When she is sick, when anyone in my family becomes ill, I am useless. My heart starts to beat fast; my hands perspire uncontrollably, fueled by the sparks of adrenalin shooting out of my brain. I lose all reason, allowing feeling to dominate my action. So I turn to my brother, as I did when Daddy had the stroke, as I do now.

But when the path is smooth, when I know my mother's heart will beat tomorrow, when her smile again will illuminate her face, then I am in control. I am the guardian of her spirit. I call her two, three times a day just to hear her voice, her "Shoiley, how *are* you?" I ask her advice, certain that she is honesty and truth. I bring her to my home and sit next to her as she folds the laundry, and feed her strawberry frozen yogurt just so I can see her smack her lips in pleasure. I buckle her in the car and drive to the supermarket where she helps me pick out the best peaches, or to Macys for bras and shoes. At night, her eyes begin to close, but she will not go upstairs. She waits until I am done making lunches and checking locks. Only then does she climb the stairs, with me, slowly, at her back.

Jack does not understand. He does not understand the thick lump in my throat that forms three times each week as I go over the Verrazano Bridge, fearful of what I will find when I get to Brooklyn. He does not understand the tears which block my vision filled with the image of her on my way back to New Jersey. When she dies—and I am afraid even to think this—I want her to die in her bed like my father, like a king. Jack says her money is hers and should be for a nursing home. Is this what she would want, or is it what Jack wants? I just don't know. What I have come to realize is that I wear my anger against Jack, against everyone, but mostly this disease, like an overcoat. Clothed in my coat of anger, I am protected against the feelings, the fears which chill my spirit. I have come to like this coat of anger.

The truth is—and we both know this—we are not arguing with each other. We are arguing with the disease which eats at her brain. We are arguing with the sadness, the frustration we feel daily. We are arguing with the pain behind our eyes which now taints every relationship, every activity we have. But we are not arguing with each other.

A nurse visits my mother, and then calls me at home. She has discovered a sacral wound near the anus, a painful bed sore. The aides had informed me of this and were treating it with ointment. But the nurse says it is infected and as big as a fist. After a few more visits, she tells me that my mother needs to see a doctor. I recall the weeks watching her slump in her wheelchair, binding her with belts so she would stay in place. Against the surface of the seat, an unspeakable pain was searing her body. The old guilt returns, stabbing my heart like a rusty knife.

I drive to Brooklyn and get into the ambulance with my mother in her wheelchair, and the aide. My mother closes her eyes and sleeps, but when she awakens, she looks right at me and then right through me. Then she screams. It is high-pitched, hysterical. It is the scream of pure terror.

We arrive at the NYU Medical Center, and I wheel my mother through the wide-aisled sterile corridor. She screams again. An Asian doctor reading a medical chart looks up and keeps walking. I begin to time the intervals between each scream, three minutes apart like labor pains. We take the elevator to the fifth floor. She screams again, and my hands remain on the wheelchair as the aide squeezes herself into a corner. An old woman and her son shift their eyes uneasily and pretend to look at the ascending floor numbers. By the time we emerge, my mother has stopped screaming, her head tilted up, staring only at the white ceiling. Aunt Naomi meets us there, and I see in her eyes that thing that I saw the day we forced my father to go to the wedding. The communal look as he ignored everyone, intent only on sucking a cube of sugar. Shock, pity? Or maybe just the realization that the ability to help those we love is as hollow as the promise of everlasting happiness. My mother screams again, and a nurse takes her into the examining room.

I do not accompany her, but tell the aide to go. I am afraid of my own reactions when I look at the wound. My aunt tells me it is not necessary, pats my hand, and sighs. There is very little we say to each other. We breathe the air saturated with the smells of alcohol and antiseptic, and that is about all we can do. I hear the screams again, and pray he is not hurting her too much. After only ten minutes, the aide wheels my mother back out. I am given a prescription, and the three of us return to the elevator. We go only two flights down, this time, for a visit with her geriatrician. She screams and we are taken right into his office. He does not examine her, however, but only shakes his head.

"I told you this would happen, right?" he says, bending his head and looking over his wire-rimmed glasses.

I remember the last thing she said to me before she stopped speaking. "The candle is going out." I look at the violet beam of light shining off the doctor's glasses, and say, "I think she knows too."

As we leave the hospital, I see a reflection of the three of us in the glass doors of the lobby. For the first time, I am grateful that my mother has lost the capacity to understand. If she did, she would have placed her hands in front of her eyes and cried.

My mother looks like a newborn lying small and curled on the white sheet, wearing only a thin cotton nightgown. Another sheet covers the lower half of her body, hiding the sacral wound. She has stopped screaming these last few days, and a serene calm has descended like a shroud over her face. I find the still visible indentation her body has made during the night and mold my own body to the spot. When I can smell the lilac of her hair, the peaches in her skin, I close my eyes and take a long deep breath. When I open them again, she is staring at me. I have never seen her eyes bluer or more beautiful.

"*Guy nesh avec fin miya*," I whisper into them, "Don't leave me."

We are, the two of us, in a cavernous room so hot that beads of water can be seen in clumps on the steel arms of the lounge chairs. She is standing at the edge, just where the shallow ends and the deep begins. She waves to me with one hand, and with the other pushes down on the thick twisted rope to steady herself. I lift my

arm to return the wave when suddenly I no longer see the sparkling white bathing cap she wears, and I realize she is under. But
then, just as quickly, she explodes to the surface like a marvelous
flying fish. And then she is down again. I realize this is no game
she is playing, that she is not submerging just to relieve herself of
the room's oppressive heat. The rope is pulling her down against
her will. It does this two more times, and each time she emerges,
my mother emits a ghastly croak as air quickly seeps into her lungs.
It is the first time that I have seen her afraid.

I am not fast enough; the water is slowing me down. I am only
nine and can't even swim, and the water is too strong and heavy.
My skinny legs push against the heave of the cool blue water until,
finally, I catch her hand and lift her up. She releases her grasp of
the rope and hugs me gratefully. "You saved me," she says, drinking in the air, "You saved me."

But then, there is a sudden rush of water and she goes down
again. Straining, I reach my fingers toward her, but grasp only the
intangible, a void.

"Mommy," I cry, "What will I do without you? Please don't leave
me!" But already the water has covered my mother's eyes, her face.
And when she floats away, I see that she is crying too.

✣ ✣ ✣

My mother is in the hospital. I am home from teaching my
morning classes when the visiting nurse calls me. Mommy is running a fever of 104, and the nurse is concerned that an infection
has set in. By the time I arrive in the emergency room, my brother
is already at her side.

"It's probably pneumonia, but they're concerned about the
infection too. The wound is pretty big," he says, stroking my mother's arm. He goes off to find our cousin, Joey, who is a nephrologist
at the NYU hospital.

"Ma, it's okay," I whisper in her ear, "we're getting you help." Her eyes remain closed as I wipe the beads of perspiration from her upper lip. A thought comes to me like a fleeting breeze, and I wonder what happened to her dentures. I must get them for her. Suddenly, I hear a high-pitched sigh like the last gasp of a dying man, and a blue cloud explodes between me and my mother.

Someone has dropped a tank of oxygen, and there is a flurry of moving gurneys as oxygen masks are thrown around the room. I pull one off a nearby table and place it quickly over my mother's mouth as I cover my own with the palm of my hand. An orderly pushes her into a corner of a nearby waiting room.

"I have asthma!" someone shouts. I don't see her or the other patients. My eyes remain only on my mother.

"I'm glad you got her out of there so fast," says Jack as he runs toward us, panting. Fire engine sirens can already be heard outside.

"Good thing we're already in a hospital," he jokes lamely, adding, "Are you okay?"

"Just fine," I answer, my heart still beating wildly in my chest.

Mommy has pneumonia coupled by a severe bacterial infection which has resulted from the sacral wound. She will have to be in the hospital for at least a week. The doctors tell us too that she will need a feeding tube; they are afraid that she will choke on her food. This means, of course, that she can't ever go back to the apartment.

"It doesn't matter anymore," says Jack, and I agree. She is beyond caring. I close my eyes momentarily and engage in a silent battle with myself. The thing is, she won't die in bed like my father. I click it off. It makes no difference now. None.

We decide that we will not intubate her if it comes to that. It is a decision we make easily, without the divisiveness which has characterized our relationship these past few months.

"It won't be a condemnation to death, but a release," advises our doctor cousin, Joey.

"We know," I reply.

Still, I wonder what, if anything, she thinks about when she is awake, eyes staring up at the ceiling. As for myself, I am no longer nervous, I am no longer fearful. There is only one emotion that is left. As Jack and I leave the building, a chilling sadness whirls around us like a storm of black snow.

It is good to see a familiar face. One of the flowers, Daisy, has returned as a private nurse to care for my mother while she is in the hospital. Like her name, she is small, unassuming, and sweet. She sits in the armchair by the window reading her Bible, and when the family visits, she pads softly out of the room for a cup of tea. She shows me how to spread lotion onto my mother's hands and feet. She helps me to modulate my voice so that it is in a soothing tone. All the things I will have to know when she is transferred to the nursing home.

"She never wanted to live like this, you know."

"I know," I say again.

When my Uncle Kalman comes, as he does everyday, he asks how my children are, how work is going. We talk around her, yet sometimes I catch her eyes open and following. I wish she would go back to sleep.

One day, I am sick. I return from the hospital with a bad cold and a hot fever sneaking into my head. I can't stop coughing. I close my bedroom door and crawl under the covers. My mother would have known what to do. She would have given me chicken soup, aspirin, a vat of hot tea, and covered me with three woolen blankets. Yes, and she would have called, nine, ten times a day. But who would help me now? Who would care if I lived or died? The cold and mucous make it easier for me to cry, and I do. Loud, woeful moans as drops of salt water fall upon my tongue. I allow myself to be sucked into the whirlpool of self-pity, my despair inconsolable.

I hear the door creak open. I look up and see Arthur. For the first time in many months, I actually see him, his face grief-stricken, his arms outstretched.

"I'm here for you," he says. I fall into his arms and cry a million tears.

✡ ✡ ✡

The Russian lady with the beehive hairdo traces the rim of the china saucer with her shiny red nail.

"How much you want?" she asks, still absorbed in the flower pattern, but raising one eyebrow nonetheless.

"One dollar." Lifting the other eyebrow, she looks up at me as if she sees ants pouring out of my mouth.

"But is not even set. Only five plates, three cups. I give you one dollar for everything," she protests, dismissing the pieces with the back of her hand.

"One dollar," I repeat evenly, as I gently remove the plate from her palm. "A dollar a piece for real china."

The woman sighs dramatically and moves on to inspect a ceramic decanter in the form of a sleeping Mexican with removable sombrero top. I turn and walk down the narrow hall toward my parents' bedroom. The recently excavated room no longer bears any semblance to the room my father took his last breath in sixteen years earlier, and where my mother a month ago was carried away on a stretcher, oblivious to the bedroom, the world many months before that. I push my back against the wall to make room for the two tall black men struggling with my parents' mattress. Saturated with the stench of alcohol and spilt medicine, it holds pockets of childhood memories. Countless evenings of family discussions planning for vacations, laughing over our foibles, the craziness in the world. Imagine that–most families talked over kitchen tables; we talked on the queen-sized bed. Even as adults in our twenties, thirties, forties, single then married, later, with children. Our parents also turned with the whims of time, the able-bodied became sick, and too soon, dying.

The bedroom looks as if it has been devastated by nuclear attack. Old photographs, bits of costume jewelry, scarves, shoes, canes, coins, even adult diapers lie strewn across the bare floor. My brother presses old honeymoon pictures of myself and Arthur into my hand.

"I thought you might want to keep these."

"She wants to give me a dollar for Mommy's English tea set," I sigh, stuffing the photos into a pocket.

"What's the difference? It'll only go to charity, anyway." He steps on an old crystal necklace, cracking it, and throws it in a plastic garbage bag drooping next to the night table.

"I know. But I hate to just give it away." I remember the way my father would haggle over each vase, set of silverware, AM-FM radio, during our Sundays on the Lower East Side. The careful records he would keep over each item, the money stored under rolled-up socks in a dresser drawer.

"Daddy always liked a good deal," I say.

My brother shrugs his shoulders and I move into the second bedroom, the one Jack lived in while in college, the one he recovered in after the accident.

A friend of the beehive lady, an older heavyset woman who heaves with each step and is constantly wiping the space between her sagging breasts, watches her son remove a faded green drape from the wall. She waddles over to me and sticks her hand between her breasts again, this time retrieving a small beaded change purse. She peels off two soggy dollar bills and places them in my palm. As I pocket the money, she taps me on the shoulder, says something indecipherable in Russian, and motions toward the small mahogany desk, night table, and matching dresser.

"Twenty dollars," I respond. She holds up five fingers.

"Twenty dollars." I walk away, feeling ill. It is as if they are going through the spoils of war, our war... The old blue sweater my father wore after the stroke. Once so meticulous in his grooming that he had several sets of cufflinks to match each suit, he would wear the sweater at the kitchen table as he slowly gulped measured spoonfuls of oatmeal, the excess dripping out of the side of his mouth. The oil painting my parents carried onto the plane coming back from Jerusalem. Sarah carrying a jug of water, too bright with its crimsons and blues over the plastic-covered gold velvet couch in the living room. The ceramic frame decorated with needles and pins which I gave my mother, just because I knew it would make her laugh. She stuck my picture in it. The elbow macaroni frame which I spray painted in silver and gold when I was in kindergarten. My picture was in that one too. The flowered cosmetic bag that held the only snapshot she had of her twin brother, the uncle I never met. The dining room chairs with the wobbly wooden legs. The old TV with the 26-inch screen. The healthcare aides usually watched soap operas on it. My mother, reduced now to a body, a thin voile of skin over a beating heart, hadn't watched anything but the walls in months. She doesn't, I don't think, even hear the radio. A picture, a purse, a life, a bed. All the same. The heavy satin brocade drapes which let the sun in during the day and shut out the street glare at night, but never the sounds of the neighbors walking above or doing their laundry below. And even when there was silence, there was no peace. The spoils of war.

The old woman is slowly coming toward me, saying something again, delving into the space between her wet breasts. With the other hand, she holds up five fingers. I shake my head from side to side and walk slowly back to my brother.

"I think I made a good deal," I whisper, more to myself than to him.

Before Jack locks the door, I pick up a pair of shoes I had set aside in the hallway.

"Aren't they a little big for you?" asks Jack, jiggling the keys in his hand. I run my finger over the chunky heel, the straight black stitches on the sides, the supple brown leather.

"I'll make them fit," I say.

✡ ✡ ✡

Jack is wiping my mother's brow with cool water when I arrive. Someone from the nursing home had called that morning to tell us she was spiking a fever and was having some difficulty breathing. Did we want her taken to a hospital?

Only two weeks earlier, we had decided to take her off the feeding tube during the day only. If she chose to eat, if she chose life, we would stand by her. If she chose the alternative, we'd be there for her too. We take turns wiping her brow, whispering into her ear. I tell her she is free to go, and I tell her not to worry. Then, Jack and I reconcile, both of us admitting we were never really angry with each other in the first place. They say she is dying of "urosepsis," a poisoning of the blood. But we know better. The source of her death was right there, always in front of us, hidden deep within that well of turmoil which began rising long, long before we were ever born.

That evening, the evening of April 1, 1999, Jack, Emily, and their two young sons, Arthur, I, and our three boys gather around the Seder table in Jack's house. As Jews do on every Passover, we recount the story of our oppression as slaves under the Pharoah, and of our journey to freedom in the land of Israel. Meanwhile, somewhere on a white bed lost only briefly in the land of life, Blima Weisstuch Russak shifts uneasily, takes one last labored breath, and begins her journey home.

Blima

We are married on April 25, 1947. It is the same month I first was taken from Mama's home, and the same month in which I regained my freedom into a world I no longer recognized. But it is the first time in many Aprils when I can freely say that, like the grass, I too am reborn.

As I walk toward the *chupa*, the Jewish canopy, with my brother Victor supporting my elbow on one side, and Ruschia on the other, I feel a happiness settle into my heart like nothing I have known before. It is like a piece of warm sun, soft like pudding, and glowing like a mother's touch. It is a survivor's kind of happiness, the sort one never experiences unless the worst has been felt. It feels wonderful, and I want to remain in the moment, hold still the hands of the clock, forever.

Chiel steps down hard and breaks the glass as all the people cheer, "*Mazel Tov!*" As he lifts the veil to kiss me before God and our well-wishers, I feel myself blush. I am Chiel's wife, I am a part of someone, and I will have a future. I look at my new husband and smile.

Never before do I remember being so doted upon. All eyes are on me as the photographer snaps pictures of me standing with Chiel under the *chupa*, clapping hands as we dance, sitting on a throne with my white bridal gown floating beneath me. If only Adele could see me now! Ruschia fixes my veil which is a long, multi-layered and very white lace. Even Chiel's fat cousin sprays me with a perfume when I walk by. As for the dress itself, it seems

to belong to another, not made for one such as I. Surely it is the
most stunning outfit I have ever found myself in. It has a wide pet-
ticoat and a scoop neck with puffy sleeves. I am swallowed up in
its layers, and am only lacking the magic wand for the role of fairy
princess. It is the first time that I, Blima, am the center of attention, adored by all. Not even did I have a womb to myself. I am
uncomfortable, but I like it. And yet, in the midst of my greatest
happiness, is the solemn voice. It is only for the moment, Blima.
Only for the moment.

Chiel and I set up a home in Lanceberg, not far from the few
cousins he has. Even though we have known each other for only
a few months, I learn that my intuition was right. He is a good
man and a good husband. Everyday he is busy at one business or
another. One day he is working with deliveries at a fruit merchant's,
the next he is sewing coats at a friend's textile plant. Many times,
I offer to work, but he prefers that I busy myself with the cooking
or planting the tomatoes and peppers on the small terrace outside
our apartment. My hands, knowing only the labor of twisting fabric, pushing in the needle, feel useless, but I do not argue. I understand him. He feels himself the man, and if he knows one thing, it
is his role to build our future.

While the sun shines, Chiel is quiet, letting his hands and legs
do the work to carry him into his future. But at night, when the
darkness seeps through the windows like a cat, his mouth pries
itself open. He talks a great deal about the war and his family. This
he does in the same detached way he spoke on the day we met. At
other times, he is sullen and I see the tinge of uncertainty in his
hazel eyes. At these times, he holds me close to him as I feel the
strength slowly seeping from my body to his.

Despite his small stature, or perhaps because of it, Chiel's viril-
ity knows no bounds. He delights openly in my breasts, my narrow
waist, and slowly I feel my shyness melt away before him. He is forever my guard, scowling at men who look in my direction a little

longer than they should. At least ten times each day, he asks if I love him. At these times, I take his hands and slip my fingers through his. His leg, like the immortal trunk of a tree, feels cool and famil-iar next to my thigh. To be wife, sister, mother to a man still so young, yet so chastened by life, is the awesome burden to which I must yield. Yet, it is almost unbearable for a shadow to consume another life within itself. Can I be all for another if I do not even know who I am? "Yes, my dear, I do love you," I say. And looking at the shy half smile of his, I am sure of it. That's when he promises me again that he will make our future, and it will come soon.

It comes sooner than I anticipate. One evening, Chiel comes home late from the textile plant. He is waving a telegraph in his hand, and rushes to embrace me.

"Do you remember my Tante Sifra and her husband whom I told you about? Well, finally, they have written and will sponsor us. Blimala, we are going to America!"

My heart jumps, but there is worry between my smiles. America is so far away, after all, a whole ocean to cross! A culture, a lan-guage which is a world apart, an ocean apart! And I, just learning to make my way in a world which I have known all my life. And, while I hardly have family left here, I have none there at all.

But Chiel and I spend a whole evening talking, and gradually each little fear subsides. He will find a job and go to school to learn English. I will make new friends, American friends who will not hate me because I am a Jew. And how many people we will meet there, Jews and even Christians, *good* Christians, Negroes, Spanish. People from all walks of life in this land where the streets are paved with gold!

Victor and Ruschia come to our home. It is only a few months since we have received permission to emigrate to America, with Chiel's *tante* and uncle as our sponsors. Ruschia is folding woolen blankets and handing them to me so that I can stack them neatly in the suitcase.

"To think," she says, fixing a corner of the blanket, "that by next month you will be living in your new home in America!"

"Oh, Ruschia, I am not so sure about this. After all, you and Victor and Kalman will be so far away. Who knows when we will see each other again?"

"Nonsense! Sometimes, Blima, you speak like a child," she replies, brusquely grabbing another blanket, "We will all be together quicker than you think once you make the arrangements for us. Why, even Kalman is convinced that maybe America is not so bad. Who knows, maybe he will even find an American bride?"

"Oh, I don't know... a whole ocean to separate us," I sit down on the bed as I start to feel the burning of tears in my eyes, "I know this is silly, but I feel like I am leaving Mama and *Tata* here, everything I have loved and known. Please, Ruschia, try to understand!"

Ruschia puts down the blanket and, taking my hand, sits down next to me.

"Believe me, Blima, you are leaving ashes only behind. Their spirit," she adds, tapping my chest gently, "is here, and you can never leave that." I gulp my sadness down, recalling the day Mama and I sat in her bedroom and the way she placed her hand on my chest and said how alike we were. Ruschia continues, "As for me, I will be glad to leave any soil that still holds the Nazi footprint." She lowers her voice and squeezes my hands between her own. "Here there is no more happiness. We must build our happiness in the future." But then she closes her eyes momentarily and pauses.

"Blima, may I ask you one favor only?" I nod, but already I am moving toward my black purse on the dresser. I remove three of the photographs and hand them to her. Ruschia runs her fingers across each picture as if she is again stroking the faces of her children. Then, she quickly places them in the pocket of her skirt.

"Ruschia," I say, still sitting down staring into the eyes of my sister-in-law and friend, "That day in Bergen-Belsen when I awoke not knowing if I would see the Devil himself, and then when I saw you–"

"I know," she answers quietly, rising as she kisses my forehead, "Let's finish packing."

The next day, as the dawn rises between the clouds, I stand shivering on the deck. Already there are lines of shadow crossing the faces of my loved ones. And, still waving in the crowd, I stand on tiptoes to see them. Suddenly, I feel a momentous force scooping me up and lifting me away as the water's spray beckons at my back. I look up. The day is gray, but there are glints of radiant sun as Chiel takes my hand and I turn to face the ocean and my future.

TODAY

MOTHER, YOU CAN

Mother, you can
shed your clothes now
the paper rag skin
slipping in the joints
a creaky skeleton
shed the deep crevice of cheek
let fall the half moon
mouth the angled nose
the pleading eye
shed the bones the
stilled heart.
And step upon that cloud
the one on the right
yes
drift higher let it carry you
up beyond the sad earth
beyond the crumbling mountains
beyond the silent horizon
higher up until
you are there.
Until you see him
your lover
hair no longer silver
smile the same
as when you met
until you see him
brother slapping knee
sneaking glances at his gold watch
sisters in a circle
saved before the fire
laughing holding you a spot
father looking stern under his hat, but
his blue eyes–your eyes–are warm.
Until you see mother
who raises both her arms
towards you–
she can reach you now
no one to hold her back
no one to grab you take you away
she can reach you now
take her hand go to her

you can now
your legs are nimble again
and your long wavy brown hair will chase behind
try your mouth
it is full like an apple
go now to her
you can, you know
go now, go home.

Shirley

This is a sad day, but it is also the day when I feel luckiest. Lucky because Betty Russak was my mother. My mother was not a famous person, but there was a warmth, a kindness about her which made her a friend to those she had never met before. My mother was not an educated person, but she was determined to see her children reach their potential in school; and in many ways she was the smartest person I've ever known. My mother was not a martyr, but she saw my father and brother through terrible illnesses and would never hesitate to give every fiber of herself to her children, her son-in-law, Arthur, her daughter-in-law, Emily, both of whom she admired, the five grandsons, Howie, Brad, Charlie, Charlie, and Sammy whom she adored above all else, and her loving and devoted brother, Karl. My mother was not an eloquent speaker; she could never make a speech in front of a group. But when she spoke, her words were always true and from the heart. My mother was not a sophisticated woman; she would always get in on the driver's side of the car even though she didn't drive, and she didn't know a computer from a television set. But she knew how to mend her grandchildren's clothes, make chicken soup, and she never minded folding towel after towel. Most of all, she made you feel as if you were the only one that mattered; and she was able to do that because that's the way she really felt. My mother was not a strong person. She cried at every sad TV show, and when she would hear of a stranger's illness or misfortune, she would sob for hours. Yet she was a woman of incredible strength. Strength enough to survive the Holocaust and the horrors of Grunberg and Bergen-Belsen. Strength to build a new life after the loss of her beloved parents, her sisters and her brother. Strength to come to a new land supported by her older brother Victor whom she looked up to and cherished with all her heart, and her younger brother Karl who was a constant source of comfort to her, and whom she adored. Strength to work side by side in launderettes and candy stores with the man who meant everything to her and to whom she was devoted till the end, my father.

This past summer, when we saw her slipping, I wanted so much to tell her what she meant to me. She knew how much my brother and I loved her, but just the same, I wanted her to hear the words. So I started thinking about all the reasons she means so much to me, I wrote them down, and when we were alone together and she could still understand what I was saying, this is what I read:

Mother—I love you. I love you because you didn't raise us by the book, but by your emotions and common sense. I love you because you were a work-ing mother way before it became fashionable, and so taught me the value of hard work and independence. I love you because you survived the loss of your parents, three sisters, a twin brother, everything you cherished, and yet you always said that Jack and I were the special ones. I love you because you didn't teach us how to play violin or give us dance lessons, but instead you told us things like "good things come in small packages," "wait until after an argument to raise your voice," and "the meaner someone is, the nicer you must be to that person." I love you because whenever I look into a mirror and see a woman in her forties with graying hair and circles beneath her eyes, you still see a teenage beauty. I love you because, no matter how upset you might be, you still smile when your children walk into the room. I love you because I never had to learn how to make chicken soup or hem a skirt—you simply wouldn't allow it—and besides, I couldn't top you anyway. I love you because you're the only one who will tell me the truth, no matter what. I love you because whenever I pick up the phone to call you, you say you were just thinking of me. I love you because you worked side by side with our father, Charlie, letting him go to school, be the boss, while you always took a backseat to everyone's successes. I love you because whenever we walked into a store or sat at a bus stop, strangers would immediately start talking to you and become your friend. I love you because you showed me how to make a marriage, telling me to wait until the husband settles down, before quietly explaining to him all the reasons why he was wrong. I love you because people are always afraid to tell you bad news since you become hysterical just by looking at pictures of people wounded or starving. I love you because you are the only one person on earth who thinks I can sing. I love you because you taught me to balance love among my children, valuing each equally, as I would each finger of my own hand. I love you because you have hated makeup and personal adornment, but you always remained so very beautiful without it. I love you because even though everyone else sees me as short, you've always made me feel tall. I love you because you are the only one who would go through each scrap in a wastebasket looking for your daughter's contact lens. I love you because only you could have been able to find that contact lens on a tiny slip of paper. I love you because even though you sometimes get lost going around the corner, and never went anywhere without your husband, you traveled alone to places like Florida and Israel. I love you because even though a stranger's suffering could make you weep, you cared for our father when he was dying, with unimaginable reserves of strength. I love you because even after I mop the floor, only you could still see dust in the corners—and only you would get down on your knees to wipe it away. I love you because your bed was never too small to allow a frightened child inside of it at night. I love you because you never forced me to have my tonsils removed because it might hurt me too much. I love you because you let us make our own choices. I love you because you truly are my best friend. I love you because we always had such fun shopping together—especially on those rare occasions when I could convince you to actually buy something for yourself. I love you because you are the only person happier than Jack or I when one of our children loses a tooth or scores a goal. I love you because when you say your grandsons are geniuses, you really mean it. I love you because you see my children through my eyes. I love you because you love all animals, and won't hesitate to sneak a scrap to one—even if someone tells you not to. I love you because even though you learned how to speak English from neighborhood chatter, you managed to become a U.S. citizen. I love you because you never failed to vote in an election, and always reminded us how proud we should be to be Americans. I love you because when you visit, you won't go upstairs to bed until I do. I love you because our voices are alike. I love you because you didn't only give me life, but you made my life worth living.

In the past few months, friends have come up to me and my brother, telling us what devoted children we are to our mother. But we never saw it that way. Because with Betty Russak for our mother, we, *we* were the lucky ones.

Emily places a plate of marzipan cookies on the wooden coffee table. It is the third night of *shiva*, the traditional period of mourning after a death. The cousins are all there. Ruschia and Victor's son, Mark, his wife DeeDee, Kalman and Naomi's children, Joey and Shaindee, and their spouses. They sit on bridge chairs and on the beige leather sofa in a semicircle, facing Jack and me. We are sitting on stiff cardboard boxes. The candles in the corner of the living room cast a warm glow behind Emily's three-foot high bronze menorah, making it, for a moment, shimmer alive. Joey, our doctor cousin, is the first to speak.

"I told Aunt Betty's doctor about her," he says, looking down at his fingernails, "He was sorry to hear it." Jack and I nod, silent. Joey continues, "Geriatricians are a frustrated lot. Their patients never have a good end, especially not with this disease...My grandmother is still alive, but her mind, well...There's only so much that can be done." I look at the glowing menorah which sends me a single spark of remembrance. My mother thought Mrs. Hershman didn't like her. But Joey's grandmother just didn't know her anymore.

My cousin, Mark, is now in his fifties, but still as darkly handsome and slender as when he lived in the Queens apartment gathering College Bowl statistics. He picks up the small stack of black and white photos which are on the table, and runs his finger gently, almost caressing each one.

"I have these at home, too," he sighs, addressing the picture more than the people around him. He flips to the large photograph on the bottom. The one of the sisters, Adele, Miriam, Brandl, my mother, and his own two sisters, the sisters he never knew.

"Do you have any photos of our grandparents?" I blurt out, suddenly. Almost as if released by a spring, the rest of the cousins inch forward, eager for an answer. Perhaps there is another piece of the puzzle? A shard of our shattered past?

Our eldest cousin looks at me curiously.

"Why would I have anything?" he asks, "It was your mother who saved all the pictures."

"What do you mean, Mark?"

"Aunt Betty kept them with her when she went to the labor camp. She only showed them to my mother when they met in Bergen-Belsen by the end of the war." I lean back, holding tightly onto the box on which I am sitting.

"She never told me," I say softly.

"If not for these, we would have only our parents' recollections," Mark adds. So it was my mother who was responsible for giving form and substance to those scraps of memory. It was my mother all along.

"Did you know that she testified for the Shoah Foundation?" Jack asks, taking the photographs from Mark, and handing them to Shaindee.

"How wonderful!" Mark, a director of a temple in Manhattan, exclaims, "Many in our congregation were encouraged to do the same thing, to document their experiences."

"I'm afraid my mother wasn't very clear, though. Her mind was so confused at the time, she was calling her brother Chiel and her sister Shirley. I guess at the very least, we have her on tape." I turn to Shaindee, who is seated next to me. She wears a long gray skirt and striped sweater. A black beret rests tilted on her short brown hair.

"Your father didn't want her to do it. He thought it would upset her too much." Shaindee nods. "Always worried," she says.

"Do you think he might ever testify, you know, to what he went through?"

The young mother of five considers then shakes her head thoughtfully.

"He keeps a lot inside," Then, as if a star fell suddenly from the sky, I recall a conversation I had with my uncle on the day of the funeral.

"Do you know what our grandfather did for a living?" I say loudly. Everyone turns. The room becomes silent except for the steady ticking of the clock on the mantle above the fireplace. When I feel the heat of their stares brush against my skin, I announce, "Grandpa owned a shoe store!" A chorus of "oh's" and "really's?" drift across the room, when suddenly Shaindee grasps my hand.

"Your mother loved shoes," she gasps, staring into my eyes.

"Yes," I say, "yes, she did." I look at my cousin who is over ten years younger than I, at her round gentle brown eyes, her dark lips filled with compassion. We don't even look alike, I think. Yet, we share the same name, the name of a grandmother neither of us has ever met.

"Do you know that you are the only female blood relative I have left?" I ask her. She says nothing, but her eyes fill with tears.

As a star-filled blackness swells outside, a soothing silence descends upon the room. Since the times we gathered for dinner as children in my Uncle Victor and Aunt Ruschia's apartment, we never saw each other except for the obligatory wedding, Bar Mitzvah, *brit*, or sadly, funeral. And yet, at that moment, we feel as close as one human being can to another. So close we have the same thought.

Jack is the first to say it.

"The way we grew up–we were so very, very lucky." And the children who never knew a grandparent, an aunt, an uncle, a sister, have to agree.

Today. I cannot sleep. I drink warm milk, stay in bed, keep the fan on, do all the things they tell me. But still, it is to no avail. I cannot sleep.

So instead, I find myself dozing at odd hours. Just before dinnertime or in the middle of a movie on TV. One evening, when Arthur is at a basketball game with the boys, I decide to partake in a guilty pleasure. I reach into the back of a cabinet, uncork a bottle of merlot and, seated in the old mauve recliner, begin to read another novel. Since beginnings are always difficult and the wine has already warmed my insides in a subtle nostalgic way, my eyelids soon grow heavy, stubbornly blackening the sharp white of the overhead light. I surrender and, still in shorts and T-shirt, fall into my bed, relishing the delicious cold as I pull the sheets over my legs.

The windows of our bedroom look onto the backyard, where there is one tree whose brittle leaves brush against the glass pane like a hoary grandfather, shaking his full tuft of gray locks in frustration. I acknowledge the tree, as I do each night, watching the

shadows of the leaves leap like orange flame across the burgeon-
ing moonlight.

It is good to dream, especially when one has not dreamt in so
long. I submerge myself indelicately into the fantasies of the night,
just as I would a novel, and wait for the unfolding.

It is not long before she comes. I can feel my face light up with
surprise, then joy. She is wearing the navy blue outfit with the
white Swiss dots which we bought together for Howie's Bar Mitzvah.
Instead of matching it to the skirt as she usually does, this time she
has on a pair of polyester pants. But there is something else too.
She carries with her a certain air, an assertiveness as she quickly
grabs my hand and we head along Pitkin Avenue. We are going
shopping again; but no, this time she knows just where she is going
and soon our shoes trample over the tinny hardness of stones and
gravel, as the sky turns a silky gray. We stop but briefly before the
house whose colors and aspect are indiscernible and melt into the
muted weeds which fill the front yard. She grasps a black handle,
which seems as if it should be locked, and flings open the door.
There, with cane in hand, is a very old man with a very long beard.
There is a round black cat sitting atop his head, which bothers him
not at all, as with the tip of his cane, he beckons us inside.

We enter a parlor where an ochre mist burns from a single tiffany shaded lamp. The first thing I notice are two little cap-haired
girls coloring the pages of a book so intensely they barely have
time to look up and smile. Another, skinnier, girl who is perhaps
a few years older, rushes past, carrying a big box camera in both
hands. Her fragile frame, it seems, cannot contain her excitement,
so I am not insulted by the fact that she does not stop to introduce herself or take our picture, as she quickly barrels out the
door. A young woman of no more than twenty is seated in a wing
chair which is decorated with faded blue flowers. Her thick chestnut hair is piled straight up in a bun which sparkles like a cup of
simmering coffee upon her head. Long lashes yield to oval brown

eyes as she looks up from her knitting and, spying us, begins to laugh, her red lips forming a perfect "O." A young man, straight-backed and stern with a full head of hair which makes him seem taller than he is, swiftly enters and begins to scold us for some unimaginable transgression before he sits and, finally, takes up the paper. There is another, an older man of perhaps fifty, who casts his eyes like a fisherman's net over us all before removing his wire-rimmed glasses and standing. Then, he politely shakes our hands and methodically begins kissing each of us in turn on the top of the head. I am momentarily dumbfounded, not knowing where I am except for the hand which leads me again as I follow, turning like a leaf in the wind.

She becomes more agitated, rushing into this room and that. We pass an old sewing machine whose spindly legs retreat from its place against the wall; in the kitchen warm white potatoes fly suddenly from a yellow bowl as a tattered apron decorated with birds spins past the window. We don't find these events startling in the least way, as we speedily go from one door to the next. Finally, and just as abruptly, she stops, looks at me, and her face goes soft until almost imperceptibly it fades. The phone rings and I wake up. It is 9 PM.

I rub the sleep from my eyes and answer it. Soon they will all be home, and almost sooner still another day will begin. In the half-light of a rising moon, I make my way, barefoot, down the stairs and then down a second landing. And there, in the small office, with the dream still vividly etched in my heart, I begin to write.

Afterward

I am Blima's daughter. I am the granddaughter of her mother, Shaindel, for whom I am named. I am the sister of her son and the mother of three of her five grandsons. And now, I am also the wearer of her shoes. They sit, made of leather, sturdy and high-heeled, at the bottom of my closet where they have been since her last, and final, illness. I have tried them on and they are a little big, so I rarely walk in those shoes. But I always wear them.

I do not need to place my feet inside my mother's shoes to wear them for I already find myself walking in the secure frame of her love and her legacy. I admit that I am still learning to fit into those shoes, and perhaps I never will.

Today, I sit next to a basket of laundry, trying to fold sense and order into my life. It is two years now since my mother is gone, and eighteen years after the death of my father. As an educator, I am constantly looking for lessons in all experiences. Yet, when I reflect on my own life, it seems only like a vast conundrum, like looking into a child's periscope of changing images, with no logic at all. What, if any, are the lessons of my life?

I don't know why the Holocaust happened. I don't think I'll ever understand that. I don't know why my mother's parents, her sisters, her twin brother, nephew and nieces were sent to die in the gas chamber, leaving only a picture to say that they once existed. I don't know why they died and, more critically, I don't know why my mother survived.

My brother found a small photograph of her taken before the war, which he enlarged and gave to me. Almost everyday, I look at the black and white photo which sits in a wooden frame on the sideboard in my dining room. I see a serious young woman, her dark hair set in curls, the bodice of her garment adorning her ample figure so that it makes an outline of a heart just below the neck, and eyes piercing, full of hope. She is quite beautiful. Could she ever have imagined the endless tunnel of agony and loss she would have to endure in those next few years? Why, *why* did my mother survive?

To say that her life in America was fruitful and productive is not enough. We were the generation who should not have been, and yet here we are alive, with children of our own. That is how one question leads to yet another. Why am *I* here? Why not Ruschia's daughters, Miriam's children, or even Brandl's, Froyim's, or Adele's? The burden of forging a legacy from the ashes, from my parents' sorrows, is not one I welcome. It would be easier, I think, to toss it away like an old winter coat. But I have no choice, and neither do my children. Nor do the children of any survivor.

I used to be embarrassed by my life. I was too spoiled, had it too easy. In my twenties, I drank wine and ate baked ziti, throwing the leftover garlic bread in the garbage. In her twenties, my mother ate frozen blades of grass, and foraged for apple peels in a pit filled with dead bodies. As a young adult, I slept in a queen-sized bed, knowing my parents were as far away as the telephone on the night table. She slept on a hard cot, squeezed against a wall, not knowing where her parents were, or even if they were alive. I yearned for a fancy dress and silk drapes. She wanted only her freedom. When I cried it was because I had lost a job. She couldn't cry at all.

How, then, could I ever measure up to my mother? As children and young adults, my brother and I treated our parents with tenderness, hiding hurtful details like those of my brother's accident from them. We revealed only the positives in our lives. While we weren't always successful, we nevertheless continued to place balm on their wounds, which were always there, if not exposed. Ours were small gestures, really, in return for what they had given us–a protected, unswerving devotion and, most importantly, an appreciation for life. I cannot remember a day when I did not know that my life as the child of survivors was blessed.

Now that both of my parents are gone, I must confront the question of the legacy I, in turn, will pass down. Somewhere in me still is the little girl who must crawl into her mother's bed, cuddling against the small of her back when the fears of the night overwhelm. But the years have taught me something. For one thing, I am no longer afraid of the unknown. My mother faced it once as a young girl, and again in her later years. For me, the unknown isn't so frightening when I consider that her essence is now a part of the thing I cannot reach. No, what scares me more are the things I know: sickness, accidents, the cruelty of men.

My mother has also given me a voice, taught me how to write. Not with commas and words, of course, but with her heart. It is a lesson which, I now know, I cannot ignore.

Most important of all, she taught me to go on. I used to think that when my mother died, my life would end too. Miraculously, it hasn't. I think that is because of the strength that she gave me, an "iron" which has kept me working and raising a family, and seen me through accident, illness, and loss. When my mother no longer had the strength, she transferred it to me. In some ways then, like her, I am a survivor too.

My Aunt Ruschia and Uncle Karl were always very dear to me, dearer still after the loss of my parents. At eighty-five, my Uncle Karl is the proud father of two, grandfather of ten, and great-grandfather of three and counting. My Aunt Ruschia lived for ten more years after the death of my mother. But I think, during those last years after she moved from Florida back to New York, we grew closer than ever. Whenever I visited her, indeed, I felt the presence of my mother, of those I never even knew. Once, when she visited from Florida, my Aunt Ruschia met me for lunch, and said something which surprised me. What she said was that I reminded her of my grandmother, my mother's mother. The first Shirley. Not only in the way I looked, my smile, my mannerisms, but in the way I was as a person.

"Your love for your family, the way you treat others. The way you listen, the way you are," Aunt Ruschia explained, adding, "Your mother noticed it, she told it to me." Tears came to my eyes as for the first time I understood why my mother survived. She had been searching for her own mother ever since she was dragged down those gray streets in Dombrowe. And before she died, my mother had found her. She found her in me.

So I do survive, but I think of my mother everyday. Her shadow comes between me and my children as I kiss their cheeks. When I am driving, I sometimes glance at the seat next to me, expecting to see her buckled in and smiling. When I enter a dressing room, I wait, thinking she will push in the door without knocking, peek in, and tell me to spin for her. At night, when everyone has gone to bed and I am seated on the couch alone, I turn to tell her about a friend or an amusing incident at work, just so I can hear her laugh. On the way to a doctor's appointment, I stop myself before calling her on the phone just to hear her reassure me, her intuitive knowing that everything will be all right. When I walk into a shop, alone, I feel her by my side, her arm linked in mine. And curiously, strangers with easy smiles and small inquisitive children approach as I stroll by myself along the aisles. At 9 PM, I listen for the sharp ring, the high-toned voice telling me, "You're the only one, the only one." In the long hours of the night, I find myself telling her of Howie's wedding, the work he is doing for the government, Brad's long hours with the team at Rutgers, Charlie's move to LA. And I feel her glancing over my shoulder whenever I taste pizza, reach for the phone, comb my hair. So, in a way, my mother is there with me. She is with me always. She is with me still.

CPSIA information can be obtained at www.ICGtesting.com
Printed in the USA
LVOW07s1523180315

431078LV00019B/1042/P